THE MIAMI CONNECTION

Journalism is his weapon. Truth is the target.

GREGOR STEEL

Bradford Press

____

1

The Interview

____

The newsroom of the *Tallahassee Gazette* carried the stale, claustrophobic scent of burnt coffee and old newsprint—a smell Max Larkin knew too well. It was the odor of stories past their prime, ambition gone sour. He stood just inside the doorway, fingers tightening on the strap of his worn leather messenger bag, resisting the urge to pivot, walk back out, and disappear into the Florida heat.

The low hum of outdated printers blended with the flat murmur of reporters' voices and the occasional ring of a desk phone. Work was getting done—sure—but not the kind he used to do. These people chased ribbon-cutting ceremonies and dog adoption fairs. He'd once chased senators into elevators, cornered crooked developers in parking garages. Now he was here, late forties, half-forgotten, half-pitied, starting over in a newsroom where half the staff looked like they'd been born after his first byline hit print.

One foot in front of the other. That's what his sponsor always said. Keep moving forward, even when the ground feels like it's giving way.

"Larkin!"

The voice cracked across the room like a snapped cable. Ed

Harper, his editor, leaned in the doorway of his glass-walled office, tapping the face of his watch with mock impatience.

"You're late."

Max adjusted the strap of his bag and offered a small shrug. "Traffic."

"At ten in the morning? In Tallahassee?" Harper's brows arched like twin question marks. "Nice try. Get in here."

No point arguing. Harper was one of the few people in journalism who still returned Max's calls. They'd known each other back when Max worked for the *Miami Chronicle*, back when his name had weight and his work had teeth. Harper had been an assistant editor then—the kind who could spot a buried lead from a mile away. Now, he was offering Max something better than a story: a shot.

Max stepped into the cramped office, noting the same mess of half-drained coffee cups, sticky notes, and dog-eared folders.

"What's the assignment?" Max asked, dropping into the cracked leather chair.

Harper didn't look up from his yellow legal pad. "Puff piece."

Of course. Max bit back a sigh. "Fantastic. Can't wait to expose the city's top gelato flavors."

Harper smirked. "This one's different. Fishing influencer. Big following. Local."

Max raised a brow. "You're serious."

"Do I look like I'm joking?" Harper finally looked up, eyes flat and pragmatic. "Three million followers. That's three million clicks. And if we're smart, we ride the wave."

Max stared. "Fishing?"

Harper slid a printout across the desk. "Jenna Morgan. Born in South Florida, raised on the water. Runs a conservation brand. Sells her own gear line. People eat it up. She's livestreaming down in St. Marks right now. You're going to talk to her."

Max scanned the one-sheet. At the bottom, Harper's handwritten note read: *Don't screw this up.*

"When's the interview?"

"Now." The word landed with newsroom finality—no negotiation.

"Why me?" Max asked.

Harper leaned back, lacing his fingers over his stomach. "Because you don't scare easy. Because she might have more to say than 'save the fish.' If she does, I want someone who knows how to listen. Go."

Max stood. The air conditioning kicked on with a tired wheeze. Out on Tennessee Street, a siren wailed, then cut off. He grabbed his bag, nodded once, and left before the old instinct to argue could find its footing.

ST. **Marks**

The drive carried him past stretches of pine forest and low marsh, the late-morning sun making heat shimmer over the two-lane road. The air here was both sharp and heavy—salt from the Gulf braided with the earthy rot of wetlands. Every so often, the trees broke, revealing flat water glittering like hammered tin, white birds lifting off in slow, startled vees.

He kept the radio off. Silence was safer than opinionated voices or songs that could drag him back to years he was done surviving.

He passed shuttered bait-and-tackle shops, their *For Sale* signs sun-bleached to gray. A diner with a rusting crab trap stacked by the door. A church marquee that read: *PRAY FIRST, THEN FISH.* The words made him want to laugh but didn't.

At the marina, the smell shifted—diesel, salt, hot rope, the faint sweetness of bait shrimp. Pickup trucks and sun-faded SUVs packed the lot, coolers bungeed in beds, long rods jutting like quills. Pelicans perched on pilings with the bored majesty of kings.

He spotted her immediately. Jenna Morgan stood at the end of a weathered dock, tan legs braced, fishing rod bent like a drawn bow. A phone sat clipped to a tripod beside her, broadcasting the moment to thousands—maybe tens of thousands—of unseen eyes.

Max stopped a few yards back, notebook in hand, watching. She wasn't posing. She wasn't faking. The shifts in her arms, the quick flicks of the reel, the set of her jaw—this was muscle memory. The fish broke the surface in a silver spray, and she laughed, the sound half triumph, half relief.

"Tagging and releasing this beauty," she told the camera, holding the tarpon so the sun lit every shimmering scale. "Healthy and strong—exactly what we want to see."

In the periphery, Max noticed a small knot of onlookers—two teenagers with skateboards, a retired couple in matching visors, and a man in a faded Gators cap whose eyes flicked to Max, then away, as if scoring some private point. The man leaned on a piling, texting with his head down for a long time.

Jenna slipped the tarpon back into the water, guiding it until it flicked and vanished. She unclipped the mic, signed off with quick, practiced words, then turned and saw Max. A small hitch crossed her expression—not recognition, but assessment.

She wiped her hands on a towel and walked toward him, the phone still tethered to its tripod, red light blinking dormant.

"You must be my reporter."

"Max Larkin," he said, offering his hand.

"Jenna Morgan." Her grip was firm, calloused—not the polished image Harper's printout implied.

"You got time to talk?"

"Fifteen minutes," she said. "Sixteen if you don't ask me to hold a fish for the thumbnail."

"Deal."

Her laugh was brief, then gone. "C'mon."

THE DOCKSIDE CAFÉ

Wide windows were thrown open to the water. Ceiling fans whispered overhead. A chalkboard listed the specials—fried mullet, smoked fish dip, Key lime pie—above a cartoon tarpon that looked like it regretted every life choice.

They took a corner table overlooking the marina. A waitress with forearms like anchor rope brought iced coffees and a basket of hushpuppies. Jenna ignored them; Max pretended to.

"So," he said, flipping open his notebook, "three million followers. That's impressive."

She shrugged. "People like fish."

"It's more than that. You've built a brand. What's the secret?"

Her eyes narrowed, a faint smile tugging at one corner of her mouth. "Why do I feel like you're trying to catch me out?"

"Occupational hazard."

She tapped a finger against the sweating glass. "Truth? I grew up on this. Dad fished. Mom ran the front desk at a marina. My first babysitter was a livewell."

"And the media side?"

"Marketing degree. UCF. Figured out early you could make a living doing what you love if you knew how to sell it. But it's not just selling—it's protecting the thing worth selling."

"Protecting how?"

She hesitated, gaze sliding to the window as a small skiff idled by with no registration numbers, the driver's buff pulled up despite the heat. Her eyes snagged on it, then returned to him.

"You ever see something that feels wrong, but saying it out loud makes you a target?"

"All the time."

A gull cried outside, sharp as a hinge in need of oil. Somewhere, a rope thumped against a cleat like an irregular heartbeat.

"A couple months ago," Jenna said, voice lower now, "out by Dog Island. Night fishing. No stars, no moon. A boat came in— wasn't a fishing boat. Big. Dark. No lights. They dropped crates into the water and a smaller boat picked them up."

"What was in the crates?"

"I don't know. But I've seen that same big boat twice since. Each time, someone in town is just... gone. Not the kind you get press conferences for. The kind you can convince yourself wanted to leave."

"You think it's trafficking."

"I think saying the word gets you noticed by the wrong people."

"Why tell me?"

"Because you're not from here. Because you used to write like you believed in something."

"Used to," he echoed.

"My dad read your Miami pieces. Said you didn't scare easy."

He waited, letting silence do its work.

She shifted. "Look, this isn't a crusade. I sell rods and sun shirts. But I fish at night. I see things I shouldn't. And lately, I feel like I'm being watched."

"By who?"

"If I knew that, I'd stop feeling crazy."

The skiff had drifted to the fuel dock but hadn't tied off. The driver's buff still hid his face. No one else seemed to notice—or maybe they'd learned not to look.

"You report any of it?"

"To who? 'Hi, Sheriff, it's me, the fish girl. I saw some crates.' "

"What about video?"

"I have some. Not of the big drop. Just a long lens clip of a handoff last week. It's dark. Looks like nothing unless you know what you're looking at."

"Can I see it?"

"Not here."

A silence settled—less empty than waiting. Max became aware of the clink of ice in other glasses, the smell of fryer oil, the steady churn of the fans.

The man in the Gators cap walked past the window without looking in. He was still texting.

Max's gut told him they were no longer just having lunch.

2

Uneasy Alliance

Jenna Morgan had always been good at wearing masks.

The phone in her hand captured the one her followers knew—the bright smile, sun-warmed cheeks, confident tone. Behind her, turquoise waves sparkled like cut glass in the late-morning sun, the kind of backdrop that made people want to believe in paradise. She leaned into the camera, wind lifting strands of her hair.

"Alright, folks, that's another one tagged and released," she said, shading her eyes. "Remember—if we don't protect our waters, nobody else will."

She signed off with a practiced wave, tapped the screen, and the smile vanished. The mask dropped.

The dock was quieter without her voice—just the slap of water against pilings and the groan of wood under her shifting weight. A gull wheeled overhead, crying sharply before disappearing toward the harbor mouth. Jenna wiped her hands on a faded towel and stared at the horizon. From here, the sea seemed endless, but lately it felt less like freedom and more like invisible walls closing in.

Too many memories lingered under those waves. Too many things she wished she hadn't seen.

She'd grown up with salt on her skin and calluses on her hands, fishing before she could ride a bike. Her father had taught her everything—how to tie a line so it would never slip, how to read the flicker of a tail beneath the surface, how to respect what the ocean gave… and fear what it could take.

The sea gives, but it can take away just as fast, he'd said more than once.

It had taken him.

The boating accident had been her baptism into loss—nineteen years old, lungs burning as she dragged herself from the wreckage, her father's body lost beneath the surface. She'd stayed off the water for years afterward, refusing invitations, selling gear she once loved. But the ocean had a way of pulling people back. At first she returned for therapy, then for work. Filming her outings had been a friend's suggestion—a way to share what she saw without feeling so alone.

What started as a handful of casual posts had exploded. Now she had millions of followers, sponsors, a boat with her name lettered across the hull in gleaming teal.

From the outside, her life looked enviable. Inside, she knew the truth: the Jenna Morgan they adored didn't exist. Not really.

The real Jenna was the one sitting at two a.m. in a dark apartment, replaying the same grainy video until her stomach turned.

In the footage, a cargo ship loomed in the black water, running dark—no lights, no markings—just a hulking shadow on the horizon. Her own whisper trembled behind the mic as she zoomed in on a smaller vessel pulling alongside. Figures moved between them, passing heavy crates. She didn't need to see what was inside to know it wasn't legal.

"Ms. Morgan?"

The voice snapped her out of the memory. She turned to find Max Larkin standing on the dock a few feet away, hands jammed into the pockets of a rumpled blazer. He looked like he'd stepped off the wrong set entirely—scuffed loafers, a day's stubble, dark eyes scanning the marina like nothing here could be trusted.

Jenna crossed her arms. "You shouldn't have followed me."

"You shouldn't have walked out in the middle of a conversation," he countered.

She exhaled, irritation sharpening her tone. Back at the café, she'd let too much slip. Instinct told her to cut him off entirely, but there was something about him—something worn and restless—that made her pause. He wasn't one of her sponsors' polished PR types. He carried a weight in his shoulders she recognized.

"You're not going to drop this, are you?"

"Not a chance," Max said.

Her gaze flicked to the parking lot, scanning for anyone lingering too long. "Not here."

They ended up in her marina office—a converted storage room just big enough for a desk, two chairs, and the smell of old salt and engine oil that never faded. Maps of the Florida coastline covered one wall, dotted with color-coded pins. Photos of her with trophy catches hung beside awards from conservation groups.

Max perched on the edge of her desk, flipping open a battered notebook. "Start from the beginning."

She stayed standing, arms crossed tight. "This doesn't leave this room."

"Scout's honor."

She arched a brow. "Yeah, you don't strike me as the Boy Scout type."

He didn't rise to it—just waited, pen poised.

"It was two months ago," she began. "I was out past Dog Island, fishing late. Sun was down. I saw this cargo ship anchored offshore —no lights, no markings. Illegal."

"What were they doing?"

"At first, nothing. Then a smaller boat pulled up. They started moving crates. Big ones. Took about an hour before both boats left in opposite directions."

"Why didn't you report it?"

Her look could have cut rope. "To who? The Coast Guard? The sheriff? Word travels in a place like this. The wrong person hears I'm talking, I end up at the bottom of the Gulf."

"And you're sure it was drugs?"

"I'm not sure about anything—except it wasn't shrimp or frozen grouper." Her jaw tightened. "And it's not just the boats. People are disappearing. A deckhand I used to hire. A charter captain out of Apalachicola. One of my sponsors' cousins. All gone."

His pen stilled mid-note. "You think it's connected?"

"I know it is." She turned toward the map, eyes tracing the coastline. "I've seen too much to pretend otherwise."

Max closed the notebook, his gaze steady. "Why tell me now?"

"Because I can't take them down alone. And you seem like the kind of guy who doesn't scare easy."

His laugh was short, humorless. "You'd be surprised."

She opened a drawer, pulled out her phone, and brought up the video.

The footage was shaky, the horizon bouncing with the boat's movement. The cargo ship loomed, a darker shadow against the night sky. The smaller boat was clearer—its crew moving deliberately as they shifted the crates.

Max leaned in. "You shot this yourself?"

"Yeah."

"Why not post it?"

She let out a humorless laugh. "Because my sponsors don't pay me to pick fights with cartels. They pay me for bikini shots and fishing tips, not crime scene evidence."

He didn't answer, still studying the frame. "Pause it."

She did. He pointed to a barely visible figure near the smaller boat's stern, holding what looked like a rifle.

"They were expecting trouble," he said.

"Or protecting their investment."

"You said people are disappearing. You think these guys are involved?"

"I think they're tying up loose ends. And I don't want to be one of them."

The air in the office thickened. The hum of the old fridge in the corner seemed suddenly loud. Max rubbed his jaw. This was no small-town human-interest piece anymore.

"We can't go to the cops," Jenna said abruptly.

"Why not?"

"Because I don't know who's clean. This kind of operation doesn't run without someone local looking the other way. Could be the sheriff. Could be the Coast Guard. Could be someone writing my sponsorship checks."

Max grimaced. "So what's the plan?"

She hesitated, tapping a finger on the desk. "I've got more footage. Times, locations, patterns. But it's not enough."

"We need more," he said.

"Which means going out there."

He blinked. "Out… there?"

"Where else? You think they'll just hand over an invoice?"

"This is insane."

"Welcome to my life."

Before either of them could say more, a muffled sound filtered through the door—voices.

Jenna froze, eyes locking with Max's. "Were you followed?"

He shook his head. "Don't think so."

The voices grew clearer—low, deliberate murmurs just outside the thin wall. Jenna's hand slid toward the fishing knife beside her tackle box.

Max moved to the door, listening. He mouthed: *Two of them.*

Her pulse thundered in her ears. Whoever was out there wasn't passing by.

They were listening.

And they knew too much.

3

Whispering Shadows

The newsroom was never truly quiet, but today it felt muted — as if the building itself were holding its breath.

Ed Harper leaned back in his chair, the cracked leather creaking under his weight. A slant of late-morning light cut across his desk, turning coffee rings on his notes into bronze halos. Phones rang somewhere on the far side of the open floor. A printer whirred and clunked. The low hum of the HVAC competed with the steady, monotonous tapping of keyboards.

It was the kind of day when the news cycle offered little to chew on — petty thefts, zoning meetings, a city council vote on recycling fees. Most of the younger reporters were out chasing scraps for the Metro section or, worse, cranking out listicles for the website.

Ed's gaze drifted to the far corner, where the ghost of Max Larkin's former glory seemed to linger like a watermark over the cubicles. Even without him in the room, Max's presence remained — a memory embedded in the walls, a name still spoken too often in whispers.

He sipped his coffee, now lukewarm. The bitterness suited the knot in his chest.

No one had expected much when Ed brought Max back —

and if Ed was honest, even he'd been only half-sure. The newsroom rumor mill had worked overtime, the younger staff tossing around words like *washed-up* and *relic* when they thought he couldn't hear. They hadn't seen Max in his prime. They didn't know.

But Ed did.

He could still picture the man Max had been — relentless, sharp, with an instinct for stories that mattered and a nose for the rot at their center. And though that fire had been buried under years of grief, booze, and regret, Ed knew it was still in there somewhere. The trouble was, Ed also knew how destructive that fire could be when Max stopped caring about the consequences.

His eyes shifted to the framed photograph propped against his lamp — a newsroom group shot from more than a decade ago. There they were: Ed and Max, side by side, ties crooked, sleeves rolled up, grinning like they'd just outwitted the entire state of Florida. Which, in a way, they had.

The third man in that photo was Daniel Reyes — campaign strategist, fixer, with a smile that never reached his eyes. That exposé had been the story of their careers… and the beginning of the end for Max.

Ed could still feel the static in the air from those months — the newsroom buzzing with adrenaline and paranoia in equal measure. Reyes had ties to a web of money-laundering schemes and cartel logistics, and untangling it had been like following a thread through a minefield.

It started small: whispers about a campaign fund with suspicious donors, an unexplained spike in polling numbers. But when Max got his hands on the first bank records, everything sharpened.

Ed had warned him then. *This guy's connected. You don't poke unless you're ready for the bite.*

Max had just smiled that cocky smile and said, *Then let's make it count.*

They had made it count — so much that Reyes's allies began to notice. The first threat was subtle: an unmarked envelope on Ed's desk containing nothing but a photo of his wife leaving her office.

Then came the calls that ended in silence. The tailing cars. The shadowy figure loitering across from Max's apartment.

Ed, ever the pragmatist, argued for handing it off — let the legal desk or the investigative pool take over. Max refused.

The deeper they dug, the darker it got. They uncovered evidence tying Reyes not just to political corruption, but to a string of fentanyl overdoses in South Florida.

That was the nail in the coffin.

The day the story ran, Max's face was everywhere — TV interviews, cable panels, reprints nationwide. It was his crowning achievement.

It was also the day the floor dropped out.

Reyes fled to Mexico before charges could land. The cartel wasn't so easily driven off. Ed still remembered standing in the hospital years later, holding a cheap bouquet, congratulating Max and Emma on the birth of their son. The joy had been pure then, untouched by the ugliness of their work.

And then, almost fourteen years later, the boy was gone — fentanyl overdose. Max had been certain it wasn't coincidence. Ed had never been able to prove otherwise.

Whether the cartel had reached that far or whether grief had warped Max's judgment didn't matter. The loss hollowed him.

Drinking dulled the pain — then dulled everything else: deadlines, instincts, opportunities. Max drifted from job to job, each ending quicker than the last. His name became shorthand for squandered talent.

But Ed had never stopped believing in the man Max could still be — though lately, he wasn't sure if he believed that for Max's sake, or to justify the risks Ed kept taking to pull him back from the brink.

That was why, when the video pinged into his inbox that morning — grainy footage of shadowed boats trading crates under cover of night — Ed had felt both dread and something he hadn't in years: possibility.

Possibility… and déjà vu.

Now, with the newsroom half-empty, Ed turned the feeling over in his mind. He should call Max. Tell him to back off before it spiraled. But trying to stop Max was like trying to stop a hurricane with an umbrella — pointless, and liable to leave you soaked. And part of him feared that Max, untethered and reckless, might actually *want* the spiral this time.

His fingers drummed the desk.

He opened the bottom drawer, pulling out a battered notepad. Faded blue ink in the corner marked a phone number. He hadn't dialed it in years. The man on the other end could open doors — or slam them shut for good.

Ed hesitated. Then, muttering a curse, shoved the pad back. Not yet.

Instead, he drafted a vague request to the Gazette's budget committee — funding for a "special project." Enough to cover Max's expenses, to give him some legal cover if the higher-ups started sniffing around.

As he typed, his mind drifted to another dimly lit office years ago — meeting a "business consultant" whose handshake carried the weight of a warning. That lead had helped them take down a corrupt sheriff running guns and drugs through the Panhandle. It had also left Ed watching his rearview mirror for six months.

History didn't repeat, he thought grimly. It just rhymed. And this rhyme was already starting to sound like a funeral march.

"Mr. Harper? You got a second?"

Ed looked up to see Tasha Greene, one of the Gazette's youngest hires, hovering near his desk. She clutched a legal pad, eyes bright with that mix of fear and eagerness he remembered from his own early days.

"What's up?" he asked.

"I, uh… heard about the project you're putting together. Special investigations?"

"Rumors travel fast."

She hesitated, then leaned in. "If you need someone to help… I'm not scared of late nights."

Her words tugged at him — a reminder of when he and Max had been exactly that fearless, certain they could expose anything and walk away clean.

"Careful," he said, forcing a smile. "That kind of talk gets you assigned to dangerous stuff."

"I can handle it," she said, chin lifting.

He didn't doubt her enthusiasm, but this wasn't a story for rookies. He waved her off gently. "I'll keep you in mind, Greene."

As she walked away, Ed wondered if she'd still be so eager once she knew what Max had stumbled into — and whether she'd still be around if the fallout spread.

By the time the sun slipped behind the downtown skyline, Ed's shoulders ached from tension. He shut down his computer, pulled on his jacket, and stepped into the corridor.

The parking lot was mostly empty. Sodium lights buzzed overhead, painting everything in harsh amber and deep shadow. The air was thick with exhaust and the faint metallic tang of the bay.

Ed unlocked his car, but before he could open the door, his phone rang.

The number was unlisted.

He hesitated, thumb hovering over ignore. But curiosity — and a thread of dread — won.

"Harper," he said.

For a moment, only static. Then a voice — low, smooth, like oil sliding over stone.

"You've been busy, Ed."

A cold shiver traced his spine. "Who is this?"

"You used to be smarter," the voice went on, ignoring the question. "Poking at things that don't concern you. Helping people who should've stayed quiet."

Ed's mouth went dry. "I don't know what you're talking about."

A humorless chuckle. "Sure you don't. Just a friendly reminder — you're not as invisible as you think. Neither is your little team."

The line clicked dead.

Ed stayed still for a moment, the weight of the phone heavy in his hand. Slowly, he scanned the lot. The pools of light from the lampposts were too far apart, leaving thick strips of darkness between the cars. His gaze lingered on each shadow, half-expecting a figure to step out.

Nothing.

Still, the sensation of being watched prickled along the back of his neck.

He got in the car, locking the doors before sliding the key into the ignition. Dashboard lights glowed pale green.

In the rearview mirror, something shifted — just a ripple of shadow where there shouldn't have been one. He blinked, and it was gone.

Ed exhaled through his nose, gripping the wheel until his knuckles whitened.

This wasn't just a story anymore.

It was the first warning shot.

And if history had taught him anything… the next one would be aimed to kill.

4

Unsettled Waters

Max Larkin sat hunched over the desk in his cramped Tallahassee apartment, the only light coming from the glow of his laptop. The blinds were half drawn, letting narrow slats of amber streetlight stripe the peeling walls. Somewhere down the block, a siren wailed and faded, replaced by the hollow thrum of a motorcycle disappearing into the distance.

The video looped again—grainy, low-res footage shot from some half-hidden vantage over dark water. Shadows moved like smudges, barely distinguishable from the ripple of the current. A dock appeared in faint outline: weathered pilings, the brief sweep of a ship's running light. Most people would dismiss it as nothing.

Max wasn't most people.

He tapped the space bar, freezing the frame. One figure stood apart from the others—silhouetted, still, watching. The glow from the running light caught the metallic glint of something in his hands. Too long, too deliberate to be a fishing pole. Not a perfect match, but Max's gut said rifle. And the stance—weight balanced, head turning in disciplined sweeps—screamed military training.

He took a screenshot, the file name defaulting to an ugly string of letters and numbers, and felt his pulse shift. This wasn't some dockside crew hustling dime bags. This was organized. Professional. Dangerous.

Max leaned back, his chair creaking. His right hand drummed the desk before finding the battered ballpoint pen he'd carried for years, clicking it over and over. The familiar itch crawled up his spine—part adrenaline, part stubborn certainty. Pull the right thread, and the whole thing might unravel.

It reminded him of Miami, when the story was everything and he could believe the work mattered enough to risk everything else. Before the shadows under his eyes felt permanent.

Memory slid in, uninvited.

The knock had come after midnight—three sharp blows that vibrated through his bones. A uniformed officer on the other side, the brim of his hat casting a shadow over eyes that wouldn't meet Max's.

"Mr. Larkin?"

Max had known before the words.

Evan had been fourteen. Bright. Sarcastic. Reckless in the way kids are when they still think they're bulletproof. But fentanyl doesn't give second chances. The cop's voice was procedural, but it caught on "overdose" and "bathroom."

The rest of that night was jagged shards—Emma's keening, the morgue's sterile chill, the antiseptic clinging to his clothes. And the guilt, settling in like a permanent houseguest.

In the weeks that followed, he'd buried himself in the only thing he knew—digging. Chasing the origin of the poison. The trail led to the cartels, to rot threaded through the state's arteries. He'd taken it to his editor with names, dates, connections. Too risky, they'd said. Too dangerous.

Emma had begged him to stop. But he couldn't. Not then. Not now.

This blurry video felt like a lit fuse. Maybe the last chance to make right the story that had been strangled in the cradle. And somewhere deep down—though he wouldn't admit it yet—he knew this trail might lead him far beyond Florida. There were bigger currents beneath the surface, pulling toward places where money and influence met in hidden rooms far from any shoreline.

He closed the laptop and stared at the slow-turning ceiling fan. He could almost hear Evan's voice—half amused, half warning—telling him he was about to get in over his head again.

Max scrolled through his contacts until he found a number he hadn't dialed in years: Hector Valdez.

Hector had been a necessary evil in Miami—a fixer who could put you in the same room as a cartel lieutenant or a dirty cop and make it look like chance. Not a friend, but an understanding: you don't ask too many questions, and you only call when you really need to.

He tapped the number. The ringtone dragged before a gravelly voice answered.

"Yeah?"

"It's Larkin."

A pause, then a low chuckle. "Thought you were dead, amigo."

"Not yet. I need a favor."

"Of course you do." The sigh on the other end was half amusement, half warning. "What kind of favor?"

"I'm looking into a shipment. Came through the coast two nights ago. Fentanyl, I think. I need names. Connections."

Silence, then, "You've got some nerve calling me with that."

"Do you know anything or not?"

"I might. But this isn't Miami, Larkin. The players here? Different. Smarter. You don't want to mess with these people."

"Just tell me what you know."

A breath. "Meet me tomorrow, nine a.m. Monroe Street Diner. Don't be late."

The line went dead.

Sleep never came. Max sat by the window, blinds tilted just enough to watch the street. Tallahassee nights had a slower rhythm than Miami, but no one should mistake that for safety.

At 2:14 a.m., a dark sedan eased down the block, headlights dimmed. It rolled past once, twice. The third time, it stopped at the corner. A silhouette in the driver's seat leaned forward, scanning. Then, slow as it came, the car drifted away.

He told himself it could be nothing. His chest said otherwise.

Morning brought no clarity. On the walk to Monroe Street, a breeze carried diesel and rain. Halfway there, the same sedan idled at a hydrant, engine running. No plates on the front bumper.

A man in a ball cap emerged from the diner's alley, sweeping the street with his eyes before vanishing into the pedestrian flow.

Inside, the diner's air was thick with frying bacon and burnt coffee. Max slid into a corner booth with his back to the wall, watching the entrance and the street.

Hector arrived on time, leather jacket creaking, eyes doing their own sweep before he sat.

"You look like hell," Hector said.

"Nice to see you too."

"No, seriously—what are you doing here?"

"I told you. Shipment. Names."

"You were right. Came in two nights ago. Same dock they've used for months. But something's changed. Heat's on. People twitchy."

"Who's running it?"

"El Cazador."

The name landed like a stone in Max's gut. The Hunter. No photos, no confirmed sightings—just wreckage in his wake.

"What's he doing here?"

"New Gulf pipeline. If he's in play, you're already out of your depth."

There was something in Hector's eyes—quick, guarded. Like he'd said too much already.

"What else?"

"That's it."

"No, it's not."

"I said that's it." His gaze flicked to a white van idling across the street. The driver smoked, face turned away. Hector's jaw worked. "And if you're smart, you'll stop asking."

"What's in the van, Hector?"

"Nothing you want to know about." Hector slid out of the booth, leaving a few bills. "Don't call me again, Larkin. This thing —it's designed to eat people alive."

He was gone before Max could push further.

Max stayed ten more minutes, pretending to scroll his phone while watching the van. Eventually it pulled away, turning down a side street.

He didn't know if Hector's warning was for him or for himself. Either way, it told Max one thing: he'd only scraped the surface. And whatever was underneath hated daylight.

Somewhere, in the quiet part of his mind, the thought returned —if this went far enough, it might take him halfway across the world. Maybe even to the kind of places where a man like El Cazador shook hands with men in tailored suits, where decisions made over a glass of whiskey rippled back to docks like the one in the video.

He tossed back the rest of his cold coffee, left cash on the table, and stepped into the pale morning sun. The air carried a faint metallic tang he'd learned to trust over the years—proof the story was real, and it was already looking back at him.

5

Dangerous Currents

The villa didn't just sit on the Yucatán coast; it clenched the cliff like a fist. White stone walls rose out of the limestone, their surfaces sun-bitten and restless with heat shimmer, the ironwork balconies casting filigreed shadows on the courtyard below. Beyond the wall and the razorwire line of bougainvillea, the Gulf spread in a blind dazzle, the surface varnished in late-afternoon gold. Behind the house, the jungle pressed close with an animal insistence—leaf-sighs, sudden thrashes, a chorus of insects drilling the hour into the air.

Miguel Ortega—El Cazador to men who spoke his name under breath—stood on the second-floor balcony and let his eyes rest on the water. He had swapped whiskey for mineral water this after-noon; the glass sweated against his palm. When decisions multi-plied, alcohol narrowed vision. He needed the opposite now: angles, edges, all variables in play.

Down in the courtyard, a bubble drifted upward like a stray moon and popped against the balcony rail. Below, six-year-old Gabriela squealed, the sound clear as a bell, and pinwheeled after the next shimmering orb. Her yellow dress flashed in the sun, sandals slapping terracotta, hair a night-black pennant. The nanny dampened a cloth at the fountain and held it ready; in this heat, joy beaded as quickly as sweat.

"Una más," the nanny said, smiling, and lifted the wand again. A stream of iridescent spheres floated into the light; the smallest burst in Gabriela's face and she laughed harder, startled and delighted.

Miguel took that laugh into him, the brief anesthetic of it. He knew what the world was—had made a private pact with the worst of it—and the sound struck him anyway, tender and unarmored. He allowed himself the indulgence of a thought: let her remain like this, reckless only with bubbles, certain of the fortress around her.

Sofia appeared beneath the archway's shadow, carrying a lacquered tray with glasses of tea that sweated profusely, ice chiming. She wore cream linen that caught the light like silk, her dark hair pulled back loosely. She set the tray down with a precise clink. Even the way she placed a glass—straightening it so condensation rings aligned with the tile's geometry—told a story: order imposed on heat and chance.

"You'll spoil her," she said, without heat.

"A father must be good at something," he answered, and looked down again as Gabriela cupped a bubble with both hands and gasped when it held, perfectly spherical for a beat, a fragile world that chose not to break.

"And Alejandro?" Sofia asked. "What must a father be for a son?"

The reflexive answer arrived already sharpened. "Exact."

Sofia lifted a brow, neither conceding nor challenging. She moved like someone who had learned a long time ago which questions were worth spending and which belonged to the silence between them.

From deeper in the villa came the comfort-sounds of ritual: knives on wooden boards, oil snapping in a pan, voices overlapping in kitchen-Spanish. The air filled with sofrito's low-simmer perfume —onion, pepper, garlic—and the lemony clean of freshly mopped tile. The brass dinner bell clanged twice. The nanny wiped Gabriela's hands. Miguel descended the stairs, letting his palm ride the cool, polished banister, and stepped into a room staged for normalcy.

The dining hall was long and old, its oak table soft with years of oil and conversation. Candles fought the remaining light and lost; their flickers were aesthetic more than functional. The walls were hung with paintings Sofia's mother loved and Miguel endured—sweeping coastal vistas, saintly faces with the flat gold leaf of devotion. A single ceiling fan drew a tired oval in the air.

Alejandro arrived from the east study precisely on time, posture like a sword, the tutor lingering in the doorway two steps back—respectful distance, concealed appraisal. The boy had Miguel's cheekbones and his grandfather's eyes: black coffee, nothing sweet in them. He took his seat without a word and unfolded his napkin with both hands.

"Papá," he said after the first bite, still looking at his plate, "are you coming to Mérida?"

"No." Miguel carved his chicken breast in clean horizontal slices. "Business here requires me."

Alejandro's fork paused, then made a small metal sound against the plate. "It always does."

That small sound pulled Sofia's gaze sideways—a quick, assessing glance at Miguel. She reached for salt and didn't use it.

"That business keeps you safe," Miguel said, and tried for calm. It came out like a warning.

Alejandro lifted his eyes long enough for Miguel to see the truth in them: the boy was keeping a ledger—hours missed, games not played, promises deferred for "business." He set his fork down, realigned the knife with the table's edge until metal and wood lay flush.

Across the table, Gabriela held up her olive-oiled fingers for inspection. "Mira, Papá! I have shiny hands."

"You have a scientist's hands," Miguel answered, and wiped them with exaggerated care. "Tomorrow," she said, "you play with me before we go."

He put his palm over her small one. "Sí, mi amor. Before you go."

Sofia's mouth softened at one corner, but her hand tightened on the stem of her glass. She looked toward the open double doors, where beyond, the Gulf had gone from molten to hammered silver, the first fingers of dusk combing highlights into the low waves. When she looked back, her face had been set to the expression she wore for guests: gracious neutrality. To Miguel, it read as: I am cataloging everything you are not saying.

When the plates were cleared—Alejandro leaving his knife aligned to the millimeter with the plate's edge; Gabriela leaving a constellation of crumbs—Miguel rose and kissed Sofia's cheek. "I will be in the study," he said.

"Of course," she answered, and the second word carried both faith and fatigue.

The study's door latched with a gentler sound than the lock deserved. Inside, the air was cooler, lemon oil and cigar leaf braided into a steady, masculine perfume. A map wall—custom commissioned, current shipping lanes overlaid in hairline gold—ran from corner to corner. A glass-fronted cabinet of ledgers and leather-bound false spines. The desk, heavy enough to require three men and a dolly to move. And small things: a dish for paperclips, a carved jaguar to worry with a thumb, an old fountain pen with a nib so fine it punished impatience.

Three men stood when he entered. Raul Vargas, square-jawed solidity, tie loosened one inadmissible notch. Behind him on the right, Eliseo—twenty-eight, baby-faced brawler, courage outpacing caution. On the left, a new hire whose name Miguel did not retain by choice. A test: if he mattered, he would earn a name.

"There's trouble on the Florida side," Raul said without preamble. Even that simple sentence sounded measured by him— words weighed, trimmed to fit.

Miguel said nothing. He crossed to the bar cart, lifted the whiskey with two fingertips and considered the bottle in the light until the amber went to orange. He poured a small measure over ice. The first crack from the glass sounded absurdly loud.

"Define trouble," he said, and took a sip. He preferred mineral water when he needed plans; sometimes plans required the small theater of whiskey.

"A reporter," Raul said. "Asking questions about shipments."

Miguel's thumb moved once along the glass, collecting condensation into a cold half-moon. "Name?"

"Not yet. He's been seen with a local woman—Jenna Morgan. Social media. Fishing influencer."

A small pause, then Eliseo, eager: "Tres millones de seguidores. She lives on the water. Kayak, boat. She films everything, patrón. People believe her."

Miguel turned just his head to look at Eliseo. "And you know this why?"

Eliseo colored. "We… monitor trends, señor. New faces near our places."

Miguel set his glass down carefully, as if the desk would punish it for arrogance. A woman who sold fish and sunshine in squares of video had wandered too close to the seam where his network lay stitched into the coast. That wasn't a coincidence; coincidence was a word used by lazy men to excuse not paying attention.

"And Valdez?" Miguel asked.

Raul's mouth tightened into a thinner line. "They approached him yesterday. He says he didn't talk."

"Says," Miguel repeated, as if tasting a note he knew from memory. Valdez sold information like bolts of cloth—always measured, sometimes cut. He stood exactly on the border between necessary and liability. "Bring him in. Tonight."

Raul nodded once, already noting the order in his head with the economy of a man who carried few words and many tasks. He didn't reach for his phone. Not yet. Miguel saw the choice—he'd wait for a beat, preserve the study's air, make the communication elsewhere. In good organizations, even small rituals were part of operational security.

The new man cleared his throat. "Patrón, there's… there's also talk of an informant." He forced the last word past his teeth like a fishbone.

The air changed. Not temperature. Something in the shape of the room—the angles grew more exact.

"From where?" Miguel asked, not moving.

"Not sure. Could be finance. Could be port crews. Someone is feeding the wrong mouths."

"Names?" Miguel said.

Raul glanced once at the new man. "Rumors only. No names."

"Then find truth," Miguel said. "Rumors are a disease. I want facts that can be cauterized." He looked at Eliseo. "You will ride with Raul. Watch how he asks questions without making noise." To Raul: "Change patterns. No regular check-ins. We constrict until we identify the leak. On Florida, double surveillance. I want the reporter and the woman watched from brim to heel. No improvisation. We document before we decide."

Raul inclined his head. Eliseo tried not to look gratified; he failed, but the effort counted. The new man practiced invisibility, which was, for the moment, correct.

They left in sequences that didn't reveal hierarchy to a listening ear in the hall: Raul first, then the unnamed, then Eliseo after a beat, letting the space between footsteps tell nothing.

Miguel remained, the whiskey involuntarily warmer. He felt for the carved jaguar and found the nose worn glossy over years of decisions. He set the glass aside and moved to the map wall. Florida was a series of hairline cuts—a coast like a mouth with too many teeth. His finger traced the Gulf route, the line that linked Veracruz to Tampa Bay's outer mouth and broke into smaller lines like capillaries feeding a limb. Each line was a promise he had made to himself long ago: control or be controlled. He chose control.

He was still at the map when Sofia's reflection bloomed in the glass like a ghost. She didn't knock, but she paused—her version of respect for rooms that were not for her.

"Gabriela is asleep," she said softly. "She wants you to know she prayed for your boats."

"Good," he said, and wished the same prayer could be ordered in cases of whiskey, delivered shrink-wrapped.

"You're sending us to Mérida." It was not a question. She already had the travel cases open on the bed.

"For a few days."

"For safety," she said, and let the word sit next to the map. "Will you come later?"

"When I can."

She looked not at him but at the band of darker water beyond the reef. "Do you remember the first time you brought me here? You told me the sea had moods. You liked the storms."

"Storms tell truths that fair weather conceals," he said.

She turned then, and the candle's guttering light wrote shadows on her face that he loved as much as he hated. "I married a storm," she said. "I knew it. But I do not want it to take our children."

It was the closest she would come to a plea. He stepped forward, took her hand, and pressed it once, a vow without language. He had kept them safe. He would keep them safe. He had built the systems for that purpose alone. The cost was not part of the vow; the cost was a private ledger.

After she left, the house changed. Not quieter—servants still crossed hallways on soft soles, a dog barked twice in the yard and was hushed—but emptier in a way that made the architecture louder. The ceilings declared their height. The tile refused to hold heat. The fan's oval grew a tick more insistent.

He called for the head of household security and gave orders like nails: travel route one to Mérida, not two; vehicles staggered; no phones in the first car, extra radio in the last; change drivers before the toll road; the children's door-to-door handled by men who looked like uncles, not soldiers. He forbid any uniform within sight of the airport. He toggled his routes in Tallahassee, sent a code to freeze a port broker's bank card for an hour—just to see who called whom when the money stalled.

By the time the cars rolled under the arch—Sofia in the second, Gabriela waving until the curve of the drive ate her hand—Miguel had a list of ten names that would have to be asked impolite questions. Hector Valdez was at the top. Not because Miguel believed

Hector had been the leak; because Hector always knew a leak's first name before it knew itself.

Alone now, he let the villa settle. He poured a smaller whiskey, set it down, didn't drink. He opened a drawer and removed a black notebook with elastic band. Inside, a grid of dates and initials; the only place he permitted handwriting with names, and even then, codes nested codes. He wrote two letters in a square and drew a small triangle beside them. The triangle meant: "watch for triangulation—two different sources meeting at a third." He set the notebook under the map with the weight of a marble paperweight shaped like a dolphin—a pointless gift from a politician's wife that made useful ballast.

His phone vibrated once on the desk, the new line. Unlisted. He let it go to the second vibration before answering.

"Ortega."

The voice was male, mid-register, cultivated. The kind of voice corporate fixers liked: low enough to soothe, firm enough to count. "The reporter knows more than you think."

Miguel didn't move. "Names."

"Later," the voice said, with the entitlement of someone too accustomed to controlling cadence. "A courtesy first. Your Florida pattern is visible. If he finds one more seam, it will come apart in his hands."

"If this is courtesy, give me contempt."

A beat. The faint scratch of breath against a mouthpiece. "You will receive a file. Consider it an adjusted weather report."

The line went dead softly, the way a theater curtain falls—not with a thud, but with suggestion.

Miguel stared at the phone without seeing it for a long beat. He pictured a reporter's face without features, only a posture: leaning over a laptop in a dark apartment, a bottle not touched tonight, a pen tapping the edge of a desk. He pictured the woman —Jenna—with a camera's false intimacy stacked like bricks around her. He thought of Tallahassee, a small capital with a big appetite for secrets, and the way politicians there let their eyes go glassy when money moved in front of them. Florida was not just a route; it was muscle and skin for men higher than him who preferred to never think about where skin ended and ocean began.

His encrypted terminal beeped, a sound he had set to mimic a dishwasher finished cycle—a domestic camouflage that made guests —friends or enemies—ignore it reflexively. He crossed to the credenza, lifted the monitor's lid, and keyed a sequence. A folder downloaded without ceremony. He clicked.

Still images appeared: a diner with a sign missing the "o" in "Monroe." A white van with a driver who knew how to turn his face three degrees from any camera's lens but not quite enough today. An older man with a rumpled blazer seated in the corner booth, back to the wall, hands around a coffee mug he didn't drink. Another shot: the street before the diner, the same man walking with his collar turned up against a breeze that carried diesel and the memory of rain.

Miguel leaned forward. Men in his business learned to recognize attributes faster than features: habit, gait, the kind of stillness a man uses when he thinks he can disappear by not moving. This one had a cop's scan without a cop's posture. He had been a man of institutions once. He had recruited his stubbornness into a profession that had no use for it anymore. He had the kind of loss that made risk taste like purpose.

A name arrived into Miguel's mind the way a fish hits a line— sudden decision after a patient wait. He did not say it aloud. He let it sit where raw names sit until they're brined and cured in confirmation.

He closed the folder and opened a different file—internal. The matrix of crews in Florida lit in his mind like a map of capillaries. He drew a finger along two names softly and then tapped a third. "Cruz," he said to the empty room, and raised a brow at his own voice—rare enough in this room to be startling.

Cruz Ruiz was ballast in Tampa, a foreman who had cultivated boredom like a bodyguard. He took no extra, asked for no special, provided nothing except efficiency. Claroscuros—the gray between lights—protected men like Cruz. But even ballast had density limits.

Miguel sent a short message to Raul: *Start with Ruiz. Ask him where boredom ends.*

He turned off the desk lamp and let twilight take the room. The Gulf outside had gone from hammered silver to cold iron. In that seam where the last light left the water, a stingray lifted like a ghost and fell back, a brief geometry of wings. He was not superstitious and refused omens. He watched anyway.

The housekeeper tapped, opened the door an inch, and announced Hector Valdez had arrived at the gate, alone, sweating. Hector always sweat when he had something to hide; the glands betrayed what his voice could mask.

"Bring him to the smaller parlor," Miguel said. "Not the study." Rooms, like glasses, were messages. He had learned early to make every inch of a house speak.

The smaller parlor held lower chairs, upholstered in cotton that seemed to catch on clothes; men sat less easily there, shifted more often, confessed faster. Miguel entered a moment after Hector, let the pause mean what it meant, and closed the door.

Hector's eyes did three quick passes: exits, mirrors, drinks. Each time his gaze caught on Miguel's face, it slid off like a moth against a pane, desperate to reach a flame it could not comprehend.

"You look healthy," Hector lied reflexively.

Miguel sat without answering. He placed a glass of water, not whiskey, on the table between them. "Tell me what you didn't say yesterday."

Hector licked his lip, considered playing dumb, then abandoned it; too costly here. "A reporter asked questions. They used the diner, the one on Monroe. He asked about routes and names. I said nothing." He raised two fingers, a schoolboy's oath and a hustler's reflex.

Miguel let silence live a full ten seconds. When sound returned, it was only the low cut of the ceiling fan. "You said nothing," he repeated, flat.

Hector swallowed. "I—" He stopped, dug in a different pocket of strategy. "The man has... reputation. He was once something. People in Miami say—"

"What do people in Miami say?" Miguel asked mildly, anticipating the answer and measuring the risk of hearing it.

"That he doesn't fall asleep," Hector said, and then hurried: "I mean—he is relentless. But… he is also—broken." The last word dared too much truth into a room that punished it.

Miguel inclined his head a fraction. "Broken men walk farther with less water."

Hector, who did not read poetry, blanched as if he had been given a test for which there was no answer. He shifted. The cotton took his suit fabric and held briefly before releasing with a small whisper. His glands worked. A drop traveled the valley beside his ear.

"Why the diner?" Miguel asked. "Why not a bar, why not a marina? Why a place with windows on the street and terrible coffee?"

Hector stared. He hadn't thought it through. That was, in part, why he survived: he did not think enough to draw bright lines behind him. "He wanted to see the street," he said, reaching belatedly for insight.

"He wanted to be seen seeing," Miguel said, and stood. "You will go home. You will tomorrow go nowhere you usually go. You will let boredom protect you for three days. If the reporter speaks to you again, you will not recognize him."

Hector bobbed his head, stood too quickly, and half bowed. He reached to shake Miguel's hand, then thought better of it. At the door, he turned, opened his mouth to add a detail he had just remembered. Miguel lifted a finger. "If it mattered, you would have remembered sooner."

Hector left with his detail still in his mouth. In cases like this, details had a way of fermenting overnight; the yeast of fear did the work, and in the morning, the truth spilled because the vessel could not contain the pressure.

Miguel walked out to the balcony again. Below, the gardeners had set sprinklers to arc across the hibiscus. In the spray, tiny rainbows formed and died. The jungle had shifted tone: night creatures had taken the mic. A single frog, impossibly loud, declared himself to the darkness.

His phone buzzed once more. A new file, the sender masked beneath a layer he recognized as government-clean, which meant nothing; masks could be bought. He opened it and watched: a grainy loop—Max in his apartment, blinds half-closed, slats of sodium streetlight striping the wall like prison bars. Max's pen tapped the desk, the sound so nearly rhythmic it could be mistaken for calm. It was not calm; it was the metronome of a man calculating how much of his life he would trade for one true answer.

Beneath the video, a single line: "Tallahassee hums when he doesn't sleep."

A flourish? A taunt? Or an ally's breadcrumb? The voice on the earlier call had said "weather report." This was barometer and wind rose.

He sent Raul a short instruction: *Proof of eyes on him. We do not blink. Use women in the market, not men in cars. He sees cars.*

He pocketed the phone and, without quite meaning to, thought of Sofia's question at dinner: what must a father be for a son? The boy was sixteen. He smelled power like other boys smelled smoke. He would reach. That was math. The thing Miguel refused to do was let some reporter's need for absolution splash the boy with the acid of consequence.

He slept three hours. In that time, he dreamed nothing—his mind had no patience for stories when it needed schedules.

Before dawn, the villa's kitchen lit quietly and the espresso machine hissed its small dragon-breath. The head of security returned from delivering the family to Mérida. "Sin problemas," the man said, and reported each segment of the drive from memory, fewer adjectives than numbers. Good. Numbers were proof; adjectives were excuses.

At six, Miguel called Tallahassee. Not a lieutenant—an old lawyer who wore respectability like a saint wore wounds: visible, useful, always earning him the right kind of pity. "The corner you own near Monroe," Miguel said without hello. "Do we still own it?"

"We represent a holding company that—"

"Answer the question," Miguel said, and the man, who believed in clean lines, obeyed. "Yes. We do."

"Then put two permits on two desks today that are not supposed to receive permits today," Miguel said. "I want to know who picks them up first."

The man hesitated for a fifth of a second. Not fear. Calculation. "They will be ready within the hour."

"Good," Miguel said. "And start two rumors that name the wrong man as right. Let's see who repeats them back to us."

By eight, he had answers: a city staffer whose brother liked cards; a port official with a new watch; a rumor that had been designed to travel uphill had instead traveled sideways—faster, more dangerous. Sideways rumors spread like oil slicks; they suffocated more fish.

At nine, the housekeeper knocked—a sound like fingertips on a lacquered box. "Señor Valdez calls from his house," she said. "He says he has remembered a detail."

"Of course he has," Miguel said. He let the call sit for two rings. "Speak," he said, when he answered.

"The reporter," Hector said, breathless with the revelation he had fermented all night, "he asked me nothing specific about the docks. He asked if I knew a woman named *Sofia*—No, not your Sofia—Sofia someone—he didn't know the last name—he said a Sofia had money moving through boats that never touch water. He said there was a code in the marina invoices."

Miguel kept his voice the same temperature as the glass in his hand. "And what did you say?"

"I said I never heard that name. I swear."

Miguel ended the call and did not let his body show the small shock that line had delivered. Not the name—Sofia was a continent of a name—but the phrasing: "boats that never touch water." That was not a phrase a normal reporter used. That was a phrase a man used when he had seen one layer beneath form, when he had noticed that companies called *Marina* did not move boats but invoices, and those invoices moved cargo that was not counted in the weight of boats but in the weight of signatures.

He set down the glass and looked at his hands. Calm. Clean. He stood and went again to the map, but didn't look at Florida this time. He looked at the Yucatán coast, then at Veracruz, then at two points that did not appear because they were not on any shipping lanes—airfields that wore cattle ranches the way a thief wore a borrowed uniform. Then he looked back at Tallahassee and thought of a diner where the "o" in Monroe was out. In absence, sometimes the most information lived.

His phone buzzed a final time. A message without sender ID. Six words: "The tide turns where rivers lie."

He stared at it until the words became shapes freed from meaning. Then he smiled a little, a bleak, true expression that rarely touched his mouth. He typed one word in reply, knowing it would reach someone who'd understand it carried both invitation and threat:

"Soon."

He placed the phone face down. Outside, the day had climbed from gold to white. Heat pinned everything. The jungle's morning hymn had quieted; even the parrots respected noon. The Gulf pretended to be still.

El Cazador did not hunt storms because he loved their spectacle. He hunted storms because they rearranged the world. If a reporter wanted to rush into the squall, he would welcome him there—not with a bullet in the first hour, but with a choice on the third day that looked like mercy and was not.

The villa breathed. Somewhere, a clock ticked. The house carried family footprints and operational secrets in equal measure, neither touching the other unless he chose.

He reached for the notebook again and drew another small triangle. Then he added a circle around it—an old mark, his own invention. It meant: *There is a second hunter.*

He didn't know yet whether the other hunter stood across the water in a rumpled blazer with a pen that would not stop tapping, or nearer, inside the rooms he owned, wearing a smile and a suit cut in Mérida. He only knew the sign on the water when he saw it: two wakes converging, surface unbroken until they met, and then—only then—the choppy tell that, for a moment, revealed the path both boats had taken.

The phone vibrated, softer this time—a courier alert. A folder at the gate, delivered by a man who had asked the guard the time in bad Yucatec Maya. The guard had been trained to note bad accents more than good passwords.

Miguel went down himself. He took the folder without touching the courier's fingers and opened it before the gate closed. Inside, a single sheet. An invoice. A marina in Tallahassee. A line item: *fuel stabilization compound*. No fuel was stabilized on that invoice; signatures were. He turned the page and found a second sheet. A child's drawing: a blue stick-figure boat with three smiling faces aboard. Crayons had pressed hard enough to leave channels in the paper.

He looked at the drawing a long time. Then he placed it gently back in the folder and walked inside.

The storm was still two days out. You learned that by smell before radar. But even now, the pressure had changed. The skin felt it.

He dialed Raul. "Move the questioning forward," he said. "Valdez second. Ruiz first. And send an old man to the market stalls by the docks in Tallahassee. He will buy tomatoes and ask 'What is the price two weeks from now?' The woman who answers a number and not a sentence is the one who knows. You will follow her to the second place she goes, not the first."

"And the reporter?" Raul asked, steady.

"We give him a line," Miguel said. "Let him think it's the river's course." He hung up and looked once more toward the Gulf, where the slick illusion of stillness held fast. For now.

The Hunter was being hunted.

It only sharpened his teeth.

————————————————

6

Unraveling Threads

————————————————

The glow from her phone screen was the only light in the room—a cold, pale rectangle that painted Jenna Morgan's face in shifting shades of blue and white. She sat cross-legged on the edge of her bed, the comforter bunched at her knees, one hand braced against the mattress to steady the faint tremor in her other.

She scrolled. Comment after comment flickered past—emojis, exclamation points, familiar usernames.

Her latest post—a quick, high-energy video of her tagging and releasing a hundred-pound tarpon—was blowing up. Views climbing. Likes piling on. Followers praising her skill, her passion, her cause. Normally, that rush would carry her. Tonight, it barely skimmed the surface. The dopamine hit didn't land.

She slowed her scrolling, searching for something she couldn't name.

Near the bottom of the feed, a single comment snagged her like a hook catching skin:

Saw a big ship docking near Gray's Reef last night. No name, no lights. You should check it out, Jenna!

Her thumb froze mid-scroll. She read it again. And again. A slow, hard pressure closed around her chest.

The timing was too perfect.

She almost typed a reply—*When? What time?*—but stopped. Anything that made her interest obvious would make it obvious to the wrong people. And the wrong people already had her name in their mouths.

She let the phone's light fade, the screen going black, until only her reflection stared back—wide-eyed, hair in messy waves, lips pressed tight.

It had been days—maybe a week—since she'd first felt it. That crawling, prickling awareness that someone was watching. Not just in public. In her own apartment. Shadows shifting at the edge of her vision. A face lingering in a passing car window. A flicker in her livestream chat that felt aimed, not random.

She'd told herself she was imagining it. But the body knew things before the mind could prove them. Her skin knew. Her gut knew. And deep in her bones, she knew she was being watched.

And she hated it. On the water, she could control the tide, the gear, the boat. On land, she was navigating a storm she couldn't track.

Her thoughts drifted to Max. He'd been cagey since their last diner meet, chasing his own leads. Promising to share when it mattered. She trusted him—mostly. But trust didn't make the air feel any lighter.

By morning, the tension had calcified into a plan. Not a good plan. But a plan.

Her office above the marina was cramped but perfect for streaming—a desk pushed toward a wide window, ring light bathing her face, tripod steady, the postcard view of docked boats behind her. She adjusted the camera, staring at her reflection in the preview screen.

This wasn't going to be her usual post about gear or sustainable fishing. This was bait.

She hit *Go Live*.

"Hey, everyone," she said, forcing warmth into her voice as the chat lit up with greetings and heart emojis. "Coming to you live from the marina, and… yeah, I've got something a little different today."

She leaned closer to the mic.

"I've been thinking about the stuff we don't always talk about out here. Not just the fishing—it's what else moves through our waters. Things you catch out of the corner of your eye. Things that… don't add up."

The comments scrolled faster.

"You guys keep sending me messages about strange ships—no lights, no markings, running quiet at night. I'm not saying it's anything. But maybe it's worth paying attention to."

Replies flooded in:

"Illegal fishing for sure."

"That's cartel stuff."

"I saw one near Bahia Honda last month."

And one that made her pulse jump: *They use Gray's Reef. Always have.*

She kept her smile fixed. "Just something to think about. Stay curious, stay safe, and keep your eyes on the water."

She ended the stream with her usual sign-off. Her hand shook as she closed the laptop.

An hour later, the call came.

"Are you out of your mind?" Max's voice cut like a blade.

"Good morning to you too," she said, leaning back in her chair.

"I saw your stream. You're poking a bear that swallows people whole."

"I'm already on their radar. Might as well use it."

"That's not a strategy. These people don't play by rules."

"Neither do I."

Silence crackled on the line. She pictured him rubbing his forehead, weighing whether to yell or admire her nerve.

"Did you at least get anything?" he asked finally.

"Gray's Reef keeps coming up. Ships at night. No lights. No names."

He swore under his breath. "Perfect. Offshore. Just what we needed."

"You in or not?"

The sun was an ember sinking into the Gulf when she met him at the marina. Her boat was fueled, the bow rocking gently. She stood with arms crossed as he approached, diesel and brine thick in the air.

"You look thrilled," he said, climbing aboard.

"You ready for some real reporting?"

He scanned the slips, eyes narrowing at the lengthening shadows. "Let's just go."

They reached Gray's Reef under a moonless sky. The air tasted metallic, the water flat and black beneath them.

Jenna throttled down until the engine was a murmur. The only sound was the slap of small waves.

Max raised binoculars. "Nothing."

"Patience, city boy."

Minutes dragged. Somewhere in the distance, a faint bass thump rolled across the water—too steady for waves, too deep for nature.

"Wait," Max said. "One o'clock."

She turned. A pinpoint of light winked in the dark. Blinked twice. Pause. Blinked again. Not navigation lights—a signal.

"That's not normal," she whispered.

He snapped photos. "We should go."

"Not yet."

But the light vanished as quickly as it came.

The ride back was wordless. Every wake felt too loud. Every shadow on the water too deliberate.

Back at the marina, the air was heavy and still. They tied off in silence, boots thudding on the dock.

Halfway to the lot, Jenna froze. "Max."

At the far end, a black car idled. Headlights on. Windows tinted so deep they mirrored the street lamps.

"It's just a car," he said, though the conviction wasn't there.

"Then why hasn't it moved?"

It didn't.

He took her arm. "Let's go."

The headlights tracked them across the lot.

Jenna slid into her seat, keys slipping in her damp palm.
"Get home safe," Max said through his open window.
"You too."
She pulled out, eyes locked on the mirror.
The black car eased from its spot and followed.
The shadows weren't just in her mind anymore.

7

Bound by Secrets

The blinds in Max Larkin's apartment were half-closed, tilted just enough to cut the afternoon glare into razor-thin slats. From his desk chair, he could watch the street below without anyone—hopefully—realizing he was watching.

He'd been at it for almost an hour.

The coffee mug on the counter had gone cold twenty minutes ago, its bitter smell turning stale in the still air. Outside, heat shimmered off the asphalt, distorting the figures of two kids on bikes weaving lazily down the block. Every so often, a car rolled past, tires whispering over the worn pavement.

Max tracked each one until it turned a corner or faded from sight.

The black sedan from last night wasn't there. Not yet.

He rubbed at the knot forming in his temple. The paranoia was creeping in—slow, measured, like a leak in the hull you didn't notice until the water was at your ankles. He'd felt it before, years ago in Miami, when he'd been living out of a hotel under an alias, trying to dodge the fallout from his Pulitzer story. And here it was again, wrapping itself around his ribs.

When he finally tore himself away from the window, it was with the reluctance of a man leaving a guard post. He sat at his desk, leaning over the chaos of open notebooks, printed screenshots, and a portable hard drive. Jenna's video footage was queued on his laptop, paused at the frame showing the faint wink of light near Gray's Reef.

He played it again, sound up.

The gentle slap of waves against her hull. The hiss of wind over the mic. Then—just for an instant—a rhythmic blink in the darkness.

He rewound. Paused. Replayed.

Every time, the light seemed more intentional. Like a signal meant for someone who knew exactly what it meant.

Beneath the video window, a list of his scribbled notes crawled across the page:

Gray's Reef – proximity to lanes → ideal drop point?

Rumors: El Cazador active again

Black car → surveillance or warning?

Unconfirmed local chatter: "silent ships"

The pieces didn't fit yet. But he knew the shape they were taking. He'd seen it before—when cartel operations hid in plain sight, moving contraband under the guise of legitimate shipping. The fronts were always clean enough for plausible deniability. The rot was underneath.

A name from his past floated to the surface: Jack Salazar.

Salazar had been his blunt instrument back in Miami, a former narcotics detective turned private investigator who operated in the gray space between law and criminality. Jack had a talent for sniffing out cartel routes no one else could find, but he'd vanished years ago after a case went bad.

If anyone could give Max clarity on El Cazador and Gray's Reef, it was Jack. If Jack was even still alive.

⬜

TRACKING him down took the better part of the day. No social media, no office listing. The Miami *Chronicle* archives had old mentions but nothing current. Finally, an ex-colleague from the paper gave him a number—no guarantee it worked—and a warning: *If he answers, he's doing you a favor. Don't waste it.*

The number rang three times.

"Yeah?" The voice was gravel and nicotine.

"Jack? It's Max Larkin."

A pause. Long enough for Max to picture the man weighing the sound of his name.

"Larkin," Jack said finally, suspicion woven into every syllable. "Didn't think I'd ever hear from you again."

"Desperate times," Max said, leaning back in his chair. "I need your help."

"You always did." A faint exhale, maybe a laugh. "What's it about?"

"Cartels," Max said, his voice dropping. "Fentanyl moving through the Gulf. I think El Cazador's in play."

The silence that followed wasn't empty—it was heavy, deliberate.

"Jesus, Larkin. You don't pick small fights, do you?"

"Never have."

Jack let the quiet stretch another beat before answering. "Meet me tomorrow. Gas station off Highway 98 near Carrabelle. Ten a.m. I'll take you from there."

"Why not give me the address?"

Jack's chuckle was low and humorless. "Because I like breathing. And because I don't put my hideout on GPS."

***

MAX DIDN'T SLEEP WELL. The night was full of false alarms—headlights flickering through the blinds, footsteps in the hall, the faint thump of music from a car idling outside at 3 a.m. Every noise scraped against his nerves.

By dawn, the sky was the washed-out gray of pre-sunrise. He packed his bag: notebook, audio recorder, extra phone battery, the camera Jenna had used on the boat. He left his apartment without looking back, though his eyes stayed busy in the mirrors all the way out of the city.

The road east was slick with dew. Patches of fog clung to low ground, curling around the base of pine trees and obscuring the horizon. Every car he passed felt like a potential tail; every stoplight was an opportunity for someone to pull in behind him. Twice, he took a random turn just to see if anyone followed.

Jenna texted him twice:

Any updates?

You're going dark on me, Max.

He thumbed back a vague reply—*Following a lead. Will circle back.*—and put the phone face-down on the passenger seat.

The gas station was the kind of place that looked like it hadn't been renovated since the '80s—faded Coke sign in the window, air pump leaning at a drunken angle, the smell of motor oil and fried chicken mingling under the morning heat.

Jack was leaning against a battered pickup, cigarette between his fingers, the rising sun throwing deep lines across his weathered face. His hair, once jet black, was now streaked with steel gray, and his eyes had the wary squint of a man who lived by scanning his surroundings first and speaking second.

"Larkin," he said, flicking the cigarette to the cracked pavement. "You look like shit."

"Thanks. You look… rustic."

Jack's grin flashed white. "Follow me."

They drove thirty minutes on a narrowing road that gave way to dirt, the canopy overhead blotting out most of the light. The forest smelled of pine sap and damp earth, the hum of insects constant.

The cabin appeared like it had grown out of the trees—small, weathered, the wood silvered by years of sun and rain. A rusting satellite dish clung stubbornly to the roof, and two solar panels leaned at precarious angles against one wall.

Inside, the air was cool and faintly musty, tinged with the smell of gun oil and old paper. Maps covered one wall, each stabbed with pins and laced with string that connected towns, ports, and unnamed offshore coordinates. Case files were stacked in precarious towers on every flat surface, their edges curled with age.

"This is where the magic happens," Jack said, tossing his truck keys onto a table scarred by decades of use.

Max's gaze swept the room. His eyes kept returning to the wall map. Pins clustered along the Gulf Coast like a rash—Tampa, Mobile, Galveston—and a single red one stuck near Gray's Reef.

"You've been busy," Max said.

"Retirement's boring," Jack replied, handing him a cold beer from a miniature fridge. "Tell me what you've got."

Max laid it out—Jenna's footage, the whispers of El Cazador, the black sedan, the unlit ships, the rumors tying Gray's Reef to something bigger.

Jack listened without interruption, leaning back in his chair, beer in hand. When Max finished, he exhaled through his nose.

"Gray's Reef," Jack said, almost to himself. "Not much traffic out there. But close enough to shipping lanes to make sense. No port authority presence. Coast Guard can't patrol it 24/7."

"You think it's a drop point?"

"Could be. Cartels love spots like that—isolated, easy to control, no prying eyes unless they're looking for you."

Max leaned forward. "And El Cazador?"

Jack's gaze sharpened. "He's a phantom. Operates out of Mexico, runs fentanyl up the coast like it's a private highway. Never touches the product himself. Never in the same place twice. But if your black car is tied to him?" He shook his head. "You're already on a list you don't want to be on."

Max felt the words settle like lead in his gut. "How do we stop him?"

"You don't," Jack said flatly. "You avoid him. Or you bury yourself so deep he forgets you exist."

"That's not an option."

Jack studied him for a beat, then got up, crossing to a metal filing cabinet in the corner. "I've got some old intel on Gulf routes. Might be out of date, but it's a starting point."

The air in the cabin shifted—barely, but enough to prick Max's skin.

A faint crunch of leaves outside. Slow. Measured.

Jack froze with his hand in the drawer.

"You expecting company?" Max asked quietly.

Jack's answer was a silent shake of the head.

They moved together toward the nearest window. Through the slit in the curtains, Max saw a flash of movement—dark shapes at the edge of the clearing. Then a car idling at the end of the dirt track. Two men standing near the hood.

Both armed.

"Shit," Jack muttered.

Before Max could reply, a pane of glass exploded inward, the report of the shot echoing through the trees. Shards glittered on the floorboards. Max hit the deck, the smell of gunpowder mixing with the sharp tang of pine sap from the shattered window frame.

Jack shoved a shotgun into his hands. "Time to go."

They crawled toward the back door as another bullet ripped through the wall. Outside, the forest was alive with shadows.

And Max knew—just as he had the night of the black sedan— that the hunt was no longer theoretical.

It had found them.

8

Watching the Watchers

The hum of Jenna Morgan's refrigerator felt too loud in the stillness.

She stood barefoot in her narrow kitchen, one hand gripping the chipped edge of the counter as if bracing for bad news. Steam rose from her coffee, curling lazily before vanishing into the air. She should drink it. She should do anything except stand there, pulse ticking in her throat.

The view beyond her window was a washed-out gray. Clouds sagged low over the rooftops, the light as thin as watered milk. On the street below, cars idled too long at the curb. Shadows pooled in the corners between buildings like damp cloth. When she turned her head, she thought she caught a flash from a windshield—quick, deliberate, gone.

Her phone vibrated against the counter. The green notification light blinked like a pulse she couldn't ignore. She unlocked it reluctantly, letting the messages spill in by the hundreds.

Most were harmless: compliments, fishing tips, invitations to livestream. But scattered among them were the ones that made her stop reading.

You okay, Jenna? Something's off.

That last stream felt… different. Are you in trouble?
You look tired. Everything alright?

They didn't know it, but her followers were circling the truth like sharks scenting blood. She was unraveling, and in this game, unraveling was dangerous.

The coffee had already cooled to lukewarm when a sharp knock broke through the quiet.

Jenna checked the peephole. Max Larkin stood there, rain in his hair, duffel bag slung over one shoulder.

"You look like hell," she said, opening the door.

"You should see the other guy." Max stepped in without waiting, the duffel landing on her table with a heavy thud.

"What's this?"

"Jack's files. Or what's left of them."

Her brows knit. "Jack?"

"A guy I worked with a long time ago."

"What happened?"

"We were ambushed. Cabin torn apart. Barely made it out."

She let out a low breath. "Jesus, Max."

"They know we're close." His eyes held hers until she had to look away.

Jenna could retreat, slip back into the curated safety of her online life. But that life already felt like a flat photograph of someone else.

"Alright," she said, straightening. "Let's figure it out."

Another knock rattled the door, harder this time. Max's hand slid toward the duffel without thought.

"It's Jack," he said, already opening it.

The man who stepped in was in his late fifties, leather jacket worn thin at the elbows, boots scuffed, jaw shadowed with stubble. His eyes scanned every corner like he was mapping vulnerabilities.

"Nice place," Jack said, voice gravel-thick. His gaze landed on Jenna. "You must be the social media queen."

She crossed her arms. "And you must be the guy who walks into my home armed without asking."

Jack chuckled, patting the holster on his hip. "Relax, sweetheart. I'm here to keep you breathing."

"Jack," Max warned.

Jack's smirk lingered, but he got to work, spreading the duffel's contents over the table—files, maps, dog-eared notebooks, photographs curling at the edges.

The three of them worked in silence at first, papers shuffling, the occasional floorboard creaking under their weight. Jenna studied Max's posture—leaning forward, elbows braced, eyes flicking quickly between documents. He looked at Jack often, like gauging how much of their past might leak out.

"How do you two know each other?" she asked.

Max gave Jack a look.

"Go ahead, Larkin," Jack said, mock-generous.

"Jack was my main source during the Reyes case in Miami," Max said. "He was narcotics, went private after. Helped me trace cartel money through seafood imports."

"Helped you?" Jack snorted. "I fed you the whole damn story."

"And I wrote it," Max countered.

Jenna tilted her head. "And after it broke?"

Jack's expression cooled. "Cartel wasn't thrilled. Larkin got a Pulitzer. I got a bullet in my car door. Figured disappearing was my best move."

"And now?"

Jack tapped a file with two fingers. "Some fights are worth picking. This one's personal."

For the next two hours, the floor vanished under a scatter of yellowed pages. Jenna crouched beside Max, tracing shipping routes marked in red ink.

"These lines," Max said, pointing to the Gulf Coast map, "aren't random. They're moving product through small boats, splintering shipments so no single hit cripples them."

Her finger stopped on a circle labeled *Gray's Reef.* "That's where we saw the signal."

"Exactly."

She sifted through photos—docks in fog, men hauling crates

before sunrise, the blurred outline of a cargo ship. "This isn't just smuggling. It's a shadow economy."

Max nodded. "And we can't hit them alone."

By the time dusk seeped into the room, Jenna's head felt heavy from hours of bad news. She slumped against the couch. "We take this to law enforcement. Coast Guard. Somebody—"

"You trust them?" Max cut in.

She hesitated. "No. But what choice do we have?"

Jack shook his head. "One wrong contact and it all burns. You need someone clean. Outside the system."

Max didn't argue, which told Jenna he agreed.

They repacked the files. Jenna noticed Max's glances toward the window, his movements slowing.

"What?" she asked.

"Probably nothing."

"Max."

His shoulders eased just slightly. "Feels like eyes on me. Everywhere lately."

"I feel it too," she said softly. "Maybe that means we're close."

"Or over our heads," he murmured.

When they left, she lingered at the door long enough to watch them split in opposite directions. The street looked calm—but it felt posed, like the air itself was pretending.

Inside, the stack of files sat in the center of her table. Proof. But proof wasn't safety.

▭

THE NEXT MORNING, the rain had stopped, leaving the air heavy and the pavement smelling faintly of oil. Max crossed the lot toward his car, running through his plan for the day: secure copies of the files, reach out to an old contact, meet Jenna that night.

Halfway there, he slowed.

A single sheet of paper was tucked beneath his windshield wiper, edges fluttering. He pulled it free—cheap printer paper, damp from the night's rain.

The message was written in thick block letters:

STOP DIGGING OR YOU'LL END UP BURIED.

The ink had blurred at the edges, but the meaning cut sharp.

Max scanned the lot. Empty cars. Closed blinds. No movement.

Then—at the far corner—a figure stood half-hidden in a stairwell's shadow. Watching. Still.

When Max turned fully toward them, the figure stepped back and vanished.

His grip tightened on the note. Somewhere close, close enough to see his reaction, someone was keeping score.

And the game had just changed.

9

At the Water's Edge

The wind off the Gulf of Mexico carried the scent of brine and diesel to the balcony of Miguel "El Cazador" Ortega's villa. Below, the sea churned in restless swells, each wave hammering the jagged rocks with the unerring rhythm of a clock counting down to something inevitable. Even over the whisper of palm fronds, the slap and hiss of water against stone was constant.

Once, that sound had been an anchor — a reminder that empires, like tides, could be mastered if you learned their patterns. Now, it felt like a warning.

He leaned against the wrought-iron railing, the salt air biting at his skin, the late-afternoon heat clinging like a second shirt. Somewhere behind him, muted music drifted from the villa's sound system — an old bolero that should have soothed him. Instead, it grated, the crooning voice stirring thoughts he'd rather keep buried.

Things were slipping.

There were whispers — a reporter digging too deep, an influencer with an audience big enough to matter. The names were new to him, Max Larkin and Jenna Morgan, but the shape of the threat was familiar. Outsiders pressing at the edges of his business, asking questions they had no right to ask.

It wasn't the questions that concerned him. It was the persistence.

And now… rumors of a leak. Someone inside feeding information to the outside. Close enough to know details that could get men killed.

Paranoia in his world wasn't a flaw — it was survival. But once it took root, it spread fast. Trust was the blood of the cartel, and Miguel could feel his own reserves thinning.

He turned from the balcony and stepped inside. The villa's study closed around him with the musk of cigar smoke, oiled wood, and old leather. Dark paneling pressed in, the light from the arched windows already fading to gold with the coming evening.

His inner circle was waiting. Raul Vargas stood at the far window, arms folded, his silhouette sharp against the sinking sun. At the long mahogany table, two lieutenants sat in silence — Enrique Ortega, wiry, shaved head, eyes like flint, and Mateo Cruz, heavier, his resting expression hovering between a sneer and suspicion.

When Miguel entered, all three men straightened. He didn't speak right away. He moved slowly across the tiled floor, each step deliberate, his gaze drifting over them, noting the tension in their shoulders, the flicker of their eyes, the stillness in their hands.

"Sit," he said.

The scrape of chairs broke the silence. Raul left the window and joined the table.

Miguel didn't take his seat immediately. He circled behind them, letting the quiet stretch until it pressed on their nerves. This was how you reminded men where power lived — by forcing them to wait while their own doubt did the work.

"The situation in Florida is deteriorating," he said at last, his voice low, smooth, steady. "A reporter is meeting with contacts, stirring questions. And there is talk of an informant."

He stopped behind Enrique, resting a hand on his shoulder. Not friendly.

"Informants," Miguel said, tightening his grip just enough to be felt, "are cancer. They feed in the dark. If they aren't cut out, they destroy everything they touch."

Enrique's jaw shifted, but his gaze stayed forward.

Miguel released him and moved to the head of the table, finally taking his seat. "Raul. Tell me."

Raul's deep voice carried no tremor, though there was weight in it. "The reporter, Max Larkin, is working with Jack Salazar — a PI who knows our routes. Salazar's been out of sight for years, but now he's back."

Miguel's eyes narrowed. Salazar. A name tied to an old near-miss in Miami — the reason Miguel had once burned a warehouse to keep the law away.

"What about Valdez?" Miguel asked.

Raul's gaze dipped. "Handled this morning. No loose ends."

The words were clean. The image was not. Valdez had been loyal. Until he wasn't.

"And Rivera?"

Enrique spoke. "Diego Rivera's missing check-ins. Asking questions about schedules. Could be nothing, but—"

"But we can't take that chance," Miguel said.

Enrique gave a curt nod.

Miguel's fingers tapped the table, the rhythm echoing the waves outside. "Bring him in. I want to look him in the eye."

Raul didn't lift his head when he asked, "And if he won't talk?"

Miguel's voice sharpened. "Then he doesn't need to breathe."

The air in the room tightened. Even Mateo, rarely silent, said nothing.

They moved through shipments, dock security, and warehouse rotations — every detail examined twice. Miguel asked the same question in different ways, watching for hesitation.

"The reporter has a partner," Raul added finally. "Jenna Morgan. She's been dropping hints online. Not direct, but enough to draw attention."

Miguel's mouth curled. "An influencer," he said, the word bitter. "And she's still breathing because…?"

"She's careful," Raul said. "We're watching. If she slips—"

"She won't slip," Miguel cut him off. "If she's a threat, she vanishes. Quietly."

Raul nodded, though his eyes stayed down.

Miguel ended the meeting with orders that left no room for interpretation. One by one, the men left until only Raul remained.

"You alright?" Raul asked.

Miguel's look killed the question. "I'll be alright when this is over."

From the window, the Gulf bled into molten gold beneath the setting sun. Beautiful. Indifferent.

Miguel found Sofia in the courtyard as dusk cooled the stone walls. Gabriela, their youngest, ran barefoot around the fountain, her laughter spilling into the air. Sofia sat on a bench, the fading light softening her face, though her gaze was distant.

"Sofia," Miguel said.

She looked up. "You look tired."

"I've been thinking."

Her brow furrowed. "About what?"

"It's time you got more involved."

She stilled. "Involved in what?"

"My work."

Her eyes hardened. "You never wanted that before."

"I didn't. But things change. There are risks now. I need you where I can see you — and I need to know you can be relied on."

Her hands tightened in her lap. "And what exactly do you want me to do?"

He pulled an envelope from his pocket, placing it in her hands. "Meeting tomorrow. Distributor. You'll watch, listen, and remind them the family is united."

"And if they ask questions?"

"You'll have answers."

Gabriela bounded over, tugging his sleeve. "Papá, play!"

Miguel brushed Sofia's hand as he rose. "Go inside. I'll join you soon."

Sofia watched him chase their daughter, her laughter echoing against the darker thoughts settling in her chest.

Hours later, the villa was silent. Gabriela was asleep. Miguel was in his study.

Sofia sat at her vanity, the envelope untouched before her. The mirror reflected a face pale and tense. Her hand trembled as she reached for her phone.

She dialed a number she had sworn never to use again.

When the line picked up, she didn't hesitate. "It's Sofia."

A low voice answered. "I told you never to call."

"I didn't have a choice. He's pulling me in. I need to know what you have on him."

A pause. "Enough. But if you're calling me, you're choosing a side."

She swallowed. "I'm ready."

The silence was heavy.

"Then you know what to do," the voice said.

She ended the call. Her reflection stared back at her — fear in her eyes, yes, but something else now. Defiance.

10

Closing the Net

The road bled into the darkness like a ribbon unraveling into nothing. Ed Harper kept his hands steady on the wheel, though the fine tremor in his fingers betrayed the effort it took. The Florida night pressed close, heavy with the smell of brine and diesel drifting inland from the Gulf. With the windows cracked, every chorus of crickets rose like static through the damp air, every rustle in the palm fronds felt amplified—conspiratorial.

He told himself not to think about the past. Not the deals. Not the people he'd burned through in the name of a story. Not the night in Miami when Cruz's shadow had crossed his path and he'd made a choice that still haunted him. Tonight had to be about control—his control.

Still, the memories clung, salt on skin.

The meeting was a gamble. Reckless. The kind of move he would have chased without hesitation twenty years ago, when his name carried weight in every newsroom from Tampa to D.C. Now, it was a faint echo, recognized only in circles where ghosts were currency.

His contact in Miami had owed him—a debt born of a buried story years back. It had taken three phone calls, a lot of silence, and a promise Ed wasn't sure he could keep to arrange this. The cartel didn't trust outsiders. They especially didn't trust washed-up reporters who had once made a living exposing them.

But Ed wasn't just any outsider. He was betting his history with Cruz would buy him at least five minutes before someone decided to put a bullet in his skull.

The GPS blinked its final turn. The asphalt thinned into packed dirt lined with mangroves. The moon was a faint smudge behind low clouds, just enough light to sketch the warped silhouette of the old boathouse at the water's edge.

He killed the headlights before pulling into the clearing. His car rolled to a stop at the edge of the lot, engine rumbling low before he cut it. Silence hit like a slap—no hum, just the hollow thud of his heartbeat.

Two black SUVs were already there, parked at deliberate angles —one facing the road, the other aimed toward the boathouse, eliminating blind spots. Their paint drank in the moonlight, windows opaque as obsidian.

Ed's pulse jumped. He reached for the briefcase on the passenger seat, feeling the weight inside—evidence, leverage, insurance if the play went exactly right.

The gravel shifted under his shoes as he stepped out. He walked toward the boathouse, each step measured, breathing slow but deliberate. The rhythm of meetings like this never changed: enter calm, stay calm, never show fear.

A shape detached from the shadows near the door. The man moved with the quiet weight of someone used to closing distance without being noticed. His leather jacket caught a dull glint from the single light above the door. A baseball cap shaded most of his face, but Ed didn't need to see the eyes.

"Harper," the man said, voice like gravel dragged across metal.

"Cruz." Ed kept his tone even, as if the years between them had folded away in an instant.

Cruz didn't smile. He turned—a silent order to follow.

Inside, the boathouse smelled of oil, mildew, and the faint ghost of fish long gone. Damp air beaded on skin, and the wooden planks underfoot groaned with every step. A single bulb hung from the rafters, its yellow light pooling in the center and leaving the corners in shadow.

Two men stood near the back wall, each with one hand resting where the bulge of a pistol pressed against a jacket seam. They didn't look at Ed directly, but he felt their eyes.

Cruz took the center table without ceremony. Broader now, heavier across the shoulders, but his aura hadn't dulled—the coiled, patient violence of a man who never rushed to pull the trigger but never hesitated when the time came. His hands bore scars that told stories no one lived long enough to repeat.

"Five minutes," Cruz said.

Ed set the briefcase down, flicked the clasps, and pulled out a photograph. A boy stared back—maybe fourteen—with hollow eyes and the face of any high school freshman, or any overdose statistic.

"This is Evan Larkin," Ed said, sliding it forward. "Max Larkin's son. Fentanyl. Ten years ago."

Cruz didn't glance at it. "And?"

"And he's one of thousands," Ed replied evenly. "Your thousands."

One of the men by the wall smirked. Cruz didn't.

"I'm not here to lecture you," Ed continued. "I know you don't care about the bodies. But you care about heat. Max isn't stopping. Neither is Jenna Morgan. And if they get what they're after, you're going to have more than me knocking on your door."

Cruz tilted his head. "You think we're scared of a reporter and a woman with a camera phone?"

"I think you should be."

Ed unfolded a map, edges worn soft. Red circles marked Gulf Coast sites—Port Aransas, Gulf Shores, Cedar Key. Beside each: coordinates, dates.

"This is part of what Max has," Ed said. "Routes. Drop points. Cargo manifests. And this—" he set a small black device beside it "—links to a secure server. One button, every major outlet in the country gets copies."

Cruz's eyes flicked to the device, then back.

"You haven't changed much," he said. "Still think you're smarter than the room."

"Maybe. But I'm still alive. That should count for something."

The silence thickened. Cruz's men shifted—one cracked his knuckles, the other adjusted his stance.

Then Ed saw it: a polished brass token, no bigger than a quarter, half-hidden under a file folder by Cruz's elbow. It bore a merchant fleet crest from Valparaíso, Chile—a shipping line Ed had seen once in a port investigation, a line the cartel had never been linked to. Until now.

He kept his face neutral, but the knowledge landed cold. This wasn't just local. It was international.

Cruz saw the glance but left the token where it was. The faintest trace of amusement flickered in his eyes—*I saw you see it.*

"You came for a deal," Cruz said. "So let's hear it."

"Back off Max and Jenna. Let them finish without interference."

"You're asking me to let them expose us?"

"I'm asking you to weigh the cost if you don't."

The pause was heavier now. Cruz's fingers drummed on the table, slow, deliberate, before he nodded to one of his men. The man stepped forward, set down a folded slip of paper, and retreated.

"This buys them a little time," Cruz said. "Not you. One wrong move, Harper, and you're done."

Ed pocketed the slip, closed the briefcase, and stood.

Outside, the air felt sharper. He reached his car, slid behind the wheel—and saw the note under the wiper.

No allies tonight. Watch your back.

The handwriting was unfamiliar.

As he pulled away, the boathouse's reflection wavered in the rearview. Ed couldn't stop thinking about that brass token.

The net was closing. And its reach was a hell of a lot wider than he'd thought.

11

Unseen Allies

The glow from Jenna Morgan's laptop screen bathed her face in cold light, throwing the rest of her apartment into shadow. Outside, the city hummed with the muffled thrum of distant traffic, the occasional horn cutting through the night air. The faint scent of brewing coffee lingered, sharp and bitter, though she hadn't touched the cup in twenty minutes.

On-screen, the comments section of her latest upload scrolled by in a relentless cascade—a wildfire of speculation, outrage, and half-formed theories.

Her video, *Beneath the Waves: Secrets the Gulf Keeps*, was less an exposé than a carefully constructed riddle. Sunlit shots of turquoise water opened the piece, waves rolling in lazy arcs. Her voiceover wrapped those images in velvet-edged steel—lyrical descriptions of the Gulf's beauty giving way to warnings about the shadows beneath. No names. No hard accusations. Just enough breadcrumbs to draw out the curious... and the informed.

The audience was reacting exactly as she'd hoped.

"This can't be real—someone fact-check this."

"If she's right, this is bigger than anyone's saying."

"Stay safe, Jenna. We're watching out for you."

Belief, doubt—it didn't matter. They were all talking. And in Jenna's line of work, silence was the real danger.

She leaned back, flexing her fingers. The rush of going live with a calculated risk always hit the same way—like a cold wind sliding under her skin. The power of her platform felt heavier now, not like influence, but like a weapon with no safety.

The buzzer to her apartment sounded, sharp enough to slice through her thoughts. She buzzed him in without asking.

Max Larkin stepped inside minutes later, the scent of damp concrete and city air clinging to his jacket. His jaw was tight, eyes scanning the room as if checking whether she'd already crossed a line he couldn't pull her back from.

"Nice to see you, too," she said, not looking up from her laptop.

He dropped a thick manila folder onto her table. The slap of it against the wood was louder than it should have been. "Do you have any idea what you've started?"

Jenna closed her laptop with deliberate calm, the click sounding final. "It's called momentum, Max. We've been shouting into a void for weeks. Now people are listening."

"Yeah, but attention cuts both ways." His voice was low, clipped. "The more noise we make, the faster they come for us."

"Let them." Her tone was iron. "The more public this gets, the harder it'll be to shut us down."

He moved to the window, pulling the curtain back a fraction and scanning the street. "You're betting they'll care enough to keep us alive."

She allowed herself a thin smile. "So far, it's working. Local news has it. A national reporter tweeted my video. Activists are digging through shipping logs for us. We're not alone anymore."

Max's shoulders eased, but only slightly. "Maybe not. But if we burn too hot, too fast, we won't last."

She nodded toward the folder. "Then let's focus. What's this?"

He sat opposite her, pulling out grainy surveillance photos and columns of shipping manifests. "Three weeks ago, a cargo transfer at Gray's Reef matched every pattern we've been tracking—big shipments broken down onto smaller boats, no paper trail. Classic ghost transfer."

Her brow furrowed as she studied the dates. "Still active?"

"I'd bet on it. But we can't prove it. Not yet."

Jenna traced a finger over a map in one of the manifests. "Then we get more eyes. I can put out a call for sightings—boats without lights, dockside activity at odd hours—"

"Not a fan," Max cut in. "You'd be asking civilians to spy on cartel operations. That's not crowdsourcing; that's painting a target on them."

"I'm asking them to notice," she countered. "We need more data points."

His hesitation lasted only a beat before he sighed. "Fine. Keep it vague. No details that lead back to us."

"Deal." She leaned back, her expression softening just enough to break the tension. "See? We can cooperate."

"Don't make a habit of it," he muttered, but a flicker of humor broke through.

That evening, Jenna recorded a new video. This one was quieter, almost hypnotic—footage of gulls wheeling over a glassy horizon, the tide whispering at the shore. She spoke about beauty, about fragility, about the quiet thefts that go unseen. Her call to action was a single line, clear and careful:

If you see something that doesn't belong, don't look away.

The flood began within the hour.

Her inbox pinged steadily—support, skepticism, the occasional crude threat. But one message froze her in place:

I've been watching this happen for years. Boats docking at night, no lights. If you're serious, I can help.

She forwarded it to Max with a single line: *We might have something.*

By morning, they were shoulder to shoulder at her kitchen table, sifting through the flood. Most leads were noise. A few... had teeth.

"This one," she said, tapping the message from the self-described witness.

"Could be bait," Max warned.

"Could be a break."

She typed quickly: *We're listening. What do you know?*

The reply came in minutes.

Attached were maps—not the rough, hand-sketched kind, but high-resolution nautical charts annotated with routes, docking times, and shipping schedules.

Max leaned in, scanning them. "This is gold. If it's real."

"It's real," Jenna said with quiet conviction. She pointed to a dock symbol marked in red. "Look here—this matches a drop point from the Gray's Reef run."

At the bottom of the email was one more line:

From a Friend Inside.

Max sat back, his gaze narrowing. "Inside what?"

Jenna didn't answer. Her mind was already moving, slotting the new data into what they knew—and what they didn't.

Max slid one of the maps closer, his brow furrowing. "Huh."

"What?" she asked.

He tapped a small, circular stamp in the corner of a manifest overlay—faint but visible when the light caught it. "This crest... I've seen it before. Ed had a run-in last week. Said Cruz was holding something with this exact mark—a Valparaíso merchant fleet emblem."

Jenna's pulse quickened. "Chile."

"Which means," Max said slowly, "this isn't just Gulf traffic. It's international."

The air between them seemed to shift, the weight of the revelation settling heavy.

Jenna closed her laptop slowly. "Then we're not just in over our heads." She met his eyes. "We're in someone else's ocean."

Neither of them spoke after that.

12

Echoes of the Past

The newsroom was nearly silent—an after-hours cavern of shadows and stale air. The few overhead fluorescents still buzzing cast a pale, unsteady glow over empty desks. Dust motes drifted in the weak light, spiraling slowly with the hum of the air system.

Max Larkin sat at his desk, his lamp's glow pushing back just enough darkness to reveal the clutter of the last few weeks—maps, half-crumpled surveillance printouts, shipping manifests, and spiral-bound notebooks scribbled with half-formed thoughts in the margins of sleepless nights. Jenna's latest online post was frozen on his laptop: a frame of still water under an overcast sky.

But Max wasn't looking at the screen. His mind was elsewhere—somewhere he couldn't step away from.

Evan's face was there again. Not the cold, drained image from the morgue, but Evan as he'd been alive—leaning over a cereal bowl, hair sticking up in every direction, wearing that frayed-cuff hoodie. His smirk held a teenage challenge, the kind that dared the world to push back.

"You're always chasing stories, Dad," Evan had once said, twirling a spoon between his fingers. "What happens when one catches you?"

Max had laughed then, dismissing it as teenage cheek. Now, in the hollow stillness of the newsroom, the question pressed down like a weight he couldn't shake.

He leaned back, rubbing a hand over his face. The ache in his chest was familiar—dull, immovable. It never left; he'd only learned how to carry it. His fingers went to his wallet, pulling out the small Chilean peso tucked behind his ID. Evan had found it once and asked about it, but Max had sidestepped the truth. Now it was more than a keepsake. It was a breadcrumb—one that could lead directly to the same cartel network bleeding into their investigation.

"You can't stop now," he murmured, pressing the worn edges of the coin between his fingers. Speaking it aloud anchored the thought.

He turned back to the mess of papers, flipping through pages with renewed purpose. Every lead, every timestamp, every route traced on a map—another inch closer to the truth.

Later that morning, the smell of fried bacon and burnt coffee hit him before the diner door had even closed behind him. The bell over the entrance jingled, blending with the low hum of regulars' chatter. His eyes went straight to the corner booth, where Jenna Morgan sat with her laptop open and a half-empty coffee mug at her elbow.

She looked up as he slid into the seat opposite her.

"You look like hell," she said, not unkindly.

"Appreciate the compliment," Max replied, deadpan.

"You sleep at all?"

"Not much. I was… thinking about Evan."

Her expression softened. She closed her laptop and leaned forward. "Want to talk about it?"

Max shook his head. "Not really. He's gone. But he'd want me to finish this."

For a moment, her gaze held his. "Then he'd be proud," she said quietly.

He offered a faint smile, but the grief in his eyes stayed.

They shifted into the work, the table soon disappearing under a scatter of maps and notes. Jenna turned her laptop toward him, pointing at satellite images of coastal routes.

"There's an old warehouse on the east side," she said, tracing a finger along a river inlet. "Technically abandoned, but close to one of the routes we think the cartel's been using. Low profile, easy to watch without being watched."

Max studied the location—rustbelt industrial sprawl, forgotten by most of the city. "You think it's safe?"

"As safe as anything else we've been doing."

"That's not saying much."

"Exactly." Her smirk faded as her tone shifted. "Max, we can't keep meeting in public. Sooner or later someone's going to notice. The warehouse gives us room to work."

He weighed it, then nodded. "Alright. We do it."

▭

THE WAREHOUSE LOOKED EXACTLY as she'd promised—corrugated siding streaked with rust, windows broken out like missing teeth. Inside, the air was cold and metallic, laced with the dry smell of old sawdust. Footsteps echoed too loudly in the cavernous space, bouncing up to skeletal rafters.

They worked without speaking much, clearing a central space and locking the entrances with heavy chains. Max set up a folding table and a pair of dented chairs while Jenna coaxed a portable generator to life, its hum filling the silence.

"This feels like the setup to a spy movie," she said.

"Let's hope it doesn't end like one."

They settled in—Jenna's keys clicking steadily while Max sifted through manifests. His gaze kept drifting to the peso coin resting beside his notebook.

Jenna noticed. "What's with the coin?"

"Long story," Max said. "Let's just say if you follow the right threads, they all pass through Valparaíso."

She frowned, but didn't press.

As dusk sank, the warehouse air grew colder. The rhythm of Jenna's typing broke under the sound of Max pacing.

"This isn't just about the cartel," he said suddenly. "It's about everyone they've touched—Evan, your family, a hundred other names we'll never know. If we can stop even a fraction of this…"

"Then we're doing it for them," Jenna said softly.

A piercing electronic alarm shattered the quiet. Jenna jumped, nearly knocking her laptop to the floor. Max was already at the control panel, killing the noise.

Floodlights blazed to life outside, bleaching the lot in harsh white. Max grabbed a flashlight and moved for the door, Jenna at his shoulder. The beam swept across cracked asphalt, catching the briefest flicker of movement along the fence—a darting shadow, fast and deliberate, gone before they could call out.

They rounded the far wall and froze. Across the corrugated siding, black paint dripped from hastily slashed capitals:

LEAVE THIS ALONE.

Beneath it, barely visible unless you knew to look, was a stenciled circle bisected by a wave—the same mark Max had seen years ago on a shipping container in Valparaíso's port.

"They know we're here," Jenna said, her voice tight.

Max's jaw hardened. "They've known for a while."

He slipped the peso into his palm, the cold metal biting his skin. Whoever had been here tonight hadn't just left a threat—they'd left a signature.

Jenna's eyes searched his. "What is it?"

"Proof," Max said. "And a promise that this just got personal."

He killed the flashlight, letting darkness reclaim the space. They weren't just chasing the truth anymore—the truth was moving toward them.

13

Fractured Loyalties

Miguel "El Cazador" Ortega sat in the grand study of his villa, where the air carried the stale weight of old cigar smoke and secrets too dangerous to speak aloud. The room was cool, but the midday heat pressed against the shuttered windows like an impatient intruder. Shadows clung to the corners, the kind that seemed to deepen the longer you stared at them.

On the desk before him lay a half-empty folder and a single object he kept close—a tarnished Chilean peso, worn smooth on one side. He turned it over in his palm, thumb brushing the faint wave-and-circle engraving, a mark few outside the highest echelon of his organization would recognize. It was a reminder of where his empire had begun—in the port of Valparaíso, on a dock where the first shipment had slipped past customs under his orders.

Back then, the mark had been a promise. Now it felt more like a curse.

The report in front of him was vague in specifics but damning in tone: gaps in communication, delays in shipments, whispers of informants within the ranks. Control—meticulous, unrelenting control—had built his kingdom. Now, hairline fractures were spreading through the foundation, the kind that started small but could topple everything if ignored.

Raul Vargas entered without knocking, his presence carrying the faint tang of diesel and the low hum of trouble. He held a tablet glowing with grainy surveillance footage.

"What is it?" Miguel's voice was low, a predator's growl in the stillness.

Raul set the device on the desk and pressed play. A coastal warehouse appeared on the screen, timestamped two nights ago. Shadows shifted along the edge of the frame—a figure, quick and deliberate, moving in and out of sight before the camera could focus.

"The alarms were tripped," Raul said. "Nothing taken. But someone was there. Watching."

Miguel's jaw tightened. "Do we know who?"

Raul's eyes flicked up. "Not yet. But it's them—the reporter and the woman. Larkin and Morgan. They're getting bolder."

Miguel leaned back, the peso still in his hand, the metal now warm from his grip. Max Larkin… that name had surfaced before in whispers from overseas ports. If Larkin had seen that mark—if he understood its meaning—then the connection to Valparaíso wasn't just history. It was a live wire, one spark away from burning the whole network.

"Double the patrols," Miguel ordered. "No one gets near our operations without us knowing."

Raul didn't move. "There's more."

Miguel's eyes narrowed. "Speak."

"There's talk among the men," Raul said. "Leaks. They think someone inside is feeding them information."

The word was poison, thick in the air. "Who do they suspect?"

"No names yet. But suspicion spreads fast. And once it takes hold…" Raul let the sentence fade, but the implication hung there —suspicion could destroy a man as thoroughly as a bullet.

That night, in a private room beneath one of Miguel's warehouses, the council gathered. The low ceiling pressed the heat down over them, and the hum of the ventilation system couldn't quite disguise the edge in every voice.

Miguel sat at the head of the table, the peso lying beside his glass like a silent witness. Raul stood just behind his shoulder.

"We have a problem," Miguel began, voice steady but cold. "Our enemies are watching. Testing. And there are whispers—of betrayal here, among us."

Eyes darted around the table. One man coughed into his fist; another shifted his chair back a fraction.

"This is not a time for weakness," Miguel continued. "I need to know who I can trust."

Ortega—one of his wiry lieutenants—leaned forward. "You believe there's a mole?"

"I don't believe," Miguel said. "I know. And when I find him, there will be no warning."

The silence after was thicker than the air. Raul broke it with clipped instructions: "Security is tightening across all fronts. Shipments, comms, personnel—nothing moves without clearance."

Miguel ended the meeting with a single nod. "Go. Watch each other."

As the men filed out, Miguel caught the briefest glance between two of them—too quick to read fully, but enough to leave a mark in his mind. Paranoia was a contagion, and he could feel its fever working through him.

Later, Raul found him back in the villa study, the fountain outside sending the sound of falling water into the silence. Through the half-open shutters, Gabriela's laughter floated in, brittle in its innocence.

"You were quiet tonight," Raul said.

Miguel didn't look up from the folder in front of him. "There's nothing to say until I have proof."

"You've been… distracted," Raul pressed.

Miguel's gaze lifted, sharp. "You think I'm losing my edge?"

"No," Raul said quickly. "But you're watching cracks form. One of them is close."

Miguel's silence was answer enough.

Raul leaned forward slightly. "This is about Sofia, isn't it?"

Miguel's grip tightened on the peso. "She's been distant. I told myself it was the strain. But if she's—"

He stopped, the thought curdling in his throat.

Raul slid a folder across the desk. "Something you need to see."

Miguel opened it. Inside—a grainy photograph of Sofia at a seaside café, her head bent close to a man Miguel didn't recognize. The angle was bad, but the man's wrist was visible. A bracelet glinted in the sun—a small medallion stamped with the same wave-and-circle design as the coin in Miguel's hand.

The air between them thickened.

"When?" Miguel asked, voice flat.

"Three days ago. Not one of ours."

Miguel set the coin down beside the photo, the two symbols facing each other like an accusation. If this man wore the mark, then he knew the old routes, the old debts—the same secrets Larkin's investigation had begun to circle.

"She's meeting with someone from Valparaíso," Miguel said quietly, the words tasting of betrayal.

Raul's expression didn't change. "What do you want done?"

Miguel's voice was calm, but the undercurrent was lethal. "Find out everything. If she's part of this leak—"

He closed his hand over the coin. "—she pays the price like anyone else."

But as Raul left, Miguel remained at the desk, the peso pressed so hard into his palm it left a mark in his skin. For the first time, he wondered if the empire he'd built had already begun to slip beyond his control—not because of his enemies, but because the rot had taken hold from within. And if that was true, then the man who had once hunted everyone else might soon find himself the prey.

14

Breaking the Surface

The marina held a kind of stillness that made sound carry farther than it should. A gull's cry from the outer pier echoed against the corrugated walls of the bait shop, and the low groan of a moored fishing trawler vibrated through the planks where Jenna Morgan sat.

Her boots dangled a few inches above the water, the cool morning air curling around her ankles. The sun was climbing, spilling gold across the surface of the harbor, breaking the ripples into scattered mirrors — beautiful, but irrelevant. Her eyes didn't follow the light. They stayed locked on the wavering reflections, as though they might rearrange into answers if she stared long enough.

She wanted to believe she was here for justice — to choke off the cartel's arteries before they pumped more poison into streets she'd never walk but knew too well from the overdose headlines. But that wasn't the whole truth.

The deeper truth was more raw.

Redemption.

For years, she'd been the Jenna Morgan her followers thought they knew — the fearless fishing influencer, smiling in every thumbnail, selling the dream of freedom on the open water. The camera never caught the looks she ignored, the odd comings and goings at private docks, the shadowy boats slipping in under no flag. She'd seen them. She'd just chosen to look away.

Now she couldn't.

The wood beneath her creaked. She turned, catching sight of Max making his way down the dock, the steady rhythm of his boots underscoring his arrival. He carried two paper cups, steam twisting upward, rich with the scent of burnt roast.

"Thanks," she murmured as he handed her one.

"You've been out here a while," he said, lowering himself to sit beside her. His frame blocked some of the wind, though the air still bit against her cheeks.

"Just thinking."

He studied her face. "About what?"

She traced the rim of the cup with a fingertip. "Why I'm doing this. Why I can't just go back to posting gear reviews and conservation hashtags."

A flicker of a smirk crossed his face. "Because you're not that person anymore."

Her eyes narrowed. "What's that supposed to mean?"

"It means you've changed," he said evenly. "And maybe that's a good thing. You're not just entertaining people anymore. You're making them pay attention."

She looked away, the tide tapping softly against the dock pilings. "I guess so."

They left the marina a few minutes later, the coffee warming her hands as they walked to the car. The ride into the city was quiet but not empty — a silence born from keeping thoughts contained.

The café was deliberately forgettable: narrow, dim, and steeped in the smell of over-roasted beans. The whistleblower was already there, tucked into a corner booth where the shadows clung to him.

He was wiry, mid-forties maybe, with thinning hair slicked straight back. His eyes, rimmed in sleepless red, scanned the room in quick bursts. His hands clamped around his cup like it was a lifeline.

"You're late," he said, voice low and rough.

"Traffic," Max replied, sliding into the seat across from him. Jenna sat beside Max, posture loose but eyes sharp.

The man's gaze flicked to her, then back. "You said this would be discreet."

"It is," Jenna said softly, leaning forward just enough to close the distance. "We're here to listen. That's all."

"You don't know what you're up against," he said. "These people... they're not just criminals. They've got protection. They can make you disappear."

"We know the risks," Max said. "But you called us."

The man swallowed. "I've been with South Coast Shipping twenty years. Dockworker to shift manager. About five years ago, things started... changing."

"What kind of changes?" Jenna asked.

"Routes altered without notice. Unmarked shipments. Docks cleared at hours that should be dead quiet. And always the same crew — men I'd never seen before, no paperwork, no IDs."

"Cartel," Max said flatly.

The man's nod was tiny but certain. "They move product through us. Mostly fentanyl. But I've seen weapons. Cash. Anything that fits in a container."

Jenna's stomach tightened. The details matched everything they'd been hearing — but here it was, clean and unvarnished from the inside.

"Why now?" she asked.

He stared into his cup, steam fogging his glasses. "Because I've seen what their drugs do. And I've seen what they do to anyone who talks. I can't keep my head down anymore."

From his bag, he slid a thick folder toward them. His hands shook.

"Shipment schedules," he said. "Six months' worth. Routes, docks, handlers. It's all there."

Max flipped it open. Every page was precise — a breadcrumb trail that could cut the cartel's reach in half if followed.

"This is dangerous to even have," Max said.

"I can't go to the cops," the man said. "Not without ending up in the river."

Jenna met his eyes. "They'll come after you."

"I know. If it stops even one shipment, it's worth it."

Back at the warehouse safe-house, the air carried a faint diesel tang from the repair shop next door. The folder's contents were spread across the steel table under the harsh lamplight.

Max leaned over the schedules, marking routes that intersected with the Valparaíso hub. Jenna placed the brass token on the map, aligning its compass rose with a circled dock number.

"You think it's more than symbolic," Max said.

"It's a key," she replied. "It got me through one door. There are more."

They spotted a shipment set for two nights from now — Dock 34, midnight offload. A perfect blind spot in the port's official rotation.

That night, they watched from the shadowed cab of Max's truck two blocks from the dock. The air was cold enough to make each breath visible. The wind brought the brine of the Pacific and the faint tang of rust.

Under the high floodlights, a small crew moved in silence. No forklifts, no idle chatter. Just the scrape of crates against metal.

Jenna caught the dull glint of brass in one man's hand. Her own token felt suddenly heavy in her pocket.

"They've got them," she whispered.

"Tokens?"

She nodded. "Keys."

They stayed until a black van rolled up, took on two crates, and slipped away into the maze of port streets.

Hours later, back in the warehouse, the photos Max had taken lay in a rough spread. The van's license plate was barely legible.

"We could run it," Jenna said.

"And light ourselves up on every system that matters," Max countered.

"So we wait."

"We watch," he corrected.

It was past midnight when Jenna's laptop flashed an intrusion alert. She dove into the code, her stomach sinking as she uncovered spyware buried deep — logging keystrokes, pulling documents, even activating their mics.

"Max."

He was at her side in seconds. "How long?"

"No idea. But look at this."

A text file hid in the code:

We know who you are. Stop now, or the world will know too.

The token sat on the desk between them, its compass rose catching the glow of the threat.

"They're not just watching," Max said. "They're telling us they're watching."

Jenna met his eyes, fear and resolve burning in equal measure. "Then we move faster."

15

Negotiating Shadows

The newsroom felt like a pressure cooker.

Ed Harper sat hunched at his desk, thumbs pressed into his temples, staring at the sprawling chaos of paper, Post-its, and half-drunk coffee cups scattered in front of him. The overhead fluorescents buzzed like a swarm of gnats. The air smelled faintly of burnt coffee and printer toner, undercut by the stale tang of too many takeout meals eaten at desks. Around him, reporters were locked in their own storms—some hunched over glowing monitors, others pacing with phones pressed to their ears.

It was barely three in the afternoon, but it felt like he'd been in this seat for a week.

From his glass-walled corner office, Ed could see the hub of activity where a cluster of reporters were watching Jenna Morgan's latest upload on a laptop, heads tilted forward in near unison. Her voice carried in fragments—sharp, controlled, laced with the defiance that had been growing since she and Max Larkin stepped into the cartel's shadow.

In another corner, the breaking news team was wrestling with a municipal scandal—just another fire to smother while the bigger blaze burned in the background. Ed had to keep both alive: the daily pulse of the paper and the dangerous investigation that could get two freelancers killed.

A young staffer, barely out of journalism school, approached clutching a printout. Her voice was tentative.

"Mr. Harper, the fentanyl deaths piece—it's ready for review."

Ed didn't look up. "Leave it on my desk."

She obeyed without protest, slipping back into the din.

He rubbed his jaw, scanning the mess in front of him—police reports, coded bank transfers, a timeline of cartel shipping movements. Every thread was fraying faster than he could tie it down. The Valparaíso token from Jenna's footage still gnawed at him—a coin-like marker with the name of the Chilean port, found in a safe house tied to Miguel Ortega. It meant international shipping lanes, foreign partners, maybe even a laundering arm buried so deep it had survived for years without exposure.

And they had barely scratched the surface.

By four, he'd gathered his most trusted investigative staff in the small, soundproof conference room beside his office. The walls were scuffed, the table dented from decades of elbows and coffee mugs. A pot of stale coffee steamed in the corner.

Linda Keating, the veteran, sat at his right—her notebook already open, pen balanced neatly between her fingers. Across from her was Kyle Rourke, the freelancer who could mine social media like a goldfield. Two others, handpicked for their discretion and stubbornness, completed the circle.

Ed leaned forward. "Two priorities: keep Jenna and Max breathing, and keep this story breathing. One dies, so does the other."

Linda's eyes narrowed. "Push too hard, they'll retaliate."

"They already are," Ed said flatly. "Jenna's been tailed twice this week. Max had his apartment tossed. We can't back off, but we can't give them an excuse to shut us down either."

Kyle tapped at his laptop, screen glowing with analytics. "Her channel's engagement has tripled since the Valparaíso token video. If we time a coordinated push—her footage, our reporting, simultaneous drops with a couple of national outlets—they can't swat it all down."

Linda frowned. "Harder to silence us, sure. Not impossible."

"Which is why we stay surgical," Ed said. "No rumor, no filler. Only what we can prove. The cleaner we are, the harder they have to work to smear us."

They mapped out a staggered release—one article per week, each a deeper incision into Ortega's network. The Chilean link would be the third drop, after it was tied to manifests and off-book bank accounts.

For a brief moment, Ed felt something rare: momentum.

The meeting broke, leaving behind the ghost of burnt coffee and the faint aftertaste of urgency.

By the time the newsroom lights dimmed for the night crew, Ed was stacking notes into folders, convincing himself he'd call it an early evening. His phone buzzed.

Unknown number.

Meet me at the usual place. I have information you'll want.

His stomach tightened. The "usual place" was a code he hadn't heard in years—a dive bar on the city's edge where regulars came to disappear.

He pocketed his phone and coat without telling anyone.

THE BAR'S sign flickered in the dark, its neon letters half-burnt out. Inside, the air was thick with stale beer and decades of cigarette smoke ground into the wood. A jukebox hummed out an old blues track no one was listening to.

In a shadowed booth sat Julio Alvarez. His hat brim cut his face in half, but Ed would've recognized that stillness anywhere. Once a cartel enforcer, later a ghost—Julio had vanished from the game years ago, leaving behind more questions than bodies.

Ed slid into the booth opposite him. "Julio."

A thin smile curved the man's mouth. "Harper. Didn't think you'd show."

"Wasn't sure I should."

Julio nodded to the bartender, who wordlessly set down two glasses of something amber.

"I don't deal in pleasantries," Ed said. "What do you have?"

Julio reached into his jacket and slid a small, weathered envelope across the table. "Enough to crack Ortega's spine in half."

Ed didn't touch it. "What's the cost?"

"No money." Julio's eyes gleamed. "I want a story. My story. The truth—that I walked away, that I've been undermining him ever since. I want the world to know I'm not the monster they think I am."

"That paints a target on your back the size of this city."

Julio shrugged. "Target's already there. This way, maybe I choose how they aim."

Ed's fingers itched for the envelope, but every instinct screamed this was another web—one that could tangle him beyond escape.

"Think about it," Julio said, leaning back. "But don't think too long. The shadows are moving faster than you are."

Ed slid the envelope into his jacket but didn't stand. "Why now? Why stick your neck out?"

Julio's smile faded. "Because your name's coming up in circles you don't want to be in. Ortega doesn't just see you as a journalist. He remembers."

Ed's brow furrowed. "Remembers what?"

"You brushed him once. Back when you thought you were chasing another story. Courthouse steps, 2003. He hasn't forgotten."

The memory flickered—a long-ago corruption case, an unremarkable man in a suit just beyond the courthouse doors. A face Ed hadn't bothered to connect to a name.

Julio's voice dropped. "The thing about shadows, Harper? They keep your shape long after you think you've left the light."

Ed left the bar with the envelope feeling like a brick in his coat. The night air smelled of salt and exhaust. Street lamps cast fractured pools of light.

Halfway home, his mirrors caught a glint—a car hanging two lengths back. No headlights. He turned twice, once down a side street, once back toward the main road. By the third turn, the car was gone. Or had simply melted into the dark.

At home, he locked the door and went straight to his desk. His hands weren't steady when he opened the envelope.

Inside—documents, photographs, a USB drive. Bank transfers, manifests, shipping routes. And in the middle, a Chilean customs document stamped with the Valparaíso seal—the same emblem etched on the token from Jenna's footage. Ortega's network wasn't just local. It was continental.

He sifted until one photo slid loose. Old, yellowing. A younger Ed Harper on the courthouse steps after his first major exposé. And in the blurred background—Miguel Ortega, watching.

Ed's pulse thudded in his ears. Julio's warning wasn't paranoia. It was history.

And now it was coming back.

16

Inner Sanctum

Max Larkin sat on the edge of his bed, elbows on his knees, the battered notebook resting in his palms like it might burn through the skin. The cheap lamp on the nightstand threw a cone of light across the pages, catching the jagged scrawl he'd been living inside for days—names, dates, coordinates, fragments of overheard conversations, snippets of text threads, hurried theories scribbled in margins.

He turned to the page where he'd written **Julio Alvarez** in thick block letters, pressing hard enough to tear the paper. The former cartel enforcer's name sat there like a bruise.

Ed hadn't given him much, only a bare-bones version—a cautious understatement that set Max's mind grinding.

"Julio's intel could tip the scales," Ed had said. "But it comes with strings attached."

Strings. There were always strings.

Max rubbed his jaw, staring at the page until the words blurred. His mind kept circling back to one thing: Julio's name, and whether this was another step toward the truth—or toward a cliff edge.

BY THE TIME Max reached the warehouse the next morning, the air was heavy with the promise of rain. The corrugated metal siding groaned in the wind, and inside, the place smelled faintly of dust, stale coffee, and the hum of electronics.

Jenna was already there, hunched over the folding table they'd claimed as their command center. Her laptop glowed in the dim light, casting an icy reflection across her face. She didn't look up when he came in.

"Morning," Max said, setting his bag down with a thud.

"You look like you didn't sleep," she replied, eyes still locked on the screen.

"I didn't," he admitted. "Too much running through my head."

She smirked faintly, but it didn't reach her eyes. "Join the club."

She swiveled the laptop toward him. "Look at this."

Max leaned over her shoulder, catching the sharp, clean scent of her shampoo beneath the warehouse's damp air. The screen was a mess of text: columns of encrypted messages threaded through timestamps and strange symbols.

"These came from the spyware we found on our devices," Jenna said. "It's not just passive surveillance—they've been using our phones and laptops as relay points. We've been part of their network."

Max's stomach tightened. "So, every time we've been talking…"

"…someone else might have been listening," she finished. "But here's the part that matters—there's a pattern in the messages. Dates, times, locations. They're coordinating something big, and it's happening soon."

"How soon?"

"A week," she said. "Maybe less."

The words landed in Max's chest like the tick of a countdown clock.

An hour later, he was leaning against the hood of his car outside, phone pressed to his ear. He hadn't spoken to Sarah Mitchell in years, but she was the only one who could help untangle this.

She picked up on the third ring. "Larkin." Her voice was wary, still sharp as glass. "Didn't think I'd hear from you again."

"Didn't think I'd have to call," Max said.

"You're in trouble, aren't you?"

"Something like that. I need to talk. In person."

She paused. "You sure you want to pull me into your mess?"

"I don't have a choice."

Another beat of silence. "Alright. Same place as before. One hour."

THE DINER HADN'T CHANGED since their last meeting—peeling vinyl booths, fryer grease baked into the walls, the low hum of a neon sign louder than the handful of regulars.

Max slid into a booth near the back, watching the door. Ten minutes later, Sarah walked in.

She'd aged, but not softened. The lines in her face looked carved by storms, not time. Her leather jacket bore the wear of more than one fight, and her gaze swept the room like she could see through every wall.

"You look like hell," she said, sliding into the seat across from him.

"Good to see you too," Max replied.

"What do you need?"

Max opened the notebook to the decrypted messages. "Cartel's moving something big. I need to know what it is, and where it's going."

She studied the page. "Where'd you get this?"

"Complicated," Max said.

"Figures." She tapped a finger along one of the lines. "This code—it's old. They stopped using it years ago. But if I can get into their system, I can track where this leads."

"Can you?"

"Maybe. But if they catch me…" She let the thought hang.

"You know what's at stake."

Her eyes met his. "Yeah. I do."

———

TWO DAYS LATER, Sarah called. "They're accelerating the timeline. Trying to flood the coast with fentanyl before anyone can shut them down. Everything's moving through a central hub—offshore platform, about twenty miles out."

Max's grip on the phone tightened. "Where?"

"Encrypted. I'm close, but it'll take time."

"We don't have time."

"I know," she said. "I'll call when I have it."

That night, rain hammered the warehouse roof in a relentless rhythm. Jenna paced the length of the room, phone in one hand, the Valparaíso token in the other.

She tossed it onto the table when she saw him. "Every lead we've chased loops back to that token."

Max picked it up. The brass was worn smooth in places, but the engraving—a stylized wave curling over a sun—was still sharp. He'd last seen one like it years ago in Valparaíso, chasing a smuggling story that had nearly gotten him killed.

"They used tokens like this to mark shipments," he said slowly. "If it's here, it's not a souvenir—it's a flag."

Jenna's eyes narrowed. "Meaning?"

"Meaning the offshore platform Sarah's tracking might not just be a hub. It could be the end point for a supply line that's been running for years."

———

AT 5:42 a.m. the next morning, his phone buzzed. Sarah's voice came fast.

"I've got it. Coordinates: twenty-two miles southeast of Key Biscayne. But Max—it's locked down tight. Armed patrol boats. Surveillance drones. You won't get near it without a plan."

Max scribbled the numbers into his notebook. "We'll figure it out."

"Be careful. They know someone's been poking around. And Max—your name's coming up in the chatter."

When the call ended, the warehouse was silent except for the low hum of Jenna's laptop. He looked down at the token in his hand, feeling its cold weight. This wasn't just about stopping the cartel anymore. It was about cutting the last thread before it strangled them all.

That evening, Jenna set a small TV on the table, tuned to a local news station. The anchor's voice was calm, but there was a cadence in her delivery that made Max's skin crawl.

"…unusual shipping activity has raised concerns among maritime officials. While no official statement has been released, experts warn of potential increases in smuggling along the southeastern coast…"

Max froze. This wasn't just news—it was a message.

"They know," he said.

Jenna frowned. "What?"

"That broadcast—it's coded. They're telling us they're watching."

Jenna's face paled. "Then what do we do?"

Max's jaw tightened. "We move faster."

He killed the TV, plunging the warehouse into a dim, electric gloom. Outside, a car rolled slowly past, headlights off, rain streaking across the windshield.

Max's hand drifted to the token in his pocket, the cold brass pressing into his palm like a reminder:

The clock wasn't just ticking—

It was almost out.

17

The Exchange

The pier groaned beneath Jenna Morgan's feet, each step pressing into weathered boards steeped in salt, diesel, and the faint sweetness of baitfish drying in the sun. She adjusted her grip on the GoPro, the cool frame biting lightly into her palm. The breeze off the Gulf snapped flags overhead and whipped stray strands of hair across her eyes—playful to anyone else, but to her it felt like static in the air before a storm.

This was supposed to look like any other day at the Gulf Coast Fishing Tournament—a festival of competition, family pride, and the kind of seafood spreads that drew tourists from three states away. And for the laughing families threading the docks, that's exactly what it was. Bright-hulled boats bobbed at their slips, sponsor logos gleaming in the sun. Vendors shouted over one another for customers, pushing fried shrimp and lemon ices. Country music spilled from tinny speakers near the weigh-in station.

But Jenna wasn't here for the fishing.

She was here to step directly into the cartel's line of sight.

The crowd's energy swirled around her, a current she didn't quite trust. She scanned faces—sun-hatted kids darting between coolers, fishermen bent over their gear, couples strolling hand in hand—and reminded herself that almost every set of eyes here was innocent. Almost.

Her pulse ticked hard in her ears. She steadied her breathing like she used to before going live on network television. This wasn't a studio. No reassuring voice in her earpiece. No producer smoothing over her pauses. Out here, she was her own anchor, her own camera operator, her own security detail.

The tiny red record light flared as she pressed the button.

"Live in three, two…" she murmured, lifting the lens to frame the marina behind her.

Her voice came out steady, practiced. "Hey everyone. Welcome back. We're here at the Gulf Coast Fishing Tournament, one of the biggest events of the season. But today, we're not just talking about fishing. We're talking about what's beneath the surface—what's threatening the waters we love and the communities we live in."

The live chat lit up in a blink.

What's she talking about?

Always loved this tournament!

Wait, is this about the drug thing she mentioned before?

She skimmed the feed without breaking stride, sneakers squeaking over damp planks. "Over the past few months, we've been uncovering some unsettling truths about what's happening off our shores—illegal shipments, dangerous substances, and the people willing to risk everything to stop them."

Her gaze kept drifting to the edges of the crowd. A man with a faded ballcap and a heavy duffel. A woman with sunglasses too big for her face, standing stock still while the tide of people flowed around her. Two fishermen leaning in close over a phone.

She panned the GoPro to take in the bright slice of coastal life —cobalt water, white hulls, children in yellow life vests—before bringing the camera back to her. "This isn't just a playground for anglers. These waters are a lifeline for entire communities. But that lifeline is under threat, and it's not just the environment at risk. It's all of us."

The comments scrolled faster now.

She's so brave for doing this.

What's she even talking about?

If this is about drugs, shouldn't the cops be handling it?

"I get it," she said, eyes steady on the lens. "Some of you might not believe me. And that's okay. But I need you to look closer. Ask the questions no one wants to answer. Why are local fishermen struggling when illegal shipments are thriving? Why are our streets flooded with poison while our leaders turn a blind eye?"

The tone in the chat shifted—less mockery, more curiosity.

Jenna moved dock to dock, speaking with a retired fisherman who'd seen his catches vanish, a bait shop owner on the brink of closing, and a little girl who dreamed of becoming a marine biologist. Each voice was another thread in the same net—loss, resilience, and the will to fight for what mattered. She wove their stories into her narrative, the subtext clear enough for the right watchers to hear.

By mid-afternoon, her live viewer count had climbed higher than she'd dared hope. A local news crew appeared, filming her as she spoke. The crowd pressed closer.

And then—something shifted.

It was subtle at first: the drop in conversation as she passed, the stillness under the music. Then came the feeling—eyes on her, steady and deliberate.

She wrapped an interview and turned toward the crowd.

That's when she saw him.

Tall. Broad-shouldered. Black jacket despite the heat. Leaning against a lamppost like he owned the dock. His posture was loose, but his eyes moved with surgical precision, sweeping the crowd until they landed on hers.

Recognition hit like a shot of cold water.

She'd seen him before—in the grainy surveillance stills Max had shown her. An enforcer for Miguel "El Cazador" Ortega's cartel.

Her hand tightened on the GoPro. She kept her face composed, kept talking, even as adrenaline roared through her veins.

"Jenna?" one of the reporters called, snapping her attention away. "You were saying something about community action?"

"Right," she said, forcing a breath. "Community action is key. Staying vigilant. Holding the right people accountable."

When she glanced back, he was still there. And now there was the faintest curve at the corner of his mouth—not a smile, but a message.

The rest of the stream passed in a blur. She hit her marks, thanked her guests, and waved off-camera before stabbing the stop button.

Her phone buzzed almost immediately.

He's here. The guy from the photos. What do I do?

Max's reply was instant.

Don't engage. Get out of there. Now.

She turned toward the lamppost.

Empty.

The noise of the tournament rushed back in—cheers at the weigh-in, laughter, the hum of engines—but Jenna's senses were locked in high alert. Every movement in her periphery was a possible threat.

She walked fast through the maze of docks toward the parking lot. Too fast. Her sneakers slapped against the boards, each step a drumbeat in her ears. Somewhere behind her, an engine revved.

She reached her car, slid inside, and locked the doors. Her chest felt tight, the air too thick.

Max's text still glowed on the screen. It should have been reassuring. It wasn't.

Because she knew exactly what had happened.

She'd sent a message to the world.

And the cartel had sent one back.

18

Uncharted Territory

Ed Harper leaned back, eyes sweeping the conference room as his team sparred over the next piece. The space was cramped, fluorescent lights humming, old paint and older carpet holding the smell of coffee and anxiety. A dozen printouts crowded the whiteboard: warehouse maps, a shipping manifest circled in red, a grainy still of a box truck, and two names underlined so hard the paper had torn. The whole room felt wired, like one bad sentence could blow the story open—or blow it up.

"This isn't just local anymore," Linda said, palms braced on the table. Her voice was flint. "National eyes are on this. Play it wrong and we lose credibility—or worse, tip off the wrong people."

"We stick to facts," Kyle countered, fingers worrying the corner of a Post-it. "But we can't strip the human cost. People need to see what the cartel's doing to their communities."

Ed lifted a hand. The chatter slowed, like a train rolling into a station. Linda's focus stayed locked, Kyle's tension sat in his shoulders, and the interns' knees jittered under the table. Thin walls carried the police scanner's murmur from two rooms away, the copy desk's muffled laughter, the squeal of a chair. Outside, sirens rose and fell.

"Anchor," Ed said. His ritual word—gravity. He tapped the whiteboard. "We can name these facts: a fentanyl supply line feeding three counties; shell companies tied to riverfront storage; seizures nowhere near matching what's moving; inspectors politely told to look the other way."

"And the two unmarked sedans across the street since yesterday," Linda added.

"Those too," Ed said lightly, though the pressure under his ribs told him otherwise. "Careful, not paranoid. Paranoid gets you sloppy."

The room exhaled together. The newsroom had adapted to risk like a swimmer to cold water—inch by inch until numbness passed for comfort.

"Structure," Ed said. "We lead with the paper trail, work out to impact. No accusing law enforcement without proof. Show how the blind spots were engineered."

"And the human element?" Kyle asked.

"We thread it—carefully. No images of kids. No gratuitous grief. The numbers speak for themselves."

Linda's gaze tightened. "We still don't have the link beyond Cold River Logistics. LLCs vanish like sugar in coffee. Taped-over DOT numbers. Whispers. But not the chain."

"I'm working on it," Ed said. His mouth was dry. "Might get it today."

"From who?" she asked.

A knock—two soft taps—cut through the hum. Ed checked the clock: 10:14. On time.

Mike Donovan stood at the door in a gray sport coat that fit better than his mood. Rain freckled his shoulders though the sidewalks were dry. The retires cop looked like a man already angling toward the exit.

"You said private," he murmured.

Mike Donovan's fall from grace had been a slow, painful unraveling. Once a rising star in the Miami Police Department, his career had been built on taking down organized crime.

"He's got too much bark and not enough leash," one of his

superiors had said after a particularly aggressive raid. Mike had made waves by calling out corruption within his own ranks, earning him as many detractors as supporters.

The final blow had come during a high-profile case involving a major cartel shipment. Mike had uncovered damning evidence that implicated a high-ranking police official, but when he tried to push it through, he was stonewalled. The case fell apart, and Mike was quietly forced into early retirement.

"Stay," Ed told Linda when she moved to go. "No shadow dance today."

Mike stepped in, unshouldered a messenger bag, and laid a manila folder and a slim hard case on the table. One hand stayed on the case, like an oath.

"Ten minutes," he said. "Fifteen if the traffic lights feel generous."

Ed nodded. "What changed?"

"Pressure," Mike said. "People who don't dial their own phones are dialing. Telling me to stop asking questions I wasn't asking."

"And the second thing?" Linda prompted.

Mike opened the folder: a subcontractor agreement, warehouse intake log, and a city permit application. "Cold River's fed by more than phantom thrift stores. Uniform contracts for Sanitation. Catering for a precinct banquet. Community grants for a 'revitalization committee' one year, 'storm drain repairs' the next."

"Storm drains," Kyle muttered.

"Nobody notices a box truck parked by a storm drain," Mike said. "Public works decal one day, charity sticker the next—no one writes down the plate."

He tapped a warehouse log entry. "Manifest says HVAC filters. They never reached the listed facility. Same truck peels off early, delivers to an unmarked site, and half the pallets land in a supposedly empty city warehouse."

Ed's eyes went to the permit. "Name?"

"Arkady Bautista," Mike said. "Because of course."

The fixer's fixer. The man who moved problems onto neighbors before they knew they had them.

Mike popped the case: a burner phone, a taped thumb drive, and a torn notebook page listing committee names, two deputy commissioners, 18th & RIVER—NO SIGN, and: WED DELIVERY WINDOW FLEXES WHEN SPEECHES.

"That's your national eyes," Mike told Linda. "Press conference means wider lanes."

"What's on the drive?" Ed asked.

"Receipts. Not the ones you want, but enough to make someone nervous. The burner's for the texts—careless on tired days."

"You stole from your own shop," Linda said.

"I redeployed," Mike replied.

Ed kept the burner in front of Mike. "If they're texting it, they're testing it. Don't give them a reason to test you."

At the door, Mike paused. "Those sedans? Not all of them are ours."

When the elevator dinged, Linda exhaled. "Proximity to danger," she said.

Ed pocketed the drive. "We start three tracks: Arkady's civic network; the municipal shell game; the logistics chain."

"And a fourth," he added. "The quiet dead."

They worked fast: public records, permits, grant minutes. Kyle began a clean, readable shell-company map. By noon they had new links—Arkady on a cold-storage permit, a grant cycling boards three times in six months, a photo of him at a "storm drain" groundbreaking.

Ed pulled out an old, isolated laptop, slid in the drive. Sloppy file names matched grant payouts. Delivery logs tagged "SPEECH DAY WINDOW OK." Photos: unmarked docks, black-wrapped pallets, Arkady in profile, timestamped.

"We hold the photos," Ed said. "Use what we can prove."

Then the texts: "no cops near river lot tonight—they're all at the podium." And: "AB says he's a Labrador."

Linda's hand on his chair was an anchor. "They're confident," she said.

Another: "he met with m.d... nothing to worry about."

At 3:41, Mike texted: *They want my phone. My bag. I'm at the river lot.* A white truck slid to the curb outside. Linda joined Ed at the window.

"Inside," Mike confirmed.

Ed's voice was calm but decisive: "Kyle—traffic cams. Linda—call Hernandez. South side of the river lot."

They took back stairs, split to separate cars, regrouped at the pier. Rain misted as they filmed from cover. The door opened. Arkady stepped out. Then Mike—no bag, no phone, expression guarded. A smaller truck backed in, pallets off-loaded. Arkady glanced toward their position—too long to be random—then returned inside. Mike lingered at a wheel well, palm flat to metal, quick movement beneath. Minutes later Ed's phone buzzed: a photo, a circled wheel well, one word: *later.*

They left as quietly as they'd come.

Back in the newsroom, Kyle scrubbed traffic-cam footage for timestamps. At 5:59, the lawyer filed. One minute of clock on their side.

Ed re-cut the nut graph, smoothed the storm-drain line, ordered the invoices for maximum impact. Sent to standards. Sent to legal. At his phone's buzz, the room seemed to tilt—another photo, another circled wheel well, this time two words:

later. tonight.

Ed stood. "We're not done," he said.

Linda met his eyes. The sedans outside turned off their wipers. The rain stopped. The door, for now, remained a door.

And the clock, for once, felt like theirs.

19

Shifting Sands

Miguel "El Cazador" Ortega sat alone in the study, the hour late enough that the villa had settled into its quieter rhythms—guards murmuring in low tones, the distant hum of the generator, the occasional bark of a restless dog somewhere along the wall.

The fireplace's embers glowed like the last coals of a war camp—fading, but stubborn. He watched them over the rim of his whiskey glass, the heat on his face doing nothing for the cold weight in his chest. Shadows gripped the corners of the room, heavy and unmoving.

On the desk, a stack of reports waited like a jury: seizure logs stamped in red, route maps with angry circles marking losses, intercepted manifests that should have been impossible to intercept.

Losses didn't rattle him. He'd built this empire knowing loss was as certain as the sunrise. What unsettled him was the silence that followed—the absence of warnings in channels that had always hummed with half-truths and rumor. No whispers in the pool halls, no coded calls from his men. Just a void, as though someone had reached in and switched off the sound.

Silence meant control. Silence meant someone inside.

His mind drifted, uninvited, to Sofia.

For years she had been the counterbalance to his world's ugliness—grace where there was brutality, calm where there was chaos. But lately, her smiles felt rehearsed, her laughter a thin surface stretched over something else. The smallest details stuck in his mind: the pause before she answered, the questions about routes she'd never asked before, the way she now checked her phone with her back turned.

The glass was half-empty before he realized it. He poured again.

That evening, he called the inner circle to the dining room.

The long mahogany table gleamed under the dim chandelier. This room had once been for celebration—meals ending in toasts and plans drawn in tequila-soaked confidence. Tonight, it was colder, its polished surface more like a judge's bench than a place for camaraderie.

Raul took his place at Miguel's right, posture rigid, eyes scanning every man present. Across from them sat Hector and Luis—familiar faces from the lean years, when the work had been dirtier and the margins thinner. But the ease that used to live in their shoulders was gone.

Miguel let the quiet stretch until it began to pinch.

"We're under attack," he said finally.

The words landed like stones. No one moved.

"Someone is dismantling what we've built. Shipments intercepted. Routes compromised. And there is talk"—he leaned forward, elbows on the table—"of a leak inside our ranks."

Hector's knee bounced under the table. "Boss, I—"

Miguel raised a hand. The motion alone shut him up. "I'm not accusing. Not yet. But if I find out anyone here is feeding our enemies…" He let the pause fill with what they already knew he was capable of.

Luis cleared his throat. "We've always been loyal. You know that."

Miguel's eyes narrowed. "Do I? Loyalty isn't talk. It's action. And lately, the action I see—or don't see—forces me to question everything."

Raul's voice was calm, steady. "The leak is the priority. Whoever's talking knows things only we know."

Miguel didn't look at him. His gaze stayed on Hector and Luis. "You'll both submit to questioning—comms, accounts, movements. If you're clean, you walk."

Their shared glance was brief, but enough to feed the gnawing in his gut.

When the others had gone, Raul remained.

"What do you think?" Miguel asked, pouring another measure.

Raul was deliberate. "They're nervous. But fear isn't guilt."

Miguel nodded slowly. "And Sofia?"

Raul's jaw tightened slightly. "You still want her watched?"

"I need to know. She's been distant. Distracted. And then there are the photos you showed me of Sofia at a café, meeting a man whose face was always obscured." The intimacy was obvious to him.

Miguel turned the laptop toward him—grainy shots of Sofia at a café, leaning toward a man whose face was always obscured. The intimacy was obvious.

Raul studied his face. His voice stayed even. "You think she's involved?"

"I think I can't afford to assume she's not."

"I put my best men on her. Quiet. No mistakes. We are quietly digging."

"Find out who he is," Miguel said. "And what she's hiding."

The next morning, the courtyard was drenched in sharp sunlight. Miguel sat at the stone table, coffee in one hand, pretending to read the paper.

Sofia emerged from the villa, silk robe tied close. Her eyes flicked toward the gate before meeting his.

"You're up early," she said.

"So are you."

She sat. "I've been thinking… maybe we should take the kids somewhere. A trip. Just us."

Miguel's gaze sharpened. "Now?"

"It could help. Put some distance between us and…" She let it hang. Her fingers tightened on the coffee cup.

"I'll think about it," he said.

Her smile was faint, fleeting.

That afternoon, Miguel convened Raul, Hector, and Velasquez over a spread-out map marked in red and blue.

Raul tapped the worst areas. "They're probing for weaknesses."

Miguel grunted. "And finding them."

Hector offered, "We can lock down remaining routes. Vetted channels only. Cut everyone else out."

Miguel's eyes slid to Raul. "Her movements?"

Raul hesitated—just enough for Miguel to notice. "We're tracking. Nothing yet."

"I want results. Quickly."

The room went still.

━━

ED HARPER LEANED over the satellite printouts Mike Donovan had brought in.

"Cold River Logistics," he said, tapping a warehouse in the image. "Keeps coming up."

Mike nodded. "It's the hub. They're feeding both ends—local distributors here, heavy hitters south of the line."

"And the seizures?"

Mike's expression hardened. "The ones that make the news are theater. The real shipments—they don't even try to intercept. Someone high up is deciding what gets hit and what passes."

Ed looked at the photo again. "If it's tied to Miguel Ortega, this isn't just a supply story anymore."

━━

THAT NIGHT, Miguel's encrypted desk phone vibrated once. No one had that number without cause.

He answered without greeting.

A low, distorted voice said, "Your problem isn't in the streets. It's in your books."

Miguel's jaw clenched. "Who is this?"

"Doesn't matter. Check the payments tied to Cold River Logistics. Same hands that took your shipments."

Cold River. The name landed like a stone in his gut.

The voice lowered further. "And the woman in your bed? She's meeting someone connected to them."

The line went dead.

Miguel stayed still, the silence in the room somehow heavier than before.

MIKE'S PHONE BUZZED. He glanced at the encrypted message, frowned.

"What?" Ed asked.

"Tip-off," Mike said. "Cold River's financials are bleeding into a shell in Mexico. And someone's watching a woman connected to Ortega."

Ed's eyes sharpened. "So it's the same pipeline."

"Same pipeline," Mike said. "Different end."

LATE THE NEXT AFTERNOON, a package arrived at the villa. No markings. No signature.

Miguel took it to the study, shut the door, and opened it slowly. Inside: a single sheet of paper, folded twice.

Stop now, or lose what you love most.

The handwriting was neat. Familiar, but he couldn't place it. A faint trace of expensive cologne lingered.

He held it over the fire until the edges curled and the words dissolved.

When Raul appeared in the doorway, Miguel didn't turn.

"Double the security," he said. "Villa. Routes. Her. Eyes everywhere."

Raul nodded. "And the threat?"

Miguel's voice was quiet but firm. "We don't stop. Not for anyone."

Raul left. Miguel reached for his phone, typing:

Prepare the other option. Quietly.

The reply came fast.

Understood.

Miguel set the phone down. Beyond the villa walls, the ground was moving. This time, he intended to move first.

20

Unearthing Allies

Max Larkin stood in front of the corkboard like a man staring at a knot he knew he couldn't untangle without cutting the whole rope. Red string ran from photo to document, document to map, map to Post-it. Every connection looked important. Every connection looked wrong.

The warehouse air was stale, the hum of the overhead lights steady enough to feel like a drill behind his eyes. They'd been living here for weeks now—sleeping in shifts, drinking bad coffee from a chipped carafe, wearing the same clothes long enough for them to feel like a second skin.

And still, the cartel was ahead of them.

He rubbed the back of his neck. They had collected mountains of information, but every time they were close to acting, the target moved. Shipments rerouted. Contacts vanished. Doors closed a second before he could walk through.

From the far table, Jenna's fingers tapped a restless rhythm against her laptop keys. The glow from the screen lit her face in pale blue, eyes narrowed as she scrolled through the flood of messages still coming in from her last livestream—the fishing tournament broadcast that had unexpectedly pulled in more viewers than anything she'd done before.

Most were curious onlookers or concerned citizens. But buried in the noise were messages that felt different. Max had learned to trust Jenna's instincts on those.

"Max," she called, not looking up.

He turned. "Yeah?"

"There's a guy here who says he used to work for the cartel. Claims he's got information. Wants to help."

He moved toward her, suspicion flaring on instinct. "Or wants to walk us into a trap."

"Could be," Jenna said evenly. "But he's not the only one. Look at this—" She angled the laptop toward him. "People who've left, people who've been hurt by them. They're scared, but they're starting to talk."

Max scanned the threads. A dozen possible leads. Each could be nothing. Each could be everything.

"Do you think any are real?" he asked.

"Only one way to find out."

They met Carlos in a café tucked into the corner of a strip mall, the kind of place that seemed too quiet for its own good. Max chose the table with the clearest line to the door. He spotted the man before the bell above the entrance had even finished ringing.

Carlos was wiry, with a nervous energy that made him look both underfed and over-caffeinated. His eyes never settled, scanning the room, the street outside, the counter.

"I got out years ago," he said in a low voice. "But I still hear things."

Max leaned forward. "What kind of things?"

"They've been moving more product than ever," Carlos said. "Trying to get ahead of the heat you've been putting on them."

"What product?"

"Fentanyl. Mostly coastal runs, but they're switching to smaller inland routes too. Safer. Less attention."

Max glanced at Jenna. Inland routes. That matched chatter

they'd picked up—routes Miguel Ortega's people were pushing to avoid heat on the ports.

Carlos's story came in jagged pieces. He'd once run logistics for a Gulf-to-Southeast route. A botched run left him with a limp and a death mark from the people he'd served. Now he kept his head down.

"Why talk now?" Max asked.

Carlos hesitated, then said, "Because I've seen what that poison does. If I can stop one shipment, it's worth it."

Jenna's pen moved across her notepad.

"Cold River mean anything to you?" Max asked casually.

Carlos froze for half a second. "I've heard it," he admitted. "Not our side. But it's used to move money. If you're looking at Cold River, you're looking at something bigger than just Ortega's boys."

Max's pulse kicked. Bigger was exactly what he feared.

IN A CRAMPED OFFICE STATESIDE, Mike Donovan leaned over Ed Harper's desk.

"Cold River's not just a shell," he said. "It's a funnel. Money from three different cartels runs through it."

Ed tapped a map. "And Ortega's inland routes line up with this?"

"Perfectly," Mike said. "Which means when he shifts product, Cold River shifts money."

ANOTHER LEAD CAME from an unexpected source—a university professor who specialized in criminal networks. The university office smelled of dust and paper—air thick with years of cataloging other people's secrets. Dr. Morales's desk was a storm of stacked books and scattered reports. Behind her, a Gulf Coast map was pocked with pins and annotated in quick, sharp handwriting.

"They operate like a corporation," she said. "One branch

exposed? They pivot. Close a port? They run through the hills. Arrest a lieutenant? Another slides in."

Max flipped through a folder she handed him. The detail was surgical—timelines of seizures, leadership changes, coded names cross-referenced with supply routes.

"How'd you get this?"

"Years of interviews, fieldwork, students embedded in affected communities. Some don't come back. Some disappear."

Jenna's eyes flicked to Max.

"What's their biggest weakness?" Jenna asked.

"You follow the dissatisfied. The trapped. The ones who want out but can't see the door. That's where the cracks are."

Max tapped a name in her report—someone in finance tied to Cold River. "You know him?"

Her gaze sharpened. "He went off-grid three weeks ago. And not by choice."

▭

DIEGO HAD BEEN HARDER to track down. He was a former driver who had spent years ferrying shipments across state lines. He had a sharp wit and a no-nonsense demeanor, but there was a heaviness in his eyes that spoke of years of guilt and regret.

They found Diego in a grease-stained garage at the edge of town. He was under the hood of a Ford when they arrived, the clink of a ratchet echoing.

"You're late," he said without looking up.

"You're hard to find," Max replied.

"That's the point."

He'd driven shipments for years until a bullet in the shoulder convinced him to walk. The cartel put his name on a list no one wanted to be on.

"You still have contacts?" Max asked.

"A few. Not reliable."

"Anything helps," Jenna said.

He pulled a folded paper from his jacket. "Last route I ran. Old, but they keep old paths alive for emergencies."

Max unfolded it—a rough hand-drawn map. One inland route was circled. It matched Carlos's description—a Cold River-linked storage yard.

"Why help us?" Max asked.

"Because I've seen kids dead from that powder. If this puts me in the ground, at least I'll have earned it."

Piece by piece, their network of allies began to grow. Carlos, Dr. Morales, and Diego were just the beginning. Each new connection added another layer to the puzzle, bringing them closer to understanding the cartel's operations.

They kept moving—dockworker, widow, others. Every meeting added a piece to the puzzle, and every name they took down could be the one already in cartel ears.

⬛

LATE ONE EVENING, Jenna pulled up surveillance stills from a trusted contact. A pier at night. Crates stacked like abandoned chess pieces. No movement.

"This was active last week," she said.

"And now?" Max asked.

"Empty."

"Or staged."

In one frame, a single light glowed from a distant warehouse.

Near midnight, Max sat alone in their warehouse, the pier images looping on his laptop. The stillness in them felt like a held breath.

His phone buzzed. Carlos's message:

Shipment rescheduled. Route unknown. Be ready.

The inland route on Diego's map flashed in Max's mind. The same shift Ed and Mike had traced to Miguel Ortega two days earlier.

The game had just moved again—and now both sides were closing in on the same piece.

21

Fragile Alliances

The fog lay heavy over the empty lot, erasing everything beyond the reach of the headlights. Jenna Morgan sat on the hood of her car, the metal leeching cold through her jeans. Twin beams carved shallow arcs into the mist, each droplet catching the light and floating like sparks in the air.

Her phone vibrated on the passenger seat — again. A steady pulse of notifications. Each ping tightened the knot between her shoulders. Any one of them could be a lifeline. Any one could be the kill shot.

Trust was currency now, and every transaction came with the risk of bankruptcy.

Carlos had sent her the location that morning: a diner clinging to a forgotten stretch of highway. "Safe enough," he'd said. She hated that phrase. Safe enough was still dangerous. And the more they pulled people into this loose coalition, the more she felt the threads shifting — ready to tighten like a noose if they trusted the wrong hands.

Carlos was late.

The fog muted everything. Somewhere in the dark, an idling

engine coughed once, then fell silent. Jenna's fingers slipped into her jacket pocket, curling around the taser's grip.

A faint glow swelled in the mist. Headlights — bobbing over uneven asphalt. Carlos's battered pickup eased into view, the light catching the dented fender she'd noticed before. She stayed on the hood until the truck stopped twenty feet away.

Carlos climbed out, scanning the lot before his boots hit the ground. Breath clouded the air.

"Sorry I'm late," he said, hands buried in his pockets. "Had to make sure I wasn't being followed."

"Were you?"

He shook his head, but the hesitation in his voice left no comfort. "Not that I could tell. But with these guys... you never really know."

The diner's neon sign stuttered above peeling paint, buzzing in the damp air. Inside, the scent of fryer oil clung to every surface. A waitress moved behind the counter without looking their way as they slid into the last booth.

Carlos unfolded a paper from his jacket — a hand-drawn map, neater than Jenna expected. Too neat.

"This is the next route," he said. "Inland. Avoids their usual choke points along the coast."

She leaned in. "Why now? They've had the coast sealed for months."

"They're panicking," Carlos said. "Pressure's building. It's longer, more exposed, but if we hit here..." He tapped a point near the map's center, "...we can make it hurt."

While he spoke, she studied him. His delivery was clean — too clean. The annotations matched in uniform handwriting, the lines drawn with precision. If this plan was so new, how had it already been rendered like a professional draft?

"And here?" she asked, pointing at a marked stretch.

He paused a beat too long. "Cold River yard. They're staging transfers there."

Her stomach tightened. Cold River was the same name

surfacing in Ed and Mike's investigation — the funnel Miguel Ortega's network used to move cartel money.

She folded the map. "I'll take it to Max."

———

MIGUEL ORTEGA STEPPED out onto his villa's terrace, the evening air still warm from the day. Raul followed, phone in hand.

"The inland plan is set," Raul said. "Bait's in place."

Miguel's gaze lingered on the horizon. "Then we wait for them to bite."

———

THE NEXT AFTERNOON, Jenna and Max found Diego at the garage where they'd first met him. He stood at the workbench, wiping grease from his fingers, the air dense with the smell of oil.

"Carlos says they're shifting inland," Jenna said. "You seen them use this route before?"

Diego frowned. "Once. Years ago. They hated it — too many moving parts. If they're using it now, it's desperation or…"

"Or what?" Max pressed.

"Or they want you there."

He pulled a worn map from the wall and set it beside Carlos's. His finger traced a narrow bridge. "If you're going to hit them, it's here. But that works both ways. They could lock you in."

Jenna and Max traded a look. No words needed.

"Then we get smarter," she said.

Two days later, she met Victor in a crowded downtown café, the hum of espresso machines blurring their words.

Victor was polished — crisp shirt, easy grin — but his eyes lagged a fraction behind the smile.

"I want to help," he said. "The things I've seen could burn them to the ground."

"Why now?"

"Timing is everything, Ms. Morgan. And this is the right time."

He spoke of shell accounts, ghost companies, offshore wires. Twice he mentioned Cold River by name. Maybe a slip. Maybe bait.

She left with a notebook full of leads and a throb behind her eyes, convinced he was holding something back.

That night in the warehouse, the blue glow of her laptop cast her in cold light. Cartel messages scrolled past as she compared Victor's claims. Her phone buzzed.

Unknown number.

Step back, or lose everything. This is your only warning.

Her pulse kicked hard. The diner. The garage. The café. Someone had eyes everywhere. She forwarded the message to Max with a single line:

We're running out of time.

By morning, the central table in the warehouse was littered with maps, photos, and coffee cups. Carlos, Diego, Dr. Morales, and Victor stood clustered around.

"This inland route is our best shot," Max said. "But if it's a setup, we're finished. We vet everyone. No exceptions."

Carlos shifted in his seat. "You think one of us—?"

"I think," Max cut in, "we don't get second chances."

No one argued. But Victor's smile was gone.

When the others left, Jenna stayed. Carlos's precise lines stretched toward the bridge Diego had marked.

She uncapped a red marker and drew a small X at the crossing. Then she opened her phone, tapped a secure contact, and typed:

Get eyes on the bridge. Now.

Her thumb hovered over *send*.

She pressed it down.

22

Deep Cover

Max Larkin adjusted the bill of his faded Twins baseball cap until its shadow cut across his eyes. In the dim sodium glow of the dockyard, the brim wasn't for sun—it was for anonymity. The night air carried a sharp mix of diesel, salt, and damp iron, the kind of smell that clung to your clothes and followed you into rooms where you'd rather not explain where you'd been.

Each step he took echoed faintly off corrugated steel walls, a hollow rhythm pulling him deeper onto a razor's edge. He'd worked undercover before, but this was different—no agency backing him, no extraction plan if it went sideways. All he had was Diego's word, a thin cover story, and his own skill at staying alive under pressure.

The cover read simple enough on paper: a down-on-his-luck smuggler who'd run Gulf ports and crooked river docks, now looking to make himself useful to small cartel crews moving product along forgotten county roads and inland waterways. Diego had supplied the background—real enough to pass a casual check—but in a world like this, credibility was cheap. Trust? That cost blood.

From the outside, the warehouse was just another tired industrial husk—metal siding, flickering lights, a chain-link fence sagging under its own weight. Inside, it was the heartbeat of a distribution network. Crates stacked in neat rows, the acrid bite of ammonia in the air, the faint metallic clink of tools. Men worked with quiet precision, every motion deliberate.

Javier ran the place. Lean, wiry, tattoos twisting up his forearms, and a long scar carved down his cheek like someone had once tried to erase him. His handshake was brief, his eyes flat.

"You're Diego's guy?" he asked, making the word *guy* sound interchangeable with *problem*.

"That's what he said," Max replied evenly. "Said you needed someone who could get the job done."

Javier's pause was deliberate, the silence testing for cracks. Finally, he said, "We'll see about that."

The crew was small. Javier at the top. Miguelito, his second—a stocky enforcer with a shaved head and restless eyes—kept everyone moving. Five others rounded it out, silent, efficient. They loaded unmarked vans, checked coded manifests, and spoke in clipped tones that carried no warmth.

Max kept his head down, ears open. He didn't ask questions, but he watched—who carried which keys, which crates left first, who hesitated when Miguelito barked orders.

For the first two days, he was just muscle—hauling, stacking, shuttling pallets across the floor. On the third night, Miguelito cornered him by the loading bay.

"What's in the boxes?" Max asked casually, as if killing time.

Miguelito's gaze sharpened. "Need-to-know. You don't."

Max shrugged, letting it slide. "Just making conversation."

The look Miguelito gave him lingered a moment too long. This wasn't casual suspicion—he was looking for an excuse.

By week's end, Max had mapped the hierarchy. Javier was deliberate and calculating. Miguelito kept order, sometimes with his hands, sometimes with the flat end of a pistol. The others followed for their own mix of reasons—money, fear, loyalty. And under it all, Max could feel the hairline fractures. Conversations that cut off mid-sentence. Glances traded in the shadows. Here, paranoia was currency.

It was a late run in the back of a van that reminded him just how narrow the margin was. He sat beside Miguelito and a younger man named Luis as they wound through a dark, tree-lined road toward a rural drop point.

"You're quiet," Miguelito said without looking at him. "Don't like talking, or got nothing to say?"

"Just focused," Max replied. "You don't make mistakes if you're focused."

Miguelito smirked faintly. "Diego said you were smart. Let's hope he's right."

The drop went smooth—too smooth. No headlights trailing them, no waiting vehicle on arrival. Still, Max couldn't shake the feeling of unseen eyes watching from the tree line.

Back at the warehouse, Javier called an all-hands. Cigarette smoke and diesel fumes thickened the air in his office.

"They're watching us," Javier said, leaning over a map. "We've lost too many shipments. One more, and they'll drop the hammer."

Miguelito muttered something low in Spanish. Two men shifted uneasily. Max kept his gaze on the map, listening.

"…her livestreams are stirring trouble," Javier said under his breath.

Miguelito nodded. "And the reporter—they're digging."

Jenna. And him. No longer off the radar.

Max's pulse stayed steady, but the air in the room seemed to thicken. This wasn't rumor—the cartel was flagging them as a threat.

That night, in his motel, he texted Jenna:

They know about us. Move carefully.

Her reply came fast: *What happened?*

They mentioned your broadcasts. They know we're digging. Stay low.

He killed the phone entirely. The safest device was the one that stayed silent.

By morning, Javier called him in. No Miguelito this time—just Javier, smoking and staring at the map.

"You know rivers?" Javier asked.

"I can get from A to B without being seen," Max said.

Javier's eyes narrowed. "There's a run inland. Off the usual roads. Bridge near the county line. You'll ride point."

The route clicked in Max's mind. Risky. Too much exposure. Which meant it wasn't just a delivery—it was a test.

Later, Miguelito stopped him in the hall. "You're fitting in," he said. "Don't mistake that for trust."

"I wouldn't dream of it," Max replied.

By nightfall, Max was certain: the bridge job wasn't about cargo. It was about flushing leaks. And he was the new face in the room.

Two hours into the run, they split into two vehicles—Max with Luis in the lead van, Miguelito in the second truck. Steel trusses loomed ahead, black against the moonlight.

Halfway across, Luis stiffened. "We got company," he said.

At the far end, a lone pickup sat with its lights off.

Miguelito's voice crackled on the radio. "Keep moving. Don't stop."

The pickup rolled forward, blocking the road. Two men stepped out, short-barrel shotguns in hand.

Luis swore.

"Out," one man ordered, tapping the van's hood with the muzzle.

Max stepped out slow, hands visible. Behind them, Miguelito's van doors opened.

From the pickup's shadow, Javier appeared. "Just making sure there aren't any… problems in the ranks."

His gaze locked on Max.

Max met it with a faint, bored smirk, even as he calculated angles—distance to the trusses, weight of the taser in his jacket, the split-second question of whether Miguelito's loyalty was to Javier or just the paycheck.

"This won't take long," Javier said. "If you're solid."

The silence stretched. The air was charged.

Max let the smirk stay. "Guess we'll see."

23

The Hidden Web

The city still wore its early-morning haze when Ed Harper turned onto the narrow side street behind the Gazette's downtown office. He'd taken the long way in—twice looping past the courthouse before convincing himself he wasn't being tailed—but the knot in his chest hadn't eased.

A silver sedan idled across from the rear lot, its engine a low hum in the cool air. The driver's face was a pale blur behind the windshield. No front license plate.

Ed killed the ignition and lingered, thumb flicking over his phone screen while his eyes stayed fixed on the sedan in the mirrors. It didn't move.

By the time he stepped out, messenger bag slung over his shoulder, the car rolled away without so much as a turn signal.

Just a car, he told himself. The thought rang hollow.

Inside, the newsroom churned with its usual chaos—phones ringing, printers coughing out pages, scanners droning from the police beat corner. But something was different this morning. An undercurrent. Conversations stilled when he passed. Heads bent closer together.

Ed threaded through the maze of cubicles toward his office, past the glass-walled conference room where the night shift's scrawl still covered the whiteboard: *possible leak in customs, missing shipment, city contracts?*

The blinds in his office were already drawn. Mike Donovan waited inside.

Mike looked like he'd been up all night—hair mussed, shirt rumpled, eyes red. He stood as Ed entered, shutting the door behind him without a word. From his coat pocket, he pulled a thin envelope and set it on the desk.

"Straight from my guy in state logistics," Mike said quietly. "You didn't get this from me."

Ed opened it. Three folded sheets slid out. The first—a grainy satellite print—showed a winding river with a narrow, unnamed bridge crossing it. The second was a partially redacted manifest, still legible enough to show shipments moving inland to staging warehouses near that crossing. The third was a list of shell companies— many of them already tied, by Ed's earlier digging, to offshore accounts.

"This is one of their backdoor routes," Mike said. "They push high-value loads across here when the main crossings are too hot. No inspections, no cameras. Just a guard who gets paid to look the other way."

Ed's pulse picked up. This matched what Max Larkin had hinted at in his last encrypted drop from deep cover. Different source, same bridge.

"You're sure it's current?" Ed asked.

Mike nodded. "As of last week. Word is something big's moving soon. Could be cash, could be product—but important enough they're pulling muscle from other ops to cover it."

Ed locked the papers in his desk. "You were never here."

A humorless smile. "That's the idea." Mike slipped out, vanishing into the newsroom's din.

Ed pulled the blinds tighter and spread the rest of his morning's haul across the desk.

The documents were a mosaic of sources:

- Bank transfer records from a retired detective with friends in financial crimes.
- Internal ledgers from a construction company, routed through an anonymous tip.
- Photos of state officials shaking hands with men on DEA watch lists.

Individually, each was damning but incomplete. Together, they sharpened into something dangerous—a lattice of connections running from cartel enforcers to boardrooms and campaign fundraisers.

At the center sat a name everyone recognized: **Vanguard Pacific**. Their CEO graced business magazine covers, cut ribbons at school openings, and funded hospital wings. Ed traced a red pen from Vanguard's offshore account to a Panamanian holding company, then to a freight broker in Laredo.

The freight broker's signature was on one of the manifests Mike had brought.

That bridge again.

"This isn't just a drug operation," Ed murmured. "It's an empire."

By midmorning, Ed had his core team in the small conference room. Linda sat at the head, flipping open her leather-bound notebook. Kyle balanced his laptop on his knees, portable hotspot already humming. Monica, an intern slipped in last, sliding a coffee toward Ed before taking her seat.

Ed shut the door and dropped a stack of files on the table. "This isn't isolated corruption anymore. It runs straight through politics, business, and law enforcement—and it's creeping into our backyard."

Linda stopped at a page of financial transactions. "Vanguard Pacific? Ed, they build schools. Sponsor hospital wings."

"They also launder money through shell companies and offshore accounts," Ed said. "And they're tied to a cartel route—a small bridge over the Rio Marillo. No oversight. Max confirmed it from inside. Mike just gave me independent proof."

Kyle pulled up a satellite image of the crossing. "If we get eyes on it, we could catch a major transfer—enough to force a federal response."

"Or enough to get someone killed," Monica said. "If Max is already in deep, they'll be watching for leaks."

"They are." Ed slid a folded note into the center of the table. Four block-printed words: **BACK OFF OR ELSE**.

The room went still.

"Found it in my mailbox last night," he said. "No envelope. No stamp. They want us to know they can walk right up to our doors."

Linda's jaw tightened. "Then we hit them harder. Rattle the cage. Make them waste time chasing ghosts so Max can feed us something big."

"That's the plan," Ed said. "We destabilize them—misinformation, false leads, all of it untraceable. Kyle, run the tech. Monica, build the human angle—families, small businesses, anyone hurt by the cartel. We make the human cost impossible to spin."

"And Vanguard?" Kyle asked.

Ed's gaze was flat. "We put them in the crosshairs. Quietly at first. Tie them to the bridge route just enough to force questions. They'll overreact, and we'll be ready."

For the next hour, the room hummed with clipped exchanges. Maps marked. Numbers traded. Timelines layered—journalistic, legal, operational. Each thread led back to the bridge.

When they broke, the coffee was cold and the air felt thin.

Ed stayed to gather the files. Outside, the newsroom's noise seemed sharper now, every phone ring a jolt.

He stepped into the street just after two, sunlight glaring off windshields. His car sat at the far end of the block.

Halfway there, he saw the silver sedan again—parked at the corner, angled toward the intersection. A figure sat behind the wheel, unmoving.

Ed didn't break stride. He unlocked his car, slid in, and pulled into traffic without looking back. In the rearview, the sedan peeled away.

Two turns later, it was gone.

At his apartment, Ed unlocked the door—and froze. The dead-bolt was still set, but the faint scent of cigarette smoke lingered.

On the kitchen counter sat a plain manila envelope. No markings, just his name in block letters.

Inside was a single photograph: Ed leaving the Gazette that morning, messenger bag slung over his shoulder. Behind him, just inside the doorway, Mike Donovan.

Three words scrawled across the bottom in red marker: **NEXT TIME, BOTH**.

Ed's hand tightened until the photo creased.

They weren't just watching. They were already inside the web.

24

Lines Crossed

Miguel "El Cazador" Ortega stood in the center of his office, the golden chandelier scattering fractured light across the polished mahogany desk. The air smelled of old leather, cigar smoke, and something harder to define—desperation that clung like humidity to skin.

At this hour, the villa's windows were black mirrors, throwing back the silhouette of a man who had built an empire out of fear and precision—and now felt both slipping.

A stack of intelligence reports sat before him, their patterns undeniable: two shipments lost in as many months, safehouses breached, routes compromised, whispers of dissent curling through the ranks like cigarette smoke.

He'd always had enemies—police, journalists, rival outfits—but this was different. The pressure wasn't just pressing from outside. It was bleeding in from within.

The desk intercom crackled. Raul's voice, clipped and grim: "We need to talk. It's about Gainesville."

Miguel's jaw tightened. He pressed the button. "Come in."

Raul entered, shutting the heavy door behind him. His eyes

looked older than they had a month ago. "The latest shipment—intercepted on the Florida route. Two drivers gone. No bodies yet."

Miguel's gaze sharpened. "How?"

"Authorities, most likely. But there's no official record yet. They're keeping it quiet, which… isn't normal." Raul hesitated. "And Miguel—this route—"

"I know the route," Miguel snapped. That corridor had been a masterpiece—built on bribes, blind customs clerks, and favors that put people in debt for life. But in the past two weeks, it had begun to fray. Someone knew exactly where to cut.

Raul's voice dropped. "That Gainesville run crossed the Rio Marillo bridge. Same crossing flagged in an American news story—buried inside a piece on infrastructure corruption."

Miguel stilled. "Who's talking?"

"Not sure yet. But it's like they're working from the inside out."

A cold certainty settled over him. This wasn't coincidence. Whoever had pushed that story had fingers deep in places they shouldn't.

"Find the source," Miguel said, his voice gravel and steel. "If this ties to the Americans, I want to know before they do."

That night, Miguel summoned his top lieutenants to the villa's private dining room. Once a sanctuary for toasts and thick steaks, tonight it felt like a war room.

Luis paced like a caged bull, muttering curses. Hector sat hunched, restless, eyes darting toward the door. Raul kept to the wall, watchful. Marcos sat at the far end, fingers drumming lightly on the table's edge, expression unreadable.

Miguel entered without a word, letting silence work before he spoke. He lit a cigar, the ember briefly lighting his eyes.

"We are under attack," he began, voice low and deliberate. "From the authorities, the media, our rivals. But that's not the real danger."

He let the pause stretch.

"The real danger," he said finally, "is in this room."

Hector's head snapped up. Luis froze mid-step. Marcos's fingers went still.

"There's a leak," Miguel continued. "Someone here is feeding information outside. Routes, schedules, safehouses. Things only we know."

Luis slammed his fist against the table hard enough to rattle silverware. "You think one of us—?"

"I don't think," Miguel cut in. "I know."

The temperature in the room seemed to rise. Hector rounded on Luis. "Maybe it's you—always running your mouth, flashing money—"

Luis lunged, his chair toppling, but Raul stepped in, planting a hand on each man's chest, shoving them apart.

"Enough," Miguel barked, smoke curling from his cigar like a warning. "Luis, Hector—you're both too loud to be clever enough for this. That leaves…" His gaze settled on Marcos.

Marcos met it without flinching. "If you're looking for someone who wants this organization to survive, you've found him. But if there's a rat, we cut his tongue out before he eats the whole body."

The line landed halfway between loyalty and threat.

Miguel leaned forward, voice dropping. "Careful, Marcos. I'm not in the mood for poetry."

By morning, tension in the villa was thick enough to taste. Guards stood tighter at their posts. Every radio call was clipped, deliberate.

That's when Javier arrived.

The lieutenant was sweating before he crossed the threshold. Miguel didn't offer a seat.

"The shipment through the new route—gone," Miguel said flatly. "Two men dead."

Javier swallowed. "Too many eyes on us. Someone tipped them. We had no choice but to abandon the—"

"You always have a choice," Miguel interrupted, his tone cold enough to frost glass. "And you chose wrong."

He nodded toward the door. Two guards appeared instantly.

"Take him outside. Make sure everyone sees."

Javier's protests echoed down the marble hall before the doors shut. Miguel didn't follow. The act wasn't for Javier—it was for everyone else.

That evening, Raul entered with a folded, damp sheet of paper. "Came through one of our lookouts in San Pedro. Risked his life to get it here."

Miguel unfolded it. The handwriting was rushed, but the meaning was clear:

Marcos is moving. Has soldiers. Promises more money, safer work. Says your time is over. Names below are with him.

Beneath were six names—three lieutenants, two mid-level enforcers, and a driver Miguel had known since the man was seventeen.

He read it twice. The ember at his cigar's tip flared, then dimmed.

"This ends now," he murmured, more to himself than to Raul.

Later, alone in his study, Miguel stared at the family photo on his desk. Sofia's smile. The kids' faces, frozen in a moment before they'd known what he truly was.

For the first time in years, something coiled in his chest. Fear.

But fear, in his world, was fuel.

He picked up the phone. "Raul. Gather the loyal men. No one leaves until this is finished."

Outside, in the villa's courtyard, the guards shifted their rifles. They could feel it too.

Something was coming.

And for the first time in a long time, Miguel wasn't certain he'd be the one left standing when it was over.

25

Silent Betrayal

Jenna Morgan sat alone in the far corner of Dockside Grind, the café's muted jazz and gentle clink of cups doing little to calm her nerves. She swirled her coffee absently, the steam rising like a veil between her and the rest of the world.

Her public day had been exhausting—the kind of smiling, sunlit performance her followers expected. She'd filmed cheerful fishing reels, posted conservation tips, even teased her next giveaway. The comment section was its usual sea of praise:

"Queen of the Gulf!"

"Those fillets look insane!"

"You're a national treasure, girl."

But the curated smile in her thumbnails wasn't the face she wore now.

Behind the posts and bright filters lived the other life—the one tethered to Max, Ed Harper, and the investigation into the cartel network threading through her own coastal community. That life had no filters. It had shadows, encrypted files, whispered warnings, and the cold knowledge that anyone around her could be watching.

She opened her laptop, pulling up the surveillance folder Max had left at the warehouse. Footage rolled by—docks, fishing piers, quiet bays—the humdrum rhythm of waterfront commerce.

Then one frame froze her blood.

It was a marina shot, long-lens, grainy. In the background—her. Standing with phone in hand, live-streaming during the fishing tournament two weeks ago. But in the foreground, stepping briefly into frame, was a man.

Not just any man.

Credence.

She knew him from local events—a friendly face who commented on her videos, reposted her gear tips, laughed at her bad bait jokes. But in the clip, he wasn't smiling. He was slipping between two men unloading unmarked crates from a van. One hand brushed a container's side, testing its weight, before he looked—directly—toward her.

Her stomach tightened. He'd seen her filming.

She rewound. Watched again. The way his shoulders squared when his eyes met the lens. The faint nod toward someone off-camera. This wasn't a curious passerby—this was a man working.

She thumbed a quick text to Max.

JENNA: *He's in the footage. From the docks. He's not just watching. He's in the operation.*

MAX: *Who?*

JENNA: *Credence. Local guy. Always reposts my stuff. Was behind me that day. He's moving their crates.*

MAX: *Don't engage. Just get me stills.*

While Jenna worked in the café, Ed Harper was three blocks away in the cramped third-floor newsroom, bent over a map of the southern shipping corridors. His desk was littered with legal pads scrawled with times, bridge names, and route numbers. The air smelled faintly of burnt coffee and toner.

Across from him, Mike Donovan tapped a ballpoint pen against the Rio Marillo Bridge icon. "This crossing—Gainesville run—that's where your last gap lines up."

Ed leaned in. "The one from the infrastructure corruption piece."

"Exactly. I just got confirmation from a source in Customs—unmarked vans have been moving through between one and three a.m. for six weeks. No inspections. All paid for."

Ed felt the electric click in his gut—puzzle pieces falling into place. "That's the same route from the missing Florida shipment Miguel's crew just lost."

Mike's brow arched. "Then somebody's hitting them on both ends."

"Or," Ed said quietly, "somebody's feeding both sides and getting paid twice."

By late afternoon, Jenna had driven to the warehouse. Max was waiting by the back door, laptop open to her footage. They watched the clip together, freezing the frame when Credence's gaze locked with her camera.

"Yeah," Max said, voice low. "That's not an accident."

"He's part of it," Jenna said. "And not just some dockhand. Look at how he checks the crate."

Max's phone buzzed. He handed it to her. The text was from Ed:

ED: *We've got a live Customs tip. Rio Marillo bridge. Tonight.*

Max looked at her. "That's your guy's route."

In the newsroom, Ed was prepping for a midnight drive north with Donovan. They'd planted a freelance stringer, Lexi—a specialist in covert photography—on the Gainesville side. She'd watch the Florida end while they staked out the Texas approach.

Back at the warehouse, Jenna paced. The footage of Credence unloading crates. The Gainesville shipment Miguel had lost. And now, a real-time tip about the bridge being hot again tonight.

"Max," she said, "what if he's there? What if I catch him again, but this time… live?"

"You're not going to the bridge," Max said flatly.

But her mind was already working—calculating angles, recalling her boat's docking point near the causeway.

That night, city lights fell away as Ed and Donovan drove south toward the border. The highway stretched ahead like a black ribbon through scrubland, headlights catching the eyes of the occasional coyote on the shoulder.

"You think your girl's footage ties in?" Donovan asked.

"If it does," Ed said, eyes fixed on the road, "this is our shot to prove the bridge is compromised."

"What if they spot us?"

"They won't." His voice carried more hope than certainty.

Jenna wasn't home. Not in the warehouse either. She was crouched behind the windbreak on her small fishing boat, camera bag wedged between her knees, lens aimed at the shadowed span of the causeway. The air was thick with brine and diesel.

At 1:47 a.m., headlights crested the bridge—two unmarked vans. No plates. No pause at the checkpoint. They rolled straight through as the guard shack's light stayed red.

Through her viewfinder, she saw him.

Credence. Riding shotgun in the second van.

Her pulse spiked. She kept filming.

On the Texas side, Ed and Donovan caught the same vans passing from their concealed pullout, cameras clicking in rapid bursts.

"Second van," Donovan murmured. "Guy in passenger seat looking straight ahead. You know him?"

Ed hesitated. "I've seen him in Jenna's files."

The vans disappeared into the night.

Jenna lowered her camera, hands trembling.

Her phone buzzed—unknown number:

Nice view from the water, Jenna. Careful you don't fall in.

She looked up, scanning the black waterline. The shore was empty.

26

Confessions and Convictions

Max Larkin stood on the marina's edge, where the pilings wore rings like old trees and the water slapped the creosote with patient indifference. Salt stung the back of his throat. Above, seagulls argued in ragged loops, their cries sharp as wire. Twenty minutes past the meet time. He kept his eyes on the horizon, where the gray water chewed the sun's reflection into shards.

He didn't check his phone. He didn't pace. His hands hung loose at his sides — harmless enough to pass, loose enough to move fast. The wind pressed against his coat, lifting the hem in a small flag of motion in an otherwise still morning.

The kid came the way skittish animals come — quiet-footed, ready to bolt. Gray hoodie, dark jeans, cap pulled so low the bill nearly grazed his nose. Dock-worker camouflage. He stopped two pilings short, as if an invisible line ran there.

"You're late," Max said without turning.

"Traffic," the kid muttered.

Max tapped the bench with a knuckle. "Sit."

The kid perched on the edge like it might lunge at him. One knee bounced. The wind caught his cap's brim and shoved it back half an inch. Two nights of bad sleep had settled into the skin under his eyes.

"You know why I asked you here," Max said.

"I don't know anything," the kid said too fast. "I just move stuff. I don't pick routes. I don't know names. I drive where I'm told."

"Last week," Max said. "Coastal run to the dry dock at Port Mary. You cleared three checkpoints you weren't supposed to. Somebody waved you through. Who gave the permission?"

The knee bounced harder. "There's a code system. You get a manifest, then a second text that overrides it. Pick up, drop off. If something goes wrong, there's a number. That's it."

"Show me the number."

The kid froze, then fished a crumpled scrap from his hoodie. He flattened it on his thigh — ten digits, Florida area code. No name. Ink fading where it had been folded and unfolded too often.

"You call this?" Max asked.

"Once," the kid said. "Crate slipped open. Blue bricks. Same kind that—" He cut himself off, throat locking. "I read your byline. I didn't know… I didn't—"

Max looked out at the water and counted four breaths before writing the digits into his notebook in block print.

"You ever meet the one in charge?" he asked.

"Not directly," the kid said. "There's a guy they call the Monk. Keeps things neat. Doesn't carry, doesn't yell. Sends different runners. They don't talk — just handoff and vanish."

"Monk," Max repeated, his tone drying the word. He drew a line from the name to the number. "Where'd you hear it? This side or across?"

The kid chewed his cheek. "Both, I think. He's the one who makes the routes invisible. Seabridge Point to inland yards. Sometimes they say Gainesville. Sometimes they call it the 'Marillo lane.' You don't say it out loud or you jinx it." A glance at the water. "But that lane's dark now. No texts about it. Locked down for something big."

Rio Marillo. The same bridge Ed and Donovan had staked out. The same run Miguel Ortega's crew had lost.

"What's coming?" Max asked.

"Flood," the kid said. "Not just fent. Guns, pressed pills, maybe cash. Deadlines moved up like there's a storm warning." He swallowed. "If they know I talked—"

"You're already on someone's list," Max said, too tired for lies. "If you're lucky, my story hits first."

He stood. The kid followed.

"Don't call that number again," Max said. "Don't answer unknowns. If someone knocks and uses your name, especially then — don't answer." He turned, then looked back. "And if you see a man who looks like he ironed the world around him, walk."

The kid blinked. "What?"

"You'll know him."

THE SAFE HOUSE slouched between mangroves and forgettable coastline. The porch screen sighed in the wind. Inside smelled faintly of coffee, laundry soap, and damp.

Jenna sat at the table, sweater sleeves pulled over her hands, stills from surveillance footage spread like playing cards. She looked up as he entered, jaw set the way exhausted people hold it to keep from breaking.

"Courier?" she asked.

Max slid the scrap of digits across to her. "Florida area code. They call him the Monk. Precise. Seabridge Point to Gainesville — the Marillo lane when they're careless. And it's gone quiet for something big."

She typed fast, fingers like wire. "Chatter on a cleanup guy in Veracruz years back. No face. He's a myth on purpose." She pivoted to another database. "The number — we can bounce it against tower dumps. Cruz's friend owes us two favors; this eats one."

"Spend it," Max said.

Her laptop hummed with backchannel searches. Max watched her instead of the screen, noting the new sweater already pilled, the shadows under her eyes.

His phone buzzed.

UNKNOWN: *YOU DIG TOO DEEP. PREPARE FOR THE STORM.*

He showed her. She said nothing, jaw tightening.

The phone buzzed again — a photo of the marina bench from twenty minutes ago, shot from behind the bait shop. The timestamp sealed the message.

Jenna closed her chat window. "Route mapping later. First we move rooms."

CRUZ'S CAR was too loud for the neighborhood; Jack's was too quiet. They arrived five minutes apart. In the kitchen, a printed map smothered the table. Jenna's laptop glowed in the center.

"We need eyes on Seabridge Point," Max said. "If there's a mixed shipment, it's inside seventy-two hours. Less if they felt heat at the bridge."

"Port security's a joke," Jack said.

"Then indirect," Cruz countered, stabbing pilot logs with a screwdriver.

Jenna didn't look up. "If Monk's people are tidy, they'll bounce, but they still have to hit a tower. We just need one that doesn't belong."

Jack gestured at Max's phone. "That marina shot? Geofence test. They wanted to see how fast you'd react."

Max said, "Gainesville and Rio Marillo lane — dark. Miguel Ortega doesn't lock down for fun."

"Or he's bleeding," Cruz said.

The name Ortega hung in the room.

Jenna's screen flickered. "Shell company tied to Seabridge Point matches the Gainesville ledger Ed traced from Vanguard."

"Two nights," Jack said. "We watch Seabridge Point and Little Talbot. No heroics."

Jenna's phone pinged — partial tower hit. Same tower as a Rio Marillo handset yesterday.

"They're touching the same glass," she said.

Max's phone buzzed again. A live location pin. Closing fast.

"That's not cops," Cruz said.

Max set the phone down, screen up. The dot slowed to 0.5 miles. The porch screen moved in the wind.

"We move," he said. "Tonight."

They left through the back. Mangroves wet with the day's breath. Shells popping underfoot. Two cars, no headlights until the bend.

Max slowed at the curve. The road ahead was empty. The pin vanished.

"They're good," Jenna said.

"So are we," he said.

They kept driving toward the causeway. Cranes at Seabridge Point stood like giants in mid-gesture.

"Tomorrow," Jenna said. "Little Talbot at two."

"Tomorrow," Max said.

His phone buzzed again — same area code, new number.

A clean hand is earned. Little Talbot. 02:00. Come alone or don't come.

"He wants proof I'll obey," Max said.

"Then we wedge the door," Jenna said.

He nodded. "And keep the hinge."

They drove on into the electric morning of the port, toward a room with one door and a man who kept things tidy. Max intended to leave it messy.

27

Tangled Truths

Ed sat alone in the back office of the newsroom, blinds drawn tight against the waning afternoon light. The desk lamp's yellow glow carved deep shadows across stacks of printed reports, marked-up photos, and half-empty coffee cups. The air smelled of paper and fatigue. Beyond the closed door, phones rang and keyboards clacked, but here the noise was muted—replaced by the hum of an old ceiling fan and the occasional pop of the baseboard as the building settled.

His fingers drummed against a **DEA** transcript, the black bars of redaction almost as thick as the lies they concealed. Every sheet in the room felt like a breadcrumb to nowhere, each lead ending in the same dead wall of "no comment" and legal obstruction.

Until now.

The report Jenna had sent sat open in front of him—a compilation of timestamps, shipping manifests, and offshore banking transactions. The kind of document you had to fight to get, and pray no one knew you had. Ed traced a line of text with his pen, and there it was: *Adrian Beltran.*

The name landed like a sucker punch.

Years ago, back when Ed still believed journalism could fix the rot if you dug hard enough, Beltran's trucking company had crossed his desk. On paper it was clean—too clean. Rapid expansion, flawless inspection records, perfect tax compliance. He'd pushed at the edges, sniffed for corruption, but an anonymous email warning him to "back off or be buried" had been enough to stop him. He told himself the trail was too thin. In truth, he hadn't wanted to see where it led.

Now Beltran was back—not in whispers, but in bold print on a ledger Jenna's contact had risked everything to pass along. Listed as a logistics facilitator for multiple cartel shipments, his cargo routes snaked through ports they couldn't touch legally.

Ed reached for the next page, but his gaze caught on a photo paper-clipped to the file. A fundraiser shot from years ago—Ed mid-toast, laughing, and there was Beltran beside him, hand on his shoulder. A snapshot of complicity he'd never intended, framed in irony. The memory stung because it was true—once, he'd known how to walk away from a story if survival demanded it. Now he wasn't sure he could.

He didn't hear the first knock. The second was sharper.

"Come in."

Linda stepped inside, closing the door behind her. Her hair was pulled back, her eyes wired with caffeine and sleeplessness.

"We've got a problem," she said, skipping pleasantries.

Ed motioned to the chair. "Get in line."

She sat, leaning forward. "Jenna's network is drawing the wrong kind of attention. We've flagged spikes from foreign servers—regions tied to cartel ops. Jack pulled dark net transcripts. They're dissecting her voice patterns, cataloguing keywords she used in the stream."

Ed straightened. "They're mapping her identity?"

"Not just hers. Yours. Mine. They're building behavioral profiles, Ed. Cross-referencing locations, associates—like they're assembling a target list."

A chill worked its way into his spine. He stood, crossed to the filing cabinet, and unlocked the bottom drawer. From the back he pulled a black case wrapped in a dust-coated towel. Inside was a burner laptop sealed in copper mesh, an unregistered flip phone, and a handful of encrypted drives.

"What is that?" Linda asked.

"A fallback kit. From when I thought disappearing might be my only option." He set the laptop down, powered it on, and typed in the old password: **REGRET2020**.

The desktop bloomed with folders: **LOSTTHREAD**, **DOXMAP**, **BELTRAN**. Ed opened the last one, scrolling through years-old emails and file dumps. One message sat at the top of the list, its subject line etched in his memory:

Your friend Beltran. Not who you think. Be careful.

The body listed holding companies, a man named Ortega, and references to deep-sea cargo routes. He'd ignored it back then. Now it read like a blueprint of everything they were uncovering.

Linda slid the printouts closer, her eyes scanning the highlighted transfers. "This one," she said, tapping a Belize account number, "matches a sub-ledger code Max pulled from the Seabridge Point manifests."

Ed looked up sharply. "Max knew of Seabridge?"

"Yeah. His courier tip and your Beltran file—they're the same route. Different front companies, same end destination."

Ed frowned.

Before he could respond, Linda's phone buzzed. She read the encrypted message aloud: "Coordinates. Bank references. And—" her brow furrowed—"*Las raíces más profundas no se ven hasta que el árbol cae.*"

"The deepest roots are not seen until the tree falls," Ed translated.

"She thinks Ortega's losing ground. Or someone wants him to," Linda said.

Ed began pacing, energy threading into his voice. "Beltran's not just a facilitator. He's a channel straight into Ortega's network. And if Max is already sniffing around Seabridge Point..."

Linda finished the thought. "Then someone's going to notice both of you."

Ed unlocked another drawer, pulling out a thick manila folder labeled **MOSAIC**. Inside were torn ledger pages, maps with smuggling routes scrawled in pen, and photos of docks at night, lit by floodlamps and shadowed figures.

"This was going to be my exposé," Ed said quietly. "Back when I thought the cost was only my job."

Linda met his gaze. "And now?"

"Now it's everything. And I'll pay it if it means dragging this into daylight."

Her phone buzzed again. She frowned, showing him the screen. This time, it wasn't Jenna.

It was a photo—grainy, timestamped twenty minutes ago. The angle was from outside, aimed up at the second-story window of Ed's office. Through the blinds, barely visible, was his silhouette, bent over the desk.

The hair on his neck rose.

Linda lowered her voice. "They're here."

28

Strategizing Survival

Jenna parked two blocks short of the warehouse and killed the engine. The evening heat clung to the car like a wet towel; the cooling metal popped in slow ticks. She kept both hands on the wheel for a count of five, listening.

In the dying light, the district looked abandoned—rows of rust-bitten roll-up doors, sun-faded signage for businesses that hadn't existed in years. But true emptiness had a sound. This wasn't it.

A gull scraped the sky with a cry too sharp for dusk. Somewhere down the block, a vehicle idled—then cut off mid-breath. Wind pushed grit across the asphalt in a low hiss.

She checked the rearview. A white work van—no logos, no ladder rack—was parked nose-out beneath a busted streetlight. It hadn't been there during her first pass fifteen minutes ago. The windshield threw back the sky like a mirror.

Her phone buzzed once in her lap. She didn't look. Instead, she reached into the passenger footwell for the folded hoodie, shaking it out and pulling it over her bright tank. The color vanished. She tugged her ballcap low, checked the tiny camera lens pinned inside the brim, then slid from the car, locking it with a soft chirp that made her jaw tighten.

The air smelled of old oil and sunburned rubber. She kept to the shadows, counting steps, letting muscle memory guide her before her mind could trip her with fear. At the corner, she paused. The van's windshield no longer reflected the sky. A silhouette now sat in the driver's seat, squared and motionless.

She looked up, as if checking the weather, then pivoted and crossed—head down, pace unhurried. No sudden angles. The warehouse waited in the second row of buildings, its cinderblock face broken by a single cracked window. A faded crown had been spray-painted over the door years ago, now blurred by sun and dust into something unrecognizable.

At the door, she reached into the rusted mailbox and found the key taped where it always was, sand clinging to it—a sign Max had already been here and re-hidden it. She stepped inside, shut the door, and breathed.

The air was thick with old work—oil, dust, and the faint algae tang of damp concrete. A bare bulb over the makeshift office cast a cone of light onto a battered metal table. Max sat behind it, elbows on his knees, a city grid map the size of a bedsheet spread across table and milk crate. His eyes took her measure before his mouth moved.

"Tail?" he asked.

"White van. Two blocks west. Could be nothing."

"Could be everything," he said without blinking.

She set her bag down, unzipped it, and slid out her laptop. The cold blue light climbed her face as she plugged into power, into the cell booster in the corner, into the world. Spreadsheets, maps, and timestamps bloomed—latticework of a conspiracy that had stopped being theory chapters ago.

"They're tracking more than our broadcasts," she said, scrolling through a feed from a follower-turned-analyst. "Movement patterns. The gap between my public appearances and shipping spikes. It's intentional now."

"We poked the bear," Max said. "Now we find the den."

Her fingers danced across the keys. In her public videos she was still breezy, still optimized for retention. But under each line was weight—a word dropped from one zip code, a phrase seeded from another, tiny pressure points meant to make the right people twitch.

"Not just rattle them," she said. "Cripple them."

Max tapped a cluster of red circles on the map. "Logistical arteries. Not the head—the legs. Cut them, and the body drops."

She cross-referenced in real time. The portable fan's hum sounded like a countdown. "This dockyard," she said, pointing to a terminal just south of the harbor. "Flagged in four logs. Incoming goods, weekend offloads. Leak it to the right office…"

"Interdiction," he said. "Surgical." He picked up a burner, thumbed in a one-time pad, sent the message. The green checkmark felt like a blade sliding a fraction deeper.

Her laptop pinged.

[SecureChannel//PartialDecryption: 17:42:09] …BELTRAN ledger lines match VANGUARD sub-ledger. Seabridge manifests show identical subcode // route: RIO MARILLO → GAINESVILLE yard → coastal transload. Cross-ref: "Monk" handler alias appears in Veracruz transcripts (2018). Source confidence 0.72.

Another fragment:

[DarkNetBoard//Scrape: 17:44:31] "…he keeps her smiling, keeps them guessing. influencer is a choke point. pull her and watch the map go quiet." Reply: "no—use her. bait."

Jenna's pulse spiked. "Ed's thread just bled into ours. Beltran, Vanguard—they're not cousins. Same family."

Max's jaw tightened. "Then that dockyard's their front porch."

Her laptop pinged again:

[PortRadio//Unverified: 17:49:03] "—pilot switch new rotation / graveyard tug double-booked / camera four stuck in loop." Reply: "leave it. loop is cleaner."

"Looped camera," she said. "Graveyard tug. Not a glitch—a plan."

He marked it. "DEA gets that one. Buys us time."

She texted Drift, an old source. *Dormant eyes near airstrip turned on. Whose hand?*

Three minutes.

Not ours. Infrared warmed two nights. No flight plan. Temporary markers. Someone's moving a runway.

She sent him coordinates; he sent back tire tracks disguised as dirt.

"Someone's ramping up," she said.

"Or about to vanish," Max replied.

Hours folded. They plotted strike zones. She seeded riddles into her next video. A coded ping to Ed would make him stand, grab a manila folder, and see the inland bridge and port as one short, lethal line.

Then her phone lit with a name she hadn't seen in months.

Mel: Call me. Urgent. Regarding Mateo.

Mel's voice was tight. "I didn't know who else to tell. Mateo's... involved. Left his planner in my car. Routes, codes... your name's in it."

"Send it."

Images flooded in—tight handwriting, color-coded tabs, red circles aligning with dockyards and old trails. One entry punched cold into her gut: *JM — Fri — South Loop — Clean handoff.*

Her initials. Her neighborhood. Tomorrow.

She sent Max a screenshot. He called before the upload finished. "That's a target plan. You're the variable."

"We move the timeline up," he said. "Tomorrow night we go dark."

Her laptop pinged with Ed's backdoor tag:

[SecureChannel//PartialDecryption: 18:31:44] Linda: "Photo —outside Ed's office, timestamp +20. They're here." Ed: "Beltran route matched to Seabridge + Marillo subcode. Vanguard broker signs Little Talbot manifest. Confirm."

"Ed's in the barrel," she said.

"And the other end's moving," Max answered.

She zoomed on the planner again. *VT—Monk — G.* An arrow from Seabridge to Gainesville, then to a yard code Donovan had flagged weeks ago.

Her phone buzzed—Drift again: *Two SUVs, no plates. One clipboard. Cameras winked twice—test.*

"Test," she echoed.

Max snapped the last Pelican case shut. "Jack and Cruz on the inlet. We take the causeway blind side. No headlights until the bend. We watch, we don't touch."

"And if Mateo shows?"

"We learn what he thinks he knows. We teach nothing."

Then—Mel again: *He came back for the planner. Asked if you were still doing 'those dock videos.' I'm leaving town.*

"Do it now," she texted.

Outside, tires whispered over grit. The white van was gone.

Her phone pulsed—courier number. *Bring the crate you opened. Or be the crate.*

She didn't answer. She started the car. Max's brake lights thought about lighting, then didn't.

The port's cranes loomed, the water black and reflective as a closed eye. Somewhere inland, a bridge held its breath.

A sound behind them—a shoe finding glass. She checked the rearview. A figure moved at the warehouse's side door, small and deliberate. It reached up and plucked the lens from the eave.

Floodlight caught the side of a face. Mateo.

Her phone vibrated one last time. She didn't look at Max—she didn't have to. They both shifted into gear.

Out on the causeway, a tug pushed a barge stacked with identical metal boxes. Every one of them harmless until you opened the wrong one.

29

Shifting Tides

The Pacific rolled against the cliffs like a slow drumbeat—steady, ancient, and as familiar to Miguel Ortega as his own pulse. Tonight, though, the rhythm felt different. Less like an ally, more like a warning that tides could turn without notice. Moonlight silvered the water, scattering a fractured reflection that refused to hold still.

Beyond the villa's open balcony doors, the wind pressed in—cool, insistent—threading through the sheer curtains as if testing the boundaries of his sanctuary. The private study smelled of mezcal, cedar, and a faint trace of salt carried inland. His father's portrait hung on the far wall, the old man's eyes a sharp, permanent accusation.

Miguel poured a shot from the jaguar-headed decanter, its ceramic glaze cool in his hand. The liquor burned a path down his throat, but the heat did nothing to steady the fine tremor in his fingers. He set the glass down with a muted clink against the mahogany desk.

A king's hands shouldn't shake. But kings didn't usually watch their kingdoms rot from the inside.

His empire—once feared, disciplined, untouchable—was unraveling. Supply lines had gone dark. Shipments vanished mid-transit.

Loyalists defected or simply disappeared, leaving only rumors behind. The old certainty—streets whispering his name in fear—was gone. Now, the whispers were about infiltration, betrayal, and about her. Sofia.

She had become more than an absence; she was a ghost threaded through every corridor, every conversation. And ghosts were harder to kill.

Two sharp knocks at the study door.

"Entra," Miguel said.

Raul stepped in, the only man still allowed to enter without waiting. Even so, caution edged his movements, as though the room itself had shifted from refuge to minefield.

"The Reynosa corridor is offline," Raul said without preamble. "No movement from Chihuahua either. Border patrol intercepted a ghost convoy last night. Empty—scrubbed clean—but the location tells us something."

"Another loss."

Raul's jaw tightened. "We're being watched. Smarter. Faster. This isn't pressure anymore—it's infiltration."

Miguel turned to the balcony, watching the waves chew at the shoreline. "And?"

Raul hesitated. "Marcos has been holding meetings. No guards. No digital trace. Deep zone. That's not his pattern."

Miguel said nothing. He crossed back to his desk and slid open the top drawer, revealing a cedar cigar box. No cigars—only folded tabs of paper, each bearing a single name. His contingencies.

"Call a meeting," he said. "Inner circle. No phones. No staff. Tonight."

[INTERCEPT: SecureChannel // PartialDecryption: 20:14:37]

ED: Source in port authority confirms—Ortega's inner council meeting scheduled. Location: villa dining hall.

LIAISON: Confirmed visual feed?

ED: Negative. Perimeter too tight. Attempting acoustic capture from offshore.

THE DINING HALL'S air hung heavy, ocean salt mingling with polished wood and the faint char of a recently doused cigar. Once, this had been Miguel's war council's sanctuary—dark jokes, easy toasts, iron loyalty. Tonight, the atmosphere was drawn taut as piano wire.

Esteban, massive as ever, leaned back at the far end, his bulk a wordless threat. Diego's fingers tapped against the lacquered surface, a nervous metronome. Marcos sat still, composed, unreadable, his expression a mask.

Miguel entered last. Eyes shifted toward him, then away.

"We are bleeding," he began, voice low but carrying. "Routes gone. Warehouses compromised. Our name once made men tremble. Now, they whisper. Who here knows why?"

Silence stretched, oppressive.

Diego finally cleared his throat. "We underestimated them. The pressure, the tech infiltration... they're not just poking—they're dissecting us."

Esteban rumbled from the far end. "Crypto's up. Diversification's working. But product still moves the streets. Flesh and powder still pay."

Marcos leaned forward, folding his hands. "We're not losing to bullets—we're losing to narratives. These influencers, these journalists—they don't just report. They shape perception. Perception drives panic. Panic drives betrayal."

Miguel's gaze narrowed. "And your solution?"

"Adapt," Marcos said evenly. "Plausible deniability. Diversify command. Stall the backlash. Offer a temporary ceasefire. Let the noise cool before we move again."

Raul scoffed from behind Miguel's chair. "You want us to grovel."

"I want us to survive."

"Survival requires strength," Raul snapped. "Anyone talking truce is already halfway to mutiny."

Heat coiled in Miguel's gut. He let the silence grow until it felt as if the walls themselves leaned in to listen.

"No one leaves this room," he said at last, "without proving loyalty."

Stillness. Sweat on hairlines. Marcos didn't blink.

Miguel let the tension stand, then cut the meeting short with a flick of his hand. "Go. Think about who you answer to."

[INTERCEPT: SecureChannel // PartialDecryption: 21:02:11]

JENNA: I've got a dock schedule. Matches Ortega's secondary routes.

ED: Feed it. If it lines up with Reynosa ghost convoy, that's leverage.

JENNA: It does. And one name overlaps—Marcos.

HOURS LATER, Miguel sat alone in the master bedroom. The wind pressed harder against the balcony doors, rattling them in their frames. The vanity still bore Sofia's presence—cosmetics, scarves, the faint trace of lavender and cedar.

He opened the drawer beneath the makeup kit. Beneath scarves and concert tickets, a false bottom. Inside: files—manifests, communications logs, shell company ledgers—all from his own archives, annotated in Sofia's hand.

He turned over a photograph: Sofia with a man in wire-frame glasses, posture relaxed, leaning toward her. Timestamp: two weeks ago. The angle was surveillance-grade.

His jaw tightened. This wasn't coincidence; it was strategy.

He slid the folder into the wall safe and spun the dial. On his encrypted phone, a courier's earlier message blinked:

Drop confirmed. All signs erased.

Miguel replied with a phrase he hadn't used in years: *Initiate contingency protocol. Phase one.*

[INTERCEPT: **SecureChannel   //   PartialDecryption: 21:47:55**]
 MIGUEL: Initiate contingency protocol. Phase one.
 LIAISON: That's an exit plan trigger.
 ED: Then he's not planning to win this fight. He's planning to survive it.

HE DIDN'T HEAR her at first, but when he turned, Sofia was in the doorway. Silk, neutral, no makeup—a ghost of the woman who once ruled dinner parties beside him.

"How long have you been there?"

"Long enough."

"You knew I'd find the drawer?"

"I knew you'd look eventually."

"You could have asked. Told me."

"You would have lied."

"I protected you."

"You caged me."

Their gazes locked, the air taut as wire.

"I saw the photos," she said evenly. "I know about your escape plan."

"You think you know."

"If anything happens to me, the documents go public—every name, every dollar, every kill order."

"You'd destroy me."

"I'd end what you've become."

For a moment, neither moved. Then Miguel saw it—not fear, not anger, but certainty. She wasn't bluffing.

"We are ash," he murmured.

"No," she said. "We're smoke. And it hasn't cleared yet."

. . .

[INTERCEPT: **SecureChannel // PartialDecryption: 22:09:13**]

JENNA: Cross-matching Marcos with Sofia. Got a hit.

ED: That ties Ortega's collapse to our leak chain. Miguel's going to know soon.

LIAISON: He might already.

MIGUEL TURNED TOWARD THE BALCONY. The tide below had shifted, currents surging against the rocks in erratic bursts. The night air carried a scent he didn't recognize—sharp, metallic, out of place.

Somewhere beyond the villa walls, a night bird called. Then another sound—too soft for a guard's step, too deliberate for the wind.

He crossed to the desk, opened the cigar box, and removed one folded tab.

The name on it was *Marcos*.

When he looked up, the balcony curtains were still swaying—though the wind had stopped.

[INTERCEPT: **SecureChannel // PartialDecryption: 22:11:42**]

FIELD OPS: Movement inside the villa perimeter.

ED: Confirm visual.

FIELD OPS: Negative. But whoever it is… they're already inside.

30

The Breaking Point

The late-afternoon sun clung to the horizon, bleeding copper light across the water as Max Larkin sat at the edge of the pier. Elbows braced on his knees, shoulders hunched, he stared at the tide as if the waves might offer an answer. The wood beneath him groaned with the slow sway of the current. Below, the ocean slapped against barnacle-crusted pilings, each thud a reminder of how time wore down anything left unguarded.

His notebook lay open across his lap, its dog-eared pages warped by years of salt air and rain. A pen dangled between his fingers, unmoving. Not a single word had landed on the page. His thoughts were gutted by a truth too heavy for language.

Two nights ago, behind a gas station lit by a flickering bulb, Max had cornered the man he'd been chasing for weeks — a courier with cartel ties, now bloodied and trembling. The man's face was a topography of bruises, his nose flattened from some earlier beating. Amid the stink of oil and dust, the courier had spoken the sentence that split Max's world in two.

"He wasn't random," the courier had rasped, coughing blood onto the gravel. "That overdose? Deliberate. A message to you. For that article on Santa Elena."

Everything had frozen then — the traffic on the highway, the night air, his own pulse. For months, Max had blamed the party scene, the lure of easy pills, his own absence. But this was worse. His son's death hadn't been chance. It had been an execution. Evan wasn't the victim of poor choices; he'd been a target.

The guilt had been suffocating when Max thought it was neglect. Now it was murder. And he'd never seen it coming.

Footsteps approached over the warped boards. Jenna sat beside him, arms folded against the sea breeze, her expression tight.

"You heard him," Max said, still watching the horizon.

"I did." Her voice was low, threaded with a dangerous calm. "This isn't on you, Max. It's on them."

"They didn't just kill my son," he said. "They turned him into a weapon against me."

"You've been exposing them for years. You think they wouldn't notice?"

"I thought—" He stopped, swallowing hard. "I thought the fight was out there. Not at my kitchen table."

Jenna studied him. "Then maybe now you fight it differently."

He met her eyes. Grief still burned there, but beneath it was steel.

"They took him from me to make me stop," Max said. "Instead, I'm going to burn them down."

[INTERCEPTED TRANSMISSION – **ENCRYPTION LEVEL 4]**
1832 HRS – SOURCE: COASTAL NODE
TARGET ALPHA (LARKIN) – in position at pier. Emotional state: elevated.
Continue observation. Orders remain: do not engage until Port Savannah window confirmed.
– SENDER: M/8

THE WAREHOUSE PASSED for a seafood distributor — faded

signage, humming forklifts, the metallic tang of ice melt. But in the back room, the disguise ended.

Maps crowded the tables, red string weaving across pins along the Eastern Seaboard. Laptops streamed grainy satellite feeds and intercepted manifests. A corkboard held rows of headshots — some crossed out in red, others marked with question marks.

Sarah handed Max a folder, her expression sharp. "We traced the bribes for those last two cargo runs. Both shell companies are in Senator Marcus Leighton's portfolio."

Max froze. "Leighton. Florida. Commerce Committee."

"Same one," Sarah said. "Maritime oversight. Perfect access."

He flipped through the pages — wire transfers, falsified pharmaceutical manifests, Cayman Islands deposits.

"This isn't just collusion," Max said. "It's infrastructure."

Janna leaned over the map. "If we leak now, they scatter. They'll scrub clean before we can follow the money."

Max shook his head. "We choke the pipeline before we go public. Make them panic. While they scramble, we dig to the root."

———

FROM HIS VILLA, Miguel Ortega leaned on the balcony rail, the wind tugging his shirt. Raul stood in the doorway with a phone.

"They know about Leighton," Raul said. "Larkin's people are moving."

Miguel didn't look back. "How close?"

"Close enough to make noise."

Miguel's gaze stayed on the horizon. "Then we give them something louder."

[INTERCEPTED TRANSMISSION – **ENCRYPTION LEVEL 4**]
1944 HRS – SOURCE: INTERNAL NODE – PACIFIC COAST
ORTEGA orders contingency escalation.
Redirect primary asset from Reynosa to Savannah node.

Confirm intercept team in place.
– SENDER: R/1

RICK NOLAN'S apartment felt like a bunker disguised as a living room. Newspaper clippings yellowed on the walls. Pushpins connected photographs, memos, and ledgers. Dust and whiskey hung in the air. Once a legend in the newsroom, Rick had vanished after his daughter's overdose. Now, he was back.

Rick handed Max a sheet. "This Belize account runs through Leighton's shell company."

Max's jaw tightened. "That's not just dirty money. That's protected dirty money."

Rick sipped his drink. "Some lines end in Washington. Others in Langley."

Max's eyes lifted to a photo of Jamie pinned above the desk. That smile gutted him all over again. Their grief was a dull, constant ache, but beneath it, their resolve had sharpened into something lethal.

"They made it personal," Max said.

"Then hit them smart," Rick replied. "Or you'll bury more than names."

Dawn broke pale over the decommissioned marina, the air heavy with salt and rust. The team gathered in a gutted boathouse, its floorboards creaking with the ghost of tides.

Sarah spread a new map. "Shipment rerouted. Private dock near Savannah. Thirty-six hours."

Max looked around at them — Jenna, Sarah, Janna—the freelancer from Mexico, three Homeland Security recruits, and a shipping whistleblower. Tired eyes, tense shoulders, unwavering resolve.

"This is our moment," Max said. "We intercept the cargo, livestream the evidence. Once it's out, they can't bury it."

Janna pulled on her gloves. "We'll need drones. Satellite backup."

Jenna added, "And a diversion big enough to keep the media busy while the feds move."

Max nodded. "I'll handle that." He unfolded a dew-blurred note from his pocket: *Prepare for the storm.*

"They know we're coming," he said. "So let's give them something to fear."

The road to Savannah cut through marshland, the horizon smeared with the lavender haze of an incoming storm. Max drove the lead SUV, Jenna riding shotgun with the map open, Sarah and Janna following close behind.

The plan was fragile but exact: get eyes on the dock, confirm the cargo, start a rolling upload before Homeland Security swept in. But twelve hours felt like minutes, every mile an echo of the courier's voice in Max's head.

[INTERCEPTED TRANSMISSION – **ENCRYPTION LEVEL 4]**

0615 HRS – SOURCE: SOUTHERN NODE

TARGET ALPHA convoy entering Chatham County perimeter.

Ortega cell in position at Dock 14.

Contingency: neutralize primary OR secure package.

– SENDER: R/1

THE PRIVATE DOCK bore no resemblance to the official port — no cranes, no customs, just squat warehouses behind rusted fencing. Miguel stood in the shadow of a refrigerated trailer, sunglasses hiding his gaze.

"Larkin's convoy is on the causeway," Raul reported. "Less than thirty minutes."

Miguel lit a cigarette, letting the wind carry the smoke over the water. "Then we make sure they leave with nothing."

Inside, under layers of frozen seafood, the real cargo waited: high-grade fentanyl pressed into counterfeit pill bottles, ready for East Coast distribution.

"Put the spotters in the lot," Miguel said. "I want their faces before they see ours."

Three blocks from the dock, Max parked in a shadowed alley. The air tasted of brine and diesel. Gulls screamed overhead.

Sarah pointed toward the chain-link fence. "Two guards at the gate. One perimeter patrol."

Max adjusted his comms. "We split. Jenna, Janna — north side. Sarah and I — south. Meet at the loading bay in ten."

"Assuming we don't get made," Jenna said.

"Then don't get made."

They moved in pairs, hugging the fence, boots crunching on damp gravel. The hum of a generator undercut the slap of waves against pilings.

[INTERCEPTED TRANSMISSION – **ENCRYPTION LEVEL 4**]

0647 HRS – SOURCE: DOCK 14 NODE

NORTH perimeter: visual on two unidentified females.

SOUTH perimeter: male/female pair, one matches TARGET ALPHA.

Await confirmation from Ortega.

– SENDER: V/9

FROM A CATWALK above the warehouse floor, Miguel scanned security feeds. Four figures moved in the shadows outside — deliberate, controlled.

Raul leaned in. "It's them."

Miguel crushed out his cigarette. "Hold the guards. I want them closer."

Max crouched behind rusted crab traps at the southern corner. Through a gap in the siding, he glimpsed pallets wrapped in plastic, export labels forged.

Sarah placed a small camera at the gap. "Uploading."

Jenna's voice crackled in his ear. "North side clear to the loading bay."

Max glanced toward the lot — and froze. A man in dark clothes stood in the shadow of a truck, watching him. Predator stillness.

[INTERCEPTED TRANSMISSION – **ENCRYPTION LEVEL 4]**
0652 HRS – SOURCE: UNKNOWN NODE
TARGET ALPHA: visual acquired.
ORTEGA: in motion.

THE SOUTHERN WALL door swung open, slicing daylight into the gloom. Miguel stepped out slowly, hands at his sides, his silhouette cut against the shadows.

Twenty yards away, Max turned to face him.

The air stretched thin, charged. Sarah's whisper was barely a breath. "Max…?"

"Stay behind me," he said.

Miguel advanced, the ghost of a smile on his lips.

The storm broke — not from the sky, but from the dockyard, where a forklift roared to life and the warehouse doors rolled upward.

Inside, under the hum of refrigeration, the shipment waited.

31

The Tipping Line

The newsroom no longer smelled like a newsroom. It smelled like a bunker—coffee left too long on the hot plate, solder from hastily rigged networking gear, and the metallic tang of Florida rain seeping through warped window frames.

Ed Harper paced between two folding tables dragged into the center of the Tallahassee Gazettel's third-floor workspace. Outside, rain tapped the glass in a slow, deliberate rhythm, like it knew something he didn't.

He didn't need a clock to know it was past midnight. The hollow-eyed fatigue on every face told him enough. Linda sat cross-legged on a swivel chair, hair pulled back, typing one-handed while sipping chicory coffee from a paper cup. Kyle hunched over a laptop, cables spilling in tangled skeins off the edge of the table.

They were already compromised. He felt it the way you feel a storm coming—not from the first flash or rumble, but from the pressure drop. Their Dropbox had been scraped. Burner phones pinged through a relay in St. Augustine. Two sources had gone dark in forty-eight hours.

· · ·

[INTERCEPTED TRANSMISSION – 00:14 EST]

Location: Unconfirmed, believed to be Veracruz safehouse.

Miguel Ortega (El Cazador): "The Tallahassee man is moving too fast."

Unknown Voice: "Let him. He's about to cross the line where the ground drops out beneath him."

ED KNEW WHAT "CROSSING THE LINE" meant. It wasn't about laws—it was the invisible threshold where you stopped being a nuisance and became a liability. Liabilities in this world didn't last long.

He leaned over Linda's shoulder. "Pull every open lead on Tallahassee lobbying firms tied to Panama. Leighton, Castor, de la Vega—anything. If there's overlap with our cartel manifests, flag it before sunrise."

"You think this is all Florida-based?" she asked without looking up.

He didn't answer. Lately, he wasn't sure where Florida ended and everything else began.

[INTERCEPTED TRANSMISSION – 00:26 EST]

Miguel Ortega (El Cazador): "When Harper connects Leighton to us, it's over."

Unknown Voice: "No. When Harper connects Leighton to them, it's over. We just have to make sure he doesn't live long enough to split the difference."

BY 02:00, the newsroom had morphed into a war room. The corkboard of community announcements was gone, replaced with a sprawling flowchart of shell corporations. The fax machine was shoved into a corner to make space for two portable servers borrowed from a university lab.

The fluorescent hum overhead was the only steady sound

besides the clack of keys. Monica had arrived hours earlier, damp from the rain, a manila folder tucked under her coat.

"It's the senator's nephew," she said, dropping the folder on the table. "Photo puts him at a cartel meet in Key Biscayne."

Ed studied the image under the harsh desk lamp. "We confirm this, we've got a direct artery from Tallahassee to Santa Elena."

[INTERCEPTED TRANSMISSION – **00:42 EST**]

Miguel Ortega (El Cazador): "If he publishes that photo, we'll have federal heat we can't pay off."

Unknown Voice: "Then burn the proof before it burns you."

AT 03:10, Ed broke his own rule about never moving without a partner. He slipped out alone into the wet Tallahassee streets, the drizzle softening every edge of the lamplight.

His destination was a dim apartment block on Gaines Street where Argo—a contact too deep in to ever be clean again—was waiting. The stairwell smelled of mildew and cigarettes. Argo stood at the far end of the hall, backlit by a cracked door's glow.

"You shouldn't have come here," Argo hissed.

"You sent the warning," Ed replied.

"And I regret it. You're marked now. So is your team."

Ed handed over a manila envelope. "What happens if this gets out?"

Argo's eyes were flat. "They hit the grid. Not everything—just enough to make people panic. Banks, cell towers, 911 dispatch. Florida first. Then the ripple goes national."

Ed felt the floor tilt under him. "And there's another file?"

"A kill switch," Argo said. "A real one. They'll hold it until you push too far. Then they drop the hammer."

[INTERCEPTED TRANSMISSION – **00:58 EST**]

Miguel Ortega (El Cazador): "He's in the wind."

Unknown Voice: "Not for long."

BY 04:00, Ed was back in the newsroom. Kyle was running a manual IP reroute. Linda napped on a couch. Monica sat beneath a desk lamp, marking affidavits with a pen between her teeth.

Ed dropped the envelope on the table and started typing. By 04:45, every verified document was uploaded to an encrypted server in Estonia. A pre-scheduled package—labeled *Domino*—was set to auto-release across multiple syndicates if they missed their next check-in.

He paused once, eyes drifting to a yellowed clipping on the wall —his first big scoop. A school board cover-up. A grieving parent. His old editor telling him, *Publish this, and you'll lose friends. But you'll make a damn difference.*

[INTERCEPTED TRANSMISSION – **01:11 EST**]

Miguel Ortega (El Cazador): "If he goes to press, there's no undoing it."

Unknown Voice: "Then make sure his press never runs."

AT 05:03, a new ping hit their off-grid terminal. Origin: a French server. Subject line:

INSIDE THE GOVERNOR'S OFFICE

No body text. No attachments. Just the implication—heavy as a loaded chamber—that what lay beyond could either blow their investigation open or burn it to the ground.

Ed stared at the screen, the air in the room growing heavier. Whatever was in that unseen file… this was the line. The tipping point.

And once they crossed it, there'd be no way back.

32

Sabotage

Rain lashed the floor-to-ceiling windows of Harper Vale's studio like a thousand bright wires, the storm smearing the skyline into streaks of neon and shadow. Thunder rolled low, a bellyful of threat that hadn't yet spoken its name. Inside: the hum of fans, the whir of drives, the steady tick of a cheap wall clock that had outlived three apartments and two lives.

Harper sat cross-legged on the hardwood in the middle of her ring of machines, palms pressed to her thighs to quiet the tremor. Screens washed her face in a carousel of color—cool VPN blues, angry notification reds, jaundiced headline yellows that misquoted her into someone else entirely. Tabs stacked over tabs until even the browser looked out of breath.

"They breached it," she said to no one, because saying it out loud kept her from pretending otherwise. "Everything."

Two weeks ago, Harper had been riding the crest of public momentum. Her exposés on the cartel's manipulation of the health care system and food supply had ignited national outrage. But now the tide had turned. It had taken less than an hour for the smear to metastasize: fake "gotcha" clips drowning search results; a synthesized voice mimicking her to friends with chilling precision;

doctored photos of her holding cash across from a man she'd never met; bot swarms with perfect grammar and surgical timing.

A pop-up bloomed on her largest monitor: **ACCOUNT UNDER INVESTIGATION.** Then three more: **ACCESS RESTRICTED. POLICY REVIEW. SUSPENDED.** Instagram. Twitter. The last of the "professional" platforms people still treated like an ID card. All gone in a chain reaction—too fast, too clean.

"They were waiting," she whispered.

She tried Max: no answer. Ed: voicemail. Jenna's burner: dead. Only one number left, one she'd promised never to use.

The line clicked on the fourth ring. "Well, well," a voice purred. "Which one of my sins just came home wearing your face?"

"Camille. I'm compromised. Deepfakes, cloned voicemail, bot swarms. Feels like they tapped the influencer backbone itself. I need extraction. Yesterday."

A low whistle. "Full-spectrum crucifixion. Somebody rich, pissed, and insomnia-proof. Drop me your hashes and node IDs. I'll ghost-shell you under a marine biology fellowship in Reykjavik and scatter your location like confetti. Twenty minutes. Chain the door twice. If I'm not me, be offended."

The line cut. Outside, the thunder went from rumor to vow. Harper shut down every networked device but her offline terminal, pulled three encrypted sticks into a Zip-seal bag, and left a note under her keyboard: **Camille has the reins. Go silent. Watch the docks.**

The hall light flickered twice when she cracked the door. The elevator down the corridor dinged and didn't open. Somewhere, a car idled where nobody parked. She double-chained the lock and left the lights on—one more false pulse for anyone watching.

[INTERCEPTED TRANSMISSION — **Miguel Ortega POV**]

SOURCE: Gulf opsec backhaul / TIMESTAMP: +00:41 GMT / CLASS: KITEWIRE

Miguel Ortega (El Cazador): Bird is out of cage.

H1: Let current carry. Nets set west-side.

Miguel Ortega (El Cazador): West is loud. I want east eyes.
H1: East closed door. No prints.
Miguel Ortega (El Cazador): Leave no prints. Watch for puffin.

FOURTEEN MINUTES LATER, Camille slipped inside—hood up, rain ghosting off her canvas jacket. "This place is a postcard for *please spy on me*," she said, kneeling by Harper's machines. A matte-black wedge in her hand pulsed test patterns across every screen.

"Kernel's not dumb," Camille said. "It's vain. Been listening for two weeks, flipped last night. Sneaky—like a cat with a bell."

"They knew what I was going to publish before I did," Harper said.

"Worse. They cataloged what you almost published. Corday."

Camille dragged a spiderweb of IP hops and shell companies onto the screen. One thread pulsed out of Washington D.C. "Corvus Strategies. Peel enough layers, it's Michael Corday. Logistics, political cover, PR throttles—he's the artery they've tied a silk tie on."

Harper's voice went flat. "Then we set a tourniquet."

From the hall: a scuff, a pause not quite long enough for coincidence. Camille counted silently, then resumed typing. "Analog," she murmured.

They packed what mattered—three sticks, two burners, a mesh pouch of coded notes—and killed the breakers. One lamp on a timer was all they left behind.

Down the back stairs, Harper's skin recorded every wrong note: a fresh shoe print at the stairwell seam; a dark smear on the rail; someone else's breath. Outside, the storm rinsed itself into mist. Camille led her to a sedan with the wrong plates.

They drove to a safehouse wedged between two dying row homes. Inside, Elias Parrish sat under a dust-ringed lamp. "Your kernel was nosy and patient," he said. "Lit up Sonora, then D.C., then Tallahassee. Overlaps Ed's trail."

"The same thing watching me was watching him," Harper said.

"Corday's the route. Miguel's the muscle. The Governor's office is the blessing. Leighton's the purse," Elias said. "It's not a conspiracy. It's an org chart."

"Org charts burn," Harper said.

Camille slid her a cover identity—Astrid Holvik, puffin enthusiast and spreadsheet hobbyist. "People trust boring," she said. "We'll be unspeakably dull."

They built a hidden broadcast in slivers: QR codes in photos, sine waves carrying coordinates, captions spelling maps by omission. A lighthouse for anyone who already knew how to look.

[INTERCEPT — **Tallahassee Gazette Secure Chat**]

ED: The moles aren't guessing anymore. Someone mirrored us in real time through Harper's back end.

ROSA: She still breathing?

ED: Find her before they do.

AT 7:00 P.M. Pacific, Jenna went live—silhouette against a blown-out skyline, voice a scalpel. She showed falsified manifests, freezer-hidden pallets, forged inspection reports. "These aren't oversights. They're weapons. Tomorrow, a shipment will arrive disguised as relief aid. Laced with fentanyl. If nothing happens by noon, you'll know where the fix lives."

A pure tone sliced the feed. Then a male voice, bleach-flat: "End your transmission. Or we will." The screen went black.

The safehouse lights hiccuped. Camille yanked every plug. "Corday flinched," she said. "When men like him panic, they overreach. Noise helps us."

[INTERCEPT — **Cartel Ops Node 4**]

V1: Blackbird chirped. Cut the dawn line.

V2: Fish still on hook?

V1: Don't pull. Let the boat drift.

[INTERCEPT — Corday Net]
OP: Soundstage spiked. Pull her mirrors.
CTRL: Doing it live. Quiet hands.
OP: Don't touch the governor feed. Not yet.

CAMILLE WAS ALREADY MOVING. "If they easy-cut the stream, they had scissors in the pipe. That means collars in the street."

They slipped into the alley's throat—bins, graffiti, the scent of motor oil. A sedan idled at the block's mouth, a figure leaned under a lamppost, and a shade lifted in a window across the way.

"Left, then right," Camille said.

They climbed a stack of shipping containers, mapping the hunt from above: sedan at the gate, men at choke points. "We're funneled," Harper said.

They dropped to the blind side and ran for the fence. Voices shouted. Feet pounded gravel. The fence tore Harper's sleeve before Camille wrenched her through.

They surfaced under an overpass, lungs burning. "Time, not safety," Camille said.

A diner gave them coffee and a booth with a wall to their backs. Harper's burner buzzed under the table—confirmation from Ed: Corday's crew had her location within five minutes of the stream.

Back at the safehouse, the air was wrong. A chair nudged two inches back. A receipt shifted. A thumbprint in dust too big to be theirs.

"My neighbor's porch cam caught a guy two doors down," Elias said quietly. "Didn't knock. Wanted us to know he could."

"They're past the keyboard," Camille said. "We're in their city now."

Harper laid her palm on the table, felt the wood's old heart steady her. "They just signed the warrant on their own future."

[INTERCEPTED TRANSMISSION — Miguel Ortega POV]

SOURCE: Gulf management relay / TIMESTAMP: +08:12 GMT / CLASS: THRESHOLD

Miguel Ortega (El Cazador): Puffin pecks glass.

H1: Window holds—for now.

Miguel Ortega (El Cazador): Let her peck. When the pane cracks, we watch whose hands bleed.

H1: And then?

Miguel Ortega (El Cazador): Then we decide who owns the house.

33

Lines in the Sand

The rain had the road pinned like a seam ripper—bright needles unpicking the night from shoulder to shoulder. Max Larkin eased off the highway into a gravel turnout, tires crunching under the low neon halo of a roadside diner's half-dead sign. *EAT* flickered to *AT*, then to *E_*, then nothing at all. The building hunched against the storm like a man who'd been hit too many times to stand tall and pretend otherwise.

He cut the engine and waited. Wipers clicked. The rain shifted —hard to soft, soft to the sly patter of drizzle. His reflection ghosted back at him in the glass: older than he remembered, lines cut deeper by the months since everything broke, chin scar catching light like a quiet lighthouse. Without moving his head, he scanned the lot: a tanker idling by the diesel pump; a compact with paper plates, nose toward the exit; a pickup angled just right to watch both the door and the corner booth. The silhouette in the cab pretended to be a coat on a hook.

Notebook and burner went into his jacket's inside pocket. He stepped into the weather, walking casual—the way men walk when they don't want to wake anything sleeping with teeth.

The bell over the diner door gave a polite chirp. Warmth met him—fry grease, coffee, the thin metal thread of an old jukebox tune. At the far end, a couple in matching fishing jackets argued gently. Mid-aisle, a trucker didn't look up—by which Max meant he'd already looked up in his spoon's reflection. The waitress clocked him and didn't smile. He appreciated that.

He took a booth with his back to the wall and a window to his left. Headlights outside stitched the rain into brief ribbons, shadows sliding their knives along the cracked tile. His right hand rested on the table, palm down; his left fished for the burner.

The text was waiting when he turned the screen over:

BLOCK-SENT: *Ink stains last longer than blood. Still want the pen?*

No signature. Didn't need one. The words smelled of saltwater, bad decisions, and a decade-old conversation in Veracruz where a man called Smitty—because no one trusted names that sounded real—had warned him tides have moods.

Max typed: **Name the place.**

A minute later: *Twenty west. The crooked finger. One bulb. Knock like you learned manners.*

The waitress set a chipped mug in front of him. "You waiting on someone?"

"Always," he said, leaving enough cash for noise and memory. One sip—burned coffee, the taste of nights where truth was a second language—and he was gone.

Outside, the pickup didn't move. Neither did the coat that wasn't a coat.

The freight depot rose from the dark like a rusted ship. Vines claimed the fence; the tower was next. A single bulb over a side door pulsed like a tired heart.

Max parked in the tower's shadow, walked slow on the gravel, and knocked three times—the way kids learn and forget until they need it again.

The door opened on a man sun-wrinkled and storm-hardened, a jagged scar tugging his mouth toward silence. Navy watch cap in the heat—a habit he couldn't lose.

"You blinked," Smitty said. Not cruel. Just ledgered.

"I didn't have the proof," Max said.

"Bullshit. You didn't have the guts."

They stood in it—two men with different ghosts. Smitty's eyes did the soldier's check: hands, beltline, eyes, posture. Then he nodded at a chair and let the door sigh shut.

The place smelled of damp metal and old rain. Two pans caught steady drips from the ceiling. A radio hissed like it half-remembered shortwave.

"You ever lose someone because you waited too long?" Smitty asked. "Not in a headline—in a kitchen. Morning coffee for two, one chair empty."

Max said nothing.

"My brother," Smitty said. "Hooked on the same stuff I used to keep from landing. I looked away long enough to call it rest. It killed him." He paced, slow, like keeping time for someone else's metronome.

"Went straight for a while," he said. "Trained badge kids. Gave them the tricks honest men need when they're outnumbered. They wanted software instead. I went under. Pulled threads until they tightened around my neck. Thought I'd let it all rot. Then your girl went on the air."

"She's not my—"

"Doesn't matter," Smitty cut in. "She lit a wet fuse. People like me started listening. People like me don't sleep well."

He pulled a matte-black drive from his jacket—small enough to lose, heavy enough to be a decision—and set it between them.

"Bill of lading manifests. Timestamps. In-line photos. Clearance codes. Next heavy load out of Yucatán. Hiding under federal tags like a priest under a borrowed name. Corday pops up at every clear-ance seam."

Corday again. The name that bled through seams, smiling like a consultant, thinking like a ledger.

"This comes with heat," Smitty said. "The kind you smell. You push this, you don't get a second chance. Neither do I."

"Why now?"

"Because the world's ending slow," Smitty said. "And I'd rather it end loud."

He slid the drive over. Max stopped it with his palm. It was warm.

Outside, something small rattled against the siding—then went quiet. The radio caught and coughed.

[INTERCEPT — **CARTEL OPS NODE 6**]

SOURCE: Inland relay / TIMESTAMP: +01:29 GMT / CLASS: SANDWIRE

V1: Choir's tuning.

V2: Pull the hymnals.

V1: Not yet. Let the soloist sweat.

V2: Copy. Mics hot.

SMITTY SCRIBBLED A THROWAWAY EMAIL, a password only three people would laugh at, and coordinates for a warehouse that wasn't on paper.

"If I don't text in twelve hours," he said, "I died exactly how I thought I wouldn't."

"Where do I send flowers?" Max asked.

"Send bullets to better men. Air to the ones in a box."

No handshake. Some agreements are too true for hands.

Max left with the drive and the paper. The pickup was gone. The compact with paper plates had moved closer to the exit.

Back at his apartment, the hall smelled of old carpet and someone else's dinner. He listened at the door until his fridge's too-loud compressor confirmed he was alone. Locks, chains, deadbolt, chock. Keys in the bowl—metal measuring the day.

He cleared the table by the window, blinds half-closed, shadows drawing invisible sides. The secure tower booted. The passphrase came by muscle memory.

The drive opened to a directory of names, numbers, clearance slips too neat to be true. Corday's fingerprints everywhere. And names—politicians, foremen, bureaucrats—some he knew, some he wished he didn't.

The burner buzzed: Jack—*Jesus, Max. This is it. Don't answer. Just move.* Jenna—*If I go live, they'll know we have it. You sure?*

He typed: *Yes.* Deleted the rest. Sent it.

The quiet leaned in. Pipes clicked. He poured bourbon and didn't drink it.

He began a contingency file:

LINES IN THE SAND: An Accounting

To be released in full if I go dark.

This is not redemption. This is a map and a fuse.

He wrote the chapters—The Promise and the Lie; The Artery with a Tie; The River and the Mouth; The Choir in the Gallery; The Dead and the Debt; The Names that Matter; What to Watch; What I Did; What You Will Do; The Fuse.

Each section a torch passed into someone else's hands.

He mirrored the file to Estonia, Iceland, a dusty box in a nonprofit newsroom. Time and pulse were the triggers.

[INTERCEPT — **CORDAY NET**]

OP: Choir boy is writing a hymn.

CTRL: Let him sing. Makes the ending cleaner.

OUTSIDE, a car door shut like a sentence ending with intent. Footsteps faded. The storm paused above the city like it was listening.

Max saved. Printed one copy. Addressed it to a name only two people knew. Wrote: *IF FOUND, READ OUT LOUD.*

He shut down the tower, left the bourbon untouched. Thought of Smitty's drive, Jenna's voice, Ed's lamp, Harper's silhouette, Miguel Ortega's name where names shouldn't be, Corday's tie on a saint's forklift mast.

The phone stayed silent. The building stayed still. The choir didn't sing.

He let the quiet hold him for a count of five, slid the second bolt home, turned off the last light, and set the burner and his notebook on the envelope like paper weighed more than it did.

The rain returned—a softer stitch, as if the sky had found a new needle.

He breathed. The file waited. The fuse lay quiet. And the line—his line—held.

34

Fragile Peace

The storm had shouldered inland by the time Ed Harper turned off Monroe and rolled past the capitol's white crown. Rain didn't fall so much as stitch the streets shut—threading cloud to pavement in vertical seams. Wipers snapped. Headlights smeared into comets. Palms bent in the wind, their fronds combed flat by weather with strong opinions.

He parked two blocks from the *Tallahassee Gazette* and killed the engine. Sat for a beat, cataloguing the details that never make the copy but decide whether you live to write it: a dark sedan idling with only parking lights; a delivery van nosed into the end of the loading zone, driver absent; a hooded figure at the bus stop, head down, shoes wrong for the weather, unmoving.

Then he stepped into the rain and let it take him. By the time he reached the Gazette's brick facade, the water had soaked through to bone—bone that remembered every bad decision and the one coming next.

Inside, the lobby smelled of wet wool and ink. Buzzers hummed. Behind smoked glass, a security guard with the habit of reading novels stripped of their jackets nodded without smiling. Ed took the stairs—habit, not bravery—and climbed to the third floor.

The newsroom's glass doors gave back a version of him he recognized only by inventory: gray at the temples, lines around the mouth from swallowing words, a left shoulder that had learned to hunch at late-night emails.

He keyed in.

The room felt like the air before a squall: static, anticipation, a hush that wasn't quiet. Desks hummed; monitors glowed with maps and spreadsheets, chat panes vanishing when you got too close. Conversations ran low and clipped, drifting into code. Somewhere a printer started and stopped, as if thinking better of it.

He ghosted through the room, checking the faces he trusted: Linda, hair in a knot that said *do not ask me for anything but the world*; Kyle with three phones and a paper notebook because paper doesn't log; Monica with her wire-frame glasses, her pen, her mercy. Their glances said what he'd taught them—fear is data, but you don't publish it.

A freckled intern tugged his sleeve. "Mr. Harmon? There's… a car outside. Been there a while."

Ed squeezed the kid's shoulder. "Call facilities. Tell them to check the gutters." An order ordinary enough to breathe.

The storm pressed at the windows. Somewhere below, a siren changed keys.

In his office, rain cut the city into slate sheets. The capitol's spire blurred into suggestion. On the desk: the secure server blinking green; a stack of blue folders full of names that didn't share space politely; a photo of his father on a beach, paper hat tilted, the man who'd taught him truth feels good until it doesn't, and you do it anyway.

He opened the secure channel. Six weeks of work spilled onto his screen—donor flows, shell companies, port clearance logs, photo captures—all braided around two names: Senator Marcus Leighton, the one the state loved; and Phoenix Group, the one it pretended not to know.

Phoenix had always been smoke: private equity moving like fog, a contractor signing NDAs with countries, an analytics firm predicting elections and sometimes "helping." Now it lived in front of him—deposits, contracts, emails trying not to be themselves. A cartel financier listed as a PAC "consultant," the way a wolf might appear on a pet adoption site as good with children.

His phone buzzed. Unknown number:

— INTERCEPT 17:11 CST | SOURCE: Harper Vale RELAY —

HV: Dock clocks moved. Watch the relief banner. Noon is a lie.

HV: Ghost nodes hot. Corday flinched.

HV: Publish like you've already been shot.

Harper's cadence, even filtered through hands he didn't know.

The second buzz landed like a tap between the shoulder blades:

Unknown Sender: *Dock 14. One hour. Come alone. Don't bring your ethics.*

Only one man alive still used that line without irony—Ray Salazar.

Ed grabbed his coat. Took the stairs two at a time.

Dock 14 never looked better in rain. The river took the weather and made it smell like metal, algae, and wood chewed by too many boots. Streetlights buzzed in angry halos. A crane groaned. The water sat low, as if mistrusting the bank.

Ray emerged first as shape, then man—thrift-store jacket, cigar as lighthouse. Ed counted other shapes: a coiled hose masquerading as shadow; the glint of a bottle in pallet gaps; the flat sliver of a phone facedown.

"You always looked like you belonged in the rain," Ray said.

"And you always looked like you knew where the bodies washed up."

Ray flicked the cigar into a puddle—hiss, gone. "Leighton piece. Tonight?"

"Yes."

Ray grimaced, pulled a flash drive from a pocket built for secrets. Black, unbranded, heavy. "Court-sealed. Depositions. Grand jury minutes. You didn't get them from me."

"What's the bill?"

"The man tied to Leighton isn't just moving cartel numbers— he's a pass-through for Phoenix Group's off-books. You think you're pulling a senator. You're picking a hive that names hurricanes."

Ed kept his face. "I've heard that rumor since I had more hair."

"You've never held the paperwork. Now you do. And these things? They want to be seen right before they decide to be ashes."

A barge horn wailed upriver. The dock shuddered.

"You came alone?" Ray asked.

"You tell me."

Ray's eyes shifted past him. "You drew a tail from the building. Don't turn. Two blocks back, cut through the antiques place with the glass swans. I'll take the other way and hope I picked the wrong enemy."

Ed smiled with his eyes. "Tired of being right and not rich?"

"All the time. Then I buy cheaper cigars."

Ray's two-finger salute vanished into the geometry of dock, crane, barge.

Back at the Gazette, the storm had eased. The third floor glowed like a ship at sea. Linda, Kyle, Monica gathered in the secure room. White-noise generator set to airplane bathroom.

Ed dropped the flash drive. "Phoenix Group's no ghost. It's a line item."

They moved like a team that knew the stakes—skepticism first, then hunger.

Linda plugged the drive into a quarantined machine. "If this is real, we go from state scandal to federal case that makes new enemies."

Kyle scribbled in his paper notebook. "Our Mexican stringers say plainclothes asked about us in a cafe. Didn't pay for their coffee. Scarier than guns."

Monica cleaned the same smudge from her glasses, put them back on. "Leighton's counsel will fish for mistakes. How's our redaction?"

"Clean," Ed said. "As clean as you can make something built by men who turned law into a private road."

Text, exhibits, photos filled Linda's screen. "Phoenix appears on a memo to modernize port inspections. Same week, Leighton's PAC gets a 'consulting donation' from a shell tied to a Cayman sublicense with a logistics firm Homeland's flagged twice. Jesus."

Kyle flipped a page. "Charity warehouse near the runway. Saint on the forklift mast. Harper's obsession."

Monica: "We are a newspaper, not a crusade."

"Sometimes the Venn diagram is a circle," Ed said.

His phone buzzed.

— INTERCEPT 20:43 EST | SOURCE: CARTEL OPS NODE 3 —

V1: Lighthouse goes hot at midnight.

V2: Let tide talk first.

V1: Choirboy at the docks?

V2: He knows the hymn. Not the echo.

Ed slid the phone away. "We push at midnight."

At 11:57, he stood behind Linda's chair. At 12:00:00, she hit **PUBLISH**.

HEADLINE: *Senator's Shadow Empire: Cartel Cash, Covert Contracts, and the Phoenix Connection*

SUBHEAD: *Exclusive investigation exposes a high-ranking lawmaker's secret ties to a transnational drug network backed by a private power bloc with global reach.*

The traffic heat-map bloomed. Syndicators pinged. Threats arrived—some in caps lock, some scented with legalese, one worse because it knew him: *How's your Detroit source doing? Still missing?*

ANOTHER INTERCEPT LIT THE PHONE:

— INTERCEPT 00:07 EST | SOURCE: Harper Vale RELAY —

HV: Relief banner moved to 10:30. Saint on the mast.

HV: Corday choking syndication. If you go down, we push your PDF.

HV: "Choir is full," Max says. I say sing anyway.

· · ·

THE NEWSROOM SHIFTED into controlled burn—Monica on the phone with a lawyer, Janna whispering to Juárez, Linda feeding mirrors until the map looked lit from within.

Ed retreated to his office, stared at his father's paper-hat grin, watched threats refresh in his inbox. A new one blinked into existence: *We remember Fall River. Do you?* Then vanished.

He messaged the room: *Phones off. Walk out in pairs. Keys left hand, not right. Breakfast here at nine.*

Drives were copied—Linda, Monica, Kyle each got one. A printed packet went into an envelope addressed to HARPER VALE / R. NOLAN / H.V. MIRRORS.

He stepped into the hallway's carpet-and-history air. The EXIT sign made its own small church. At the landing, the dead stairwell camera glowed red.

Downstairs, the guard's chair was empty, paperback open to an underlined sentence: *No one is ever as anonymous as they think.* The lock had a fresh nick.

Outside, the sedan's parking lights blinked once. The driver lit a cigarette.

His car's side mirror was wrong. Seat pushed back a notch. Two wet footprints by the door—headed away.

He didn't startle. The fear rose, and he pressed it down with the only thing that worked: *We publish. We come back. We do it again.*

He turned toward the coffee shop with lights still on. He'd sit until sky admitted morning. Kyle would pick him up at six. They'd eat eggs that weren't eggs.

His phone buzzed:

— INTERCEPT 01:19 EST | SOURCE: Harper Vale RELAY —

HV: They cut one mirror. We lit three more.

HV: Don't walk alone. Max says the fuse is primed.

HV: See you on the other side of noon.

Ed gripped the coffee shop's door. Warm air came out to meet him like a dog, hopeful.

Behind him, the sedan's taillights flared once, then darkened.

The fragile peace he'd bargained for—a last story without

bodies—collapsed without a sound. In its place: a wet street, a straight line, a morning coming like a verdict.

He stepped inside, shook off the rain, and ordered two breakfasts he wouldn't eat. Took the corner booth, back to the wall, eyes on the door. Watched the window until it watched back.

35

The Coup

The storm didn't arrive—it swallowed.

Lightning flared white along the veranda's arches, turning the villa's cliffside gardens into x-rays of themselves—palm ribs, bone-white statues, roses thorned like barbed wire. Thunder followed late, a rolling verdict that shook the glass and rippled the bourbon in Miguel Ortega's hand.

In his study, a ring of monitors pulsed cold, surgical blue against mahogany panels. Each feed was a heartbeat—irregular, uncertain. Safehouses in Colima, the container stack in Manzanillo, the desert vaults in Baja. One by one, the screens slipped to snow, then to black. Not a cascade of failures. An erasure.

The house knew before he did. Sound leaked out of the corridors like air from lungs. The machine hum dropped a register and held there. A radio cracked somewhere far off, then remembered to be quiet. Lightning flashed again and the saints in oil looked, for once, like men.

"Sir, we've lost Zapopan," Mateo said from the door—vest crooked, sidearm drawn, sweat beading despite the chilled air. Loyal to the bone, because he never pretended otherwise. "Cameras are

181

down across the grid. Simultaneous. They hit command. Not a glitch."

Miguel lowered the bourbon without looking, turned to the wall of dead screens like a general staring at a battlefield gone blind. "Who's inside?"

"Valdez with twelve," Mateo said. "But… Marcos is with them."

Of course.

Marcos Navarro: the boy from dust and broken glass, taught to turn a bribe into a bridge and a bridge into a trap. Miguel had lifted him out of Culiacán's teeth, taught him the grammar of power—command softly, pay once to own forever, kill without anger, remember the receipt. Until the boy learned a new language: succession, evolution, pain as policy.

Miguel had measured the danger in his cadence—speaking not to him but over him, to an audience that didn't yet exist. Quiet reversals. Meetings unlogged. Plans rewritten mid-stride. He'd chosen not to see it. The way men ignore water climbing a step.

He'd been wrong.

A tremor came through the floorboards—a bass note under the storm. Distant gunfire. Not close. Not far enough.

"Evac route," Miguel said, already moving for the bookcase.

"North helipad's under fire," Mateo said. "South tunnel's green. Two men at the hatch. We go now."

Miguel pressed his thumb to the sensor beneath San Pedro's carved bust. The shelf sighed open. Behind it: a matte pistol, an encrypted sat phone, and the leather-bound book that had outlived three wars and a government—offshore accounts, keys, the lattice-work of favors, names of men who smiled in public and breathed in private.

He took all three.

"Lock the study," he said. "Two minutes. If I'm dead, burn what's left."

No reply. Loyalty doesn't waste words.

They stayed out of the main corridor, took the service passage that smelled of polish and old bread. The hidden door to the tunnel took a palm, a code, and a prayer. Steps carved a century ago dropped into red emergency light, making the walls look like they were bleeding. Dust rose and hung, weightless.

Halfway down the second flight, a silenced shot cracked around the bend. Mateo jerked, stumbled, hand pressed to a wound that hadn't existed a second before. Blood misted the stone, black under the red light. He fell the way bodies decide.

Miguel slid into an alcove. Another silenced shot chewed the step where his ankle had been. Three sets of footfalls. Tactical. Night optics. Not street hitters—shaped people.

His fingers found the grooves along the wall. The first switch killed the red lamps, dropping the tunnel into mountain black. The last thing he saw was Mateo's eyes—angry the body had failed the work.

The second switch was older. Somewhere beyond the wall, gears clashed. At the attackers' feet, the floor unlocked like a mouth.

Two men fell into the pit—one screamed, one didn't. The third skidded, cursed in Spanish warped by a northern accent, and fired blind.

Miguel put three rounds where a man would be. The third dropped like cutlery on tile. Miguel moved.

The air warmed as he ran. The book under his arm felt like an organ. The sat phone, a stone. At the hatch, the lock stood open. He slid through into storm air thick with jasmine and burning.

The estate blazed. The helipad strobed in rain. The southern wing belched flame, the pool steamed like a god's bath.

He cut through the gardens. Statues blackened by heat watched him pass. Roses lay trampled, red on wet stone.

Then he saw them.

Marcos, lit by fire and storm, ringed by a dozen young men with clean guns and cleaner faces. His hands were empty—someone else carried for him now. He stood in Miguel's stance.

Miguel didn't announce himself.

"Wings are locked," Javier said into his mic. "Teams suppressing extrinsics. Primary target—"

"—is me," Miguel said.

A dozen rifles turned. Safeties clicked.

Marcos's face emptied further. "Boss," he said—in the past tense.

Lightning stitched the hedges white. In that flash, Miguel counted three to Marcos's left who could move, two to the right who thought they could. Javier didn't flinch.

"You learned well," Miguel said. "It's what I wanted. To be surpassed. Not like this."

"Like this was always the way," Marcos said, stepping forward. "I bring the house into the new century. You built it for a world that still read newspapers."

"And you want one that prints only your picture."

"I want a world that obeys the gravity of reality. You taught me gravity. I'm using it."

Miguel held the pistol low. He was about to speak when a new problem entered in silk and a brooch.

Sofia crossed the ruined arch in a fog-colored robe, smoke curling in her hair, rosewater at her throat. The brooch was heavy with an older name.

"Take me to Marcos," she said, like a queen asking for a light.

The circle let her in, closed again.

"Sofia," Marcos said.

"Marcos," she said.

They traded lines like knives. She handed him a wax-sealed envelope, made him step closer. Lightning lent him light. His face paled.

Javier's name appeared over and over in what he read—calls to Colombia, payoffs to Medellín, the kind of promise men keep to protect their knees.

"You lie," Marcos said.

"I preserve," Sofia said. "Miguel built a room men wanted to enter. You broke the door and think that's the same thing."

"You're bargaining."

"I'm annotating."

Her gaze slid to Miguel: *I am not yours. I am not his. I will outlive this.*

"Bring her," Marcos told Javier.

Sofia passed Miguel without looking.

Miguel took three steps left. A young man lifted his rifle. "Easy," Miguel said. The barrel wavered.

"You taught me to build networks," Marcos said.

"You learned to sever," Miguel said.

"Endurance is an old man's romance."

"And pain is a boy's arousal."

Lightning cracked again. The helipad faltered, the generator caught.

A voice on a walkie: "We had him in the tunnel. Two down. Third quiet. Lost visual in the garden."

Marcos kept his eyes on Miguel.

"You've taken something large," Miguel said. "Find out what it cost."

He fired at the pergola's base. Old wood gave. The structure collapsed, forcing the flank to scatter. Smoke billowed. Saint Jude toppled.

Miguel walked toward the hedges without hurry. Boys followed momentum into mistakes. Javier shouted too late.

His phone buzzed:

[INTERCEPT — Harper Vale RELAY | +00:41 GMT]

HV: Southern grid dark. Not weather. Switch hit.

HV: Phoenix liquidity dump. This isn't a coup—it's a cut.

HV: "Phase Omega" mean anything?

He cleared the hedge and was gone into the service lane. The Jeep was missing. Two ponchoed guards died quickly.

The old airstrip waited three kilometers down a forgotten road.

In the hangar, he bypassed the plane for the radio. Ledger and sat phone on the bench. Three slow presses, one fast.

"This is Ortega," he said. "Phase Omega."

Accounts would drain. Boats would vanish. Contracts collapse. Insurance photos turn to heat. The rooms that bent governors would deliver their weight to new desks.

Miguel tied the book shut.

· · ·

[INTERCEPT — **GULF Gazette | 00:14 EST**]

ED: Phoenix Cayman arm zeroed.

ROSA: That's not a coup. That's an exit wound.

BACK AT THE VILLA, Marcos stood in stormlight. Sofia, on the veranda, told him why he'd lost: *You mistook fear for loyalty.*

Down the cliff road, a small engine caught. In Tallahassee, a headline detonated. A senator's phone buzzed.

On the airstrip, the bulb burned out.

Miguel stepped into the storm's throat—ledger gone, phone silent. No crown. No house. A different kind of weight.

He smiled once, brief and private, the way men do when they've lost something large and found something sharp.

Ghosts don't die. They change hunting grounds.

36

Stand or Fall

Morning came down like a verdict—ash-gray, airless, the kind of sky that looks less like weather and more like consequence. Max Larkin stood beneath it, breathing gasoline and damp cement. The wind brought nothing—no salt, no cut-grass relief—just the stale breath of a city holding itself still.

He rolled his cuffs under the sleeves of the threadbare coat that had crossed borders and bad ideas: Haiti's tear at the hem, Lebanon's coffee stain ghosting the pocket, a Tijuana graze the doctors called "lucky." The coat had earned retirement. So had Max. But the war had come home and refused to leave, and he didn't know how to do anything but walk toward it.

He crouched behind the jag of a half-demolished wall, peering through a window carved by rebar and explosives. Across the lot, the warehouse beat with idle engines. Reefers exhaled white vapor. Semi-trailers idled like penned herd animals—nervous, flaring, impatient. Men moved in lanes as clean as code: clipped hand signals, hidden Kevlar under charity-branded windbreakers. Logos lied on the crates: relief aid, agricultural equipment, disaster-response kits. The lie was well-designed. The lie had a marketing team. Inside every crate—poison.

Max watched with double vision: the micro choreography of today, and the macro machine stretching from these docks to villages without names. His tablet's map mirrored it—nodes and branches, hubs and spokes. Fentanyl was the product, yes, but the bloodstream was money, influence, borders that bent to order. He'd explained this in panels, in print, in metaphors he no longer trusted. Now he could smell it.

His earpiece clicked. Jenna's voice—low, steady—settled his own tempo. "North camera loop's live. South gate bribe's been cashed. Local PD's on 'traffic control' two blocks out—which is code for don't call us. Federal partners say ten minutes before the window closes. Your call."

"Copy." He scanned the tablet—static map, current nodes, a blinking satellite image of a tug easing into an unlisted berth. The last five days had been a controlled fall: movement, disinformation, burned sources, false routes. But last night's courier—a man with no name and eyes fixed on the ground—had delivered something rare: a ledger. Not just shipments. Not just banks. Names, dates, amounts —the difference between a school and a war.

One pseudonym surfaced like a watermark: *El Blanco.* Vargas faction's internal handle. Three payments in the last quarter to defense and logistics officials in Honduras and El Salvador. The numbers were careful. The dates were prayers.

Max felt his jaw set. He didn't think of Evan—Evan arrived on his own, as grief does. Fourteen. A hospital room where antiseptic lost to reality. A coroner calling it an acute overdose, as if death were a single moment. Evan had not died of a moment. He had died of a system.

Max stood. A small decision in a large book.

"You've got both entries?"

"North and south," Jenna said. "Claymore staged in the blind. Interdiction team's two streets out. Once we blow the whistle, it keeps blowing."

"Good." He watched a forklift trundle a pallet of "water filters" past Bay Three. Gloves too new for a man who worked with his hands. "We break their spine."

A beat—calculation, not hesitation. "You sure?"

"I stopped being sure a long time ago." He exhaled. "Do it."

The assault arrived like a tide remembering gravity. Engines and idle chatter became flash and concussion. Stun grenades flayed the shadows. Commands barked in two languages. Boots hit concrete in threes and fours. A premature shot—its owner dropped fast. Another tried to make a point and paid in seconds.

Max moved with the team, camera slung, tablet tight to his ribs. He wasn't filming for clicks. He filmed because truth without record is an empty threat. The center of the room fell to men with zip ties; the edges, to blood.

Behind a caged wall past a door that failed at being a door: the control room. No windows. Two racks of servers, a bank of ledgers because paper doesn't ping, and one man—thin hair, cheap watch, bad iron job on his shirt. Manny Rivas. Max knew the face from a buried compliance newsletter.

Hector's hands shot up like muscle memory. His eyes moved like a man mapping exits.

"I'm just numbers," he whispered.

"You watched them," Max said.

Max set a portable drive on the table. "You're going to give us everything. Stall, you disappear slow. Help, you breathe fresh air today."

Manny sat. Typed. Code spilled—transactions, shell companies, routed IPs from countries where paperwork is sport. Another window opened with codenames pretending to be random.

"Which banks?" Max asked.

"All of them. But think less bank, more man who golfs with the man who owns the bank. That's where flags disappear. If I name them, they'll know."

"They already know," Max said. "They're looking for us."

"Names like fog," Manny said. "Caligo. Chorus. Monastery. Caligo keeps reappearing. Not a person."

"Then define Caligo."

"The umbrella. Private meetings where politics and commerce

decide who gets the aisle seat. The part of the map with no border. I'm not supposed to know. Numbers know anyway."

The puzzle clicked—not solved, just dangerous.

Manny's upload bar ticked past fifty percent.

"We're not just cracking a cartel," Max told Jenna. "We're exposing a shadow government. Fentanyl's just the carrier."

"Then we move," she said. "Before they cauterize."

[INTERCEPT: **KITEWIRE | +09:20 GMT]**

V1: Choir lost the first chair.

V2: New conductor?

V1: Boy raised the baton, strings missing.

V2: Ghost in the balcony.

TWO HOURS LATER, the safehouse was the kind of quiet that lies. A motel off an unloved interstate—curtains and deadbolts over décor. Surveillance blankets over windows. Burners charging on a buzzing strip.

Janna typed like sleep would cost them the war. Smitty watched, hawk-like. Jenna mapped coordinates over manifests, turning the ledger into a language.

Max, on a bed with a history, ran Manny's dump for the tenth time. One word circled itself: *Caligo.* He circled it again.

"What the hell is Caligo?" he asked softly.

"Fog," Janna said. "Latin. Owl genus. Power word for men who like sounding educated while breaking things."

"Phone," Jenna said, sliding his burner. A courier's three-line text: location, time, phrase—*grand navarre - east wing - closed door trade.*

Smitty rubbed his beard. "Two outlets got chatter floods. Puerto Rico's silent. Not offline—silent. That's worse."

Janna stopped typing. "They're closing ranks. Run it now or watch someone else mangle it."

Max stood. "Grand Navarre tonight. Closed-door security-briefing-slash-trade-wine-and-cheese. Catering invoice has a shell tied to Sofia."

"Vargas?" Jenna asked.

"Ortega," Smitty said. "Widow. Not so dormant."

The name woke the room.

"Max," Jenna said, tired but sharp. "You go in clean. We keep you clean. Do your job inside."

"What job?" Smitty asked.

Max held up the ledger. "Put a face on Caligo."

THE GRAND NAVARRE'S lobby was built to make men feel inevitable—marble that lied prettily, brass that faked age, staff trained not to blink. Max wore a navy suit that looked tailored. Stubble gone. Badge passable.

Rain turned from consequence to theater. Jenna's camera tracked from the van. Janna and Smitty ghosted through the bar.

In the elevator, his reflection was a man harmless until he wasn't. East wing: carpet swallowing footsteps, chandeliers showing off, two security men in suits too proud.

"Press," Max said, flashing the badge with a half-smile that says *let's both own this mistake.* The taller guard nodded. The shorter clocked Max's scuffed shoes, decided not to care.

Ballroom doors loomed. Laughter bled under them—measured, careful. Max thought of Evan by accident.

"Last chance to leave a hero," Smitty said in his ear.

Max pushed through.

The room was a choreography of deals—clusters, circles, corners. A dais no one respected. Champagne, badges, polished smiles.

And there—Sofia Ortega. Stunning dress, pearls, brooch. The room leaned without knowing. She spoke with the gravity of choice.

Jenna's text: invoice, shell company, Sofia's ghost signature behind a logistics firm with a saint on its mast. The saint from the yard. Click. Cost incoming.

Senator Leighton intercepted—border security made flesh. He shook Sofia's hand like a peer.

The ledger's circle around *Caligo* burned in Max's head. *Caligo* wasn't a person—it was a table where cartel, corporate, and elected hands moved levers together.

"Max, they clocked you on fourth-floor cam," Jenna warned. "Two waiters with no drinks. One guy at service. Exit now or freeze."

He didn't.

Sofia looked at him—placed him. Recognition of the moment, not the man. Her smile said: *We're finally in the same sentence.*

Max moved toward her.

[INTERCEPT: BACKROOM | 12:06 EST]

ED: Navarre flagged. Caligo appears as catering vendor.

ROSA: That's cover.

ED: Publish at noon plus thirty.

"They made you," Jenna murmured.

Sofia's smile was the absence of a frown.

"Ms. Ortega," Max said.

"Mister Larkin," she said—without introduction.

"Press," he said.

"We are all press now," she replied. "We press what we need, the world prints what it can afford."

"I brought a record to a conspiracy," he said.

Leighton smiled for cameras that weren't there. "Audit and oversight are democracy's bones."

"You sell bones by the crate," Max said.

The service door shifted. Smitty in his ear: "New team. Not waiters. Move it."

Sofia watched the tremor in his hands and learned something she'd suspected.

"What is Caligo?" Max asked.

"Climate," she said.

"Who controls the climate?"

"People who understand weather."

"El Blanco?"

"A ghost. Your country has given us so many. We owe you one."

"You're using relief routes for poison," Max said. "Building a pipeline that looks like charity."

"You think you'll walk out with a story," she said.

Jenna's voice: "Max. Out. Now."

He stayed.

The room shifted. Security angled. Sofia inclined her chin— punctuation to a year's sentence.

Her smile softened, without kindness.

[INTERCEPT: GLASSBIRD | +14:32 GMT]

HV: Fog rolling in. Caligo on the floor.

UNKNOWN: Lights out or lights on?

HV: Both.

Darkness enveloped the room. Random lights from phones gave the room a soft glow. Max slipped out the catering door unnoticed.

37

Echoes at the Threshold

The storm followed him in like a stray with bad intentions.

Max Larkin let the wipers freeze mid-swipe, watching rain river the windshield into crooked panes. A sodium streetlamp hummed like a bad mood, flickering hard enough to strobe the chain-link fence. At the strip's end, the warehouse crouched—long, ribbed, blank metal door, no number. An address that only exists for people already paid to find it.

He didn't get out. Not yet.

He let the scene breathe: shallow troughs where a body could flatten, roofline gaps where a cigarette would betray an amateur, an alley seam just wide enough for a man to wait and call it patience. Years of stakeouts had burned the checklist into him: never trust first pictures; killers live in the margins.

Lightning flared beyond the harbor, turning corrugated roofs into bones for a blink. Thunder took its time like verdicts do.

Rain hit like cold nails when he stepped out. The coat collar helped until it didn't; water found the seam and walked his spine.

Boots over slick gravel. The dumpster's rot-sour breath of diesel and fruit. A beer can bent into a figure-eight. At the door, he let his ears work: the not-sound first—air shifting when someone moves and decides not to. Reflection pooled at the curb caught a tall, lean shape angled to watch both entry and far corner.

Jenna.

Two steps sideways, another angle, then he opened the door.

Cold bit harder inside. Concrete swallowed the desk lamp's weak cone, spat back shadow. Rain on corrugate ticked a steady metronome over smaller sounds: heel pivot, zipper teeth, paper deciding whether to tell the truth.

Jenna's nod: clear enough; hand near exit.

Delgado clutched his leather briefcase to his ribs, as if willpower could prevent theft. Smitty kept to a column's shadow, hood up, windbreaker flapping just enough to fake invisibility.

This wasn't a briefing. This was eve-of-war, where voices stay low out of respect for the cost of noise.

Satellite maps spiderwebbed in red and blue. Photos with names scrawled in margins, some faces X'd thick and final. Laptops chewing encrypted chatter in vertical rain. The dented lamp lit their most dangerous relic: a print stack of clean money made dirty by purpose.

A Panamanian "energy consulting" firm with a name only a bored lawyer could love. Funds that snaked through three time zones, wore two passports, and took communion—finally—in a campaign account woven into state machinery. If you didn't suspect rot, you'd call it immaculate.

Max read until the lines fuzzed. Capitol soil. All this time they'd been cutting weeds while the roots hugged the pilings.

"They were always in it together," he said. "We trimmed lies. The roots are under the capitol stairs."

Smitty's eyes did a slow exit-check before coming back. "This is the sort of thing that gets folks unalived before breakfast."

"Or before lunch," Delgado said, not joking.

Jenna tapped the lamp. "This turns the wheel—if we can make it breathe. Governor's shop will law you to death, smear you to paste, bot you into oblivion. And that's the opening act."

"I'm not scared of lawyers." Max let the raw edge stay in his voice. "I'm scared of forgetting why I started."

Jenna's look softened. "Evan."

Max nodded once. Sleep came in jagged pieces now—Evan's laugh behind a door he couldn't open, his wife's silhouette in windowglass, the antiseptic sawdust of a hospital room lodged in his throat.

He tapped Delgado's timeline. "Marstone Advisory. Born six months before Javier Marín evaporates. Same month shipments pivoted north to Route 26."

"That's when highway eyes went dark," Jenna said. "Someone upstairs pulled the plug. Ghost road."

"Trujillo," Max said. "Deputy Secretary of Transportation then. He's the hinge. I want his phone breadcrumb, his Zoom smiles, his church seat, his side door. Who he pays, who pays him."

Delgado's fingers flew. Columns multiplied.

"You sure?" Smitty asked. "This trigger? No safety. No do-overs."

"I've never been more sure."

Jenna's exhale was steady. "Then we go all in."

[INTERCEPT: **MILLHOUSE | 07:12**]

bonehouse check: target one + flock inside. paper's live. keep yokes loose. no birdcage yet.

FORTY-EIGHT HOURS BLURRED. Time stopped making shapes.

Max met a retired clerk in a strip-mall café that used to be a pawnshop. Pale, wiry, eyes of a man who'd once believed rules applied to him. The folder he slid across the laminate table was a shield.

"You didn't get this from me. I kept a copy for when the sky turned Old Testament."

Memos with Trujillo's signature, margin notes clearing shipments with "no eyes."

Smitty's trail led to a logistics retiree in a ranch house undecided about abandonment. Freight moves like this don't happen by accident, son. They happen because a suit says this lane is a whisper, not a shout. Names "forgotten," habits remembered.

Jenna and Delgado coordinated encrypted transmissions. Three outlets agreed to mirror, one wanted more time, one wanted it softer. Jenna said no.

Shadow tails multiplied. The silver Toyota. The hotel clerk with the too-casual questions. Midnight text on a burner: *you can still fold your hand.* He let it sit, unopened.

Back at the bone-cold warehouse, another map went up. Lines insisting on meaning. Evan arriving in his head at a red light—grief using traffic as humiliation.

[INTERCEPT: **SOAPBOX | 14:45**]

courier made the handoff. paper's wandering. tails keep drift— don't spook herd. no leash pulls till tollbooth.

THEY CONVERGED in Jenna's loft the night before detonation.

"I tied in with Ed," Jenna said. "Tallahassee Gazette hits lead at six. Two mirrors at six-fifteen. Master goes to offshore crate. Skeleton keys dance."

Smitty paced. "Enough to move the mountain?"

"It's truth," Max said. "They can't bury it forever."

He typed the last line: *This is not an accident. It's a machine. And it's time to shut it down.* SEND.

Progress bar crawled: 1%... 47... 100.

Everything died. Lights. Screens. The building's deep, ugly thunk.

"EMP?" Max asked.

Jenna had the router's back off. "No. Grid-snip. Precision."

Amber emergency strips lit. Towers winked like confused stars.

On the dead screen, letters typed themselves: *your hearse is triple-parked, newsboy.*

"Pack what breathes, burn what doesn't," Jenna said.

They left in three vehicles, headlights low, roads that forgot they were roads.

Before the warehouse communion—before the clerk's trembling hands, before the lights went out—the storm had sent a scout: a sheet of paper taped to a lamppost three blocks from their first meet. He'd noticed it without noticing. Now it was back: a charity logo that meant relief to strangers and cover to men who knew. The machine was never shy. Just polite in public.

He thought of the Grand Navarre's marbled lie, of Sofia's smile stamped across his day like a watermark. Of Miguel's empire cracking like plaster. Of the boy with the baton who had raised nothing and everything at once. Of Caligo—the fog that is a table, the table that is a government without a flag.

Rain thickened, shrinking visibility to a ribbon. The bridge deck threw watery light against his windshield, strobing. For a second he was seventeen again—stealing his father's truck, driving to the county line out of principle, heart knocking a rhythm under the dash. For a second he saw Evan's hands on a game controller, thumbs moving like they were decoding a life. For a second he wanted to pull over and be a different man. For a second he didn't.

He drove.

They'd set the warehouse to look like memory—and it worked. After the clerk handoff, the concrete seemed older, the lamp's cone meaner. Smitty stood in the same spot because he understood what repetition did to fear. Jenna had added a new map and a photo strip that pushed Caligo from rumor into shadow.

Delgado spun his laptop around, accounting miracles rendered bloodless on-screen.

"Marstone's subs pinwheel into six accounts—three through Belize, one the Caymans, one through a Tallahassee credit union with a board member whose brother married into the Trujillo family. Last one's a decoy—it cycles back to a PAC that hates drugs so much it sleeps with them."

Jenna dabbed a red pen at a node. "Cross here with Route 26… watch the dust settle. The highway cams weren't out—they were rerouted to a closed loop. The only eyes were paid to see nothing."

Smitty snorted. "Law calls it compliance. Street calls it bought."

Max traced the chain from pretend energy firm to a smiling yard sign. "We can't just publish. We have to show it. A ledger's nothing without the breath that goes with it."

"Ed's packaging the human side," Jenna said. "The mother who couldn't bury her son because the county 'lost' evidence. The nurse who clocked six relief pallets with the wrong weight profile. We're backing the spine with bone."

Delgado clicked. A photo: Senator Leighton shaking a hand that didn't want to be photographed. The other face was cropped, but the brooch in frame was all the ID they needed.

Max felt the floor tilt. "Sofia."

Jenna swore, softly. "We don't have forty-eight hours. We have twelve."

Smitty's face emptied. "You light that fuse, you'd better be ready to lose the house."

"House is already on fire," Max said. "We're deciding who gets to run through with water."

[INTERCEPTED TRANSMISSION – **18:03**]

HANDLE: SALTLINE

eye on the loft. birdhouse got candles only. squad three reports kettle scream broke mid-pour. grid bite confirmed.

HANDLE: MILLHOUSE

copy. no pull yet. let 'em cook. we want the scatter, not the fire.

NIGHT BEFORE THE UPLOAD, they made last calls and burned the rest.

Max took his one allotted whiskey like medicine and let it sit in his ribs. Jenna stood at the window, watching the city pretend it couldn't be paused. Smitty disassembled a phone and put it back together with less in it. Delgado wrote names on a scrap of paper, folded it, and slid it into his shoe.

Max wrote the close—the sentence he might never see in print.

This is not an accident. It's a machine. And it's time to shut it down. He typed it three times in three drafts in three places, in case fate worked as a copy editor.

SEND.

The progress bar crawled with bad grace, like it knew the room was rooting against it. At 100%, everything died. The building made the sound a body makes when the next breath doesn't come. Outside, the city stumbled, then relit with apology-colored light.

On the dead screen, letters appeared slow and deliberate: *you missed last call, pressman.*

"What do we do?" Delgado asked, voice too loud in the thin light.

"The same thing we were going to do," Jenna said. "We go."

They went.

RULES OF FLIGHT:
 —Never take the straight line if you want to stay unmeasured.
 —Leave what can hurt you if found.
 —Take what can hurt them if lost.
 —Trust paper over electricity.
 —Trust faces least of all.

Max drove east, bridge humming its old tune. The storm peeled into sheets. The night breathed danger and inevitability in equal shares. One eye on the lane, one on the glass.

The burner buzzed—small, obscene. Instinct overruled principle.

Your root's in the mansion. Trujillo's just the bark.

He half-smiled. Rot loved a metaphor. The capitol dome miles away became a tree—roots woven into foundations, drinking from pipes, breaking stone because roots do. Hands on levers, names on brass, a portrait gallery that could be mistaken for family to anyone who couldn't count.

Evan. The last voicemail unheard because there'd be "a better time." The ER doors he'd walked through with a press badge like it meant something.

Knuckles tightened on the wheel. "Okay," he told the empty car.

━━

THE SAFEHOUSE WAS in a cul-de-sac that forgot its own name. Slow pull-in, low lights. The garage door rose discreetly. Inside smelled of cardboard, dust, and an old tenant's good idea.

Jenna was there, hair rope-wet, eyes dry. Smitty came in through the kitchen with the kind of quiet you learn in the military or burglary. Delgado followed with a tote heavier than it should be.

"No tails," Smitty said. "Either they fell off, or they're better than me. Don't know which I hate more."

Jenna spread printouts on the floor—tables were for civilized arguments. "The bark is the bark. The root is the mansion."

Delgado scowled. "Governors don't take cash. They take gifts dressed as favors dressed as infrastructure."

"Then we don't accuse," Smitty said. "We reveal."

Max sat on the floor, letting the chill keep him awake. "We prove the soft corruption that carries the hard. Consulting. Advisory. Stewardship. Words that make men feel noble while they load poison on trucks."

Jenna tapped a donor list. Two shell companies already mapped. Phoenix's ghost arm pledging through a third. A Friday photo op with the governor and a 'public-private logistics consortium'—Marstone in the footnotes.

"They'll let us take the picture for them," Delgado said.

"You ready to blow a hole you can't stand after?" Smitty asked.

"I stood on a pier today and watched a woman who collects empires smile like she'd already signed my obituary," Max said. "I've been ready since before I knew."

The house answered with a deep, alien hum. Jenna's eyes went up. Smitty shifted weight. Delgado closed the laptop like closing a child's eyes.

"Grid probe," Jenna said.

"Move before they bite," Smitty replied.

In the hours before dawn, they worked like people who had stopped negotiating with sleep.

Smitty printed a floor plan of the governor's events hall—gifted to them by the architects who had posted their portfolio online with pride. Jenna drafted copy that named no names but showed every hand. Delgado wrote a script that would read clean to the casual eye and cut deep for the one man who knew what it meant. Max wrote the lead he'd been composing in his head for a month, underlining one sentence twice: *This is not an accident. It's a machine.*

At 04:47, the city's lights flinched, then pretended nothing had happened. Somewhere, a substation operator blamed a squirrel—because humans need stories.

At 05:12, a white van parked two doors down. It left three minutes later after no one came out to greet it.

At 05:59, Jenna handed Max a burner with a single number preloaded. "Ed," she said. "On a line that can take a punch."

Max stared at the phone, feeling the distance between the boy he'd been and the man holding it. He thought of Fall River, of the whistleblower he hadn't double-sourced out of arrogance, of the disappearance that followed. Of promises made and debts unpaid.

"Time," Jenna said gently.

"Time," he echoed, and called.

Ed answered on the third ring, voice roughened by fatigue and purpose. "You alive?"

"For now," Max said.

"Good. The switch is armed. We go on the minute. Any last sins to confess?"

"Later. I need a favor—hold the second graph two paras longer. Let the governor's office deny the wrong thing first."

Ed grunted. "You're cruel."

"I'm tired."

They didn't say goodbye. Goodbyes sounded too much like endings, and this wasn't one.

At 06:00, the *Tallahassee Gazette's* homepage decided it was done being cautious. At 06:02, the mirrors lit. At 06:06, the first denial hit the inbox wrapped in patriotism. At 06:09, a bot farm mistook a metaphor for treason and went to work. At 06:11, a lawyer threatened to call someone's mother. At 06:14, a junior staffer somewhere typed *what is Marstone* into a search bar and began an education.

At 06:17, the safehouse lights blinked and came back like a man who'd forgotten his keys.

At 06:18, three knocks hit the front door—confident, deliberate, the kind of knock used by people unaccustomed to hearing "no."

No one moved.

The knocks didn't repeat. Tires rolled. The white van didn't return.

Smitty exhaled. "They're poking, not punching."

"For now," Jenna said.

Max's phone buzzed—a message from a number that changed digits like it wanted to be a cipher: *nice story. nasty roots. bark won't hold come noon.*

He typed nothing. He didn't need to. They were already moving toward the mansion, whether they wanted to or not.

The warehouse wasn't safer by morning, but it was familiar, and familiarity is a kind of armor. They reconvened to plan the next three hours—attack and defense braided into one move.

Delgado dropped a fresh printout: donations mapped to contracts mapped to "task forces" that looked like oversight but worked as escort services for money. "This is where we draw blood," he said. "We show how 'public-private partnership' means 'private hands in public pockets.'"

Jenna circled three names. "We hit the deputy, the chief of staff, and the governor's fixer who doesn't exist. Leave the governor's name out of the top, put it in the photos. Let the readers do the math. People remember math they solve themselves."

Smitty's grin was thin. "You kids are mean. I like it."

Max watched rain stripe the window and thought of the sound a rope makes when it starts to fray. He felt the chapter turn in his bones.

"You okay?" Jenna asked. She always asked.

He smiled without teeth. "Ask me tonight."

"Tonight," she said.

Lightning straightened the shadows for a heartbeat. Thunder rolled in late. Somewhere, an ambulance took the shoulder. Somewhere else, a banker skipped breakfast. The city weighed the benefits of pretending.

He smiled without teeth. "Ask me tonight."

HE WENT ALONE to the café again—ritual as shield. The clerk was there, hands less steady, eyes more certain.

"It's not going to stop," the man said. "Men like that don't go to bed because you told the truth. They buy better pillows."

Max opened the folder the man slid over—supplementary memos, the kind kept out of pride in the drafting. A Post-it carried a line he'd seen before, now in a new throat: *Marstone—speaker luncheon comp—Gov's residence (private)*. A week from Friday. The place where power lived. The bark was RSVP'd.

"Thank you," Max said.

The clerk pinched the bridge of his nose. "I had a boy. He left and came back and left again. The second time, he didn't come back. I never learned how to bury an absence. Do something with this that hurts."

Max touched the man's forearm—brief, the way men permit each other. "I'm trying."

He left through a side door, letting the alley swallow him. A silver Toyota rolled past slow enough to be obvious. He looked at the driver; the driver didn't look back. New tail. New patience.

He texted nothing and walked to where his car wasn't until the Toyota lost interest or reported it.

THE LOFT WAS GONE to them, but Jenna ghosted its network footprint, watching the last two days of surveillance like bad art.

"They were inside before the upload," she said. "They watched you write the closing line."

Smitty shook his head. "That's a hell of a thing to do to a writer."

Max laughed once, without kindness. "I've had worse edits."

Delgado lifted a legal pad. "Ready to cut the voiceover for the noon update?"

"Ready."

They recorded in a bathroom for the sound. Max spoke into the lens—machine, money, Route 26, Marstone, special logistics. He didn't say governor. The photos would.

When it was done, Jenna scrubbed two breaths from the audio. "Better."

His phone buzzed mid-sip of coffee that had decided to be tragic. The message was shorter this time: *move your feet.*

He did.

Halfway to another safehouse, the city stuttered again. Lights hiccupped. A traffic signal decided twice. Sirens braided in three directions. The storm steadied.

From the bridge, the capitol dome glimmered dully through the drizzle. A tree came to mind—roots in the basement, bark on the lawn, lobbyists chattering like squirrels. He laughed, surprised.

At the safehouse, they watched the noon feed—Ed's lede had landed like a right hook. The governor's office denied the wrong paragraph, corrected itself, and looked worse. Local anchors smiled the smile reserved for train wrecks. The mirrors held. The bot-farm howled.

"Hold your breath," Jenna said. "Here comes the counterpunch."

It arrived as a hole in the grid—two blocks wide, three seconds long. The house blinked to candlelight, then back. A polite knock touched the door.

No one answered. When it didn't come again, they slipped out the back, leaving the house like a shed skin.

Max's burner buzzed—a message from nowhere: *The connection you seek sits in the governor's mansion. Trujillo is only the beginning.*

He read it aloud without meaning to. Smitty rolled his shoulders. Delgado muttered a prayer. Jenna's eyes went cold and bright.

"Then we stop being polite," she said.

"We were polite?" Smitty asked.

"For journalists," Jenna said.

The storm had left the sky and entered the room.

"Stand or fall," Max said.

"Stand," Jenna replied.

"Stand," Smitty echoed.

Delgado nodded. "Stand."

They didn't shake hands. They didn't say *let's go*. They just went.

Back to the warehouse—ritual as armor, some rooms holding courage like a charge. The lamp's cone was the same. The cold was the same. The plan hadn't changed. Only the cost.

They spread the new photos, the memos, the Post-it. Jenna circled the mansion in blue—red was already taken by blood. Smitty outlined public-event entry points—public means cameras, cameras can save you and get you killed. Delgado drafted the next drop in bullet points—bullets travel straight.

Max stood at the edge of the table, saw Evan as he always would, and pressed a hand flat over the Marstone page—silent promise.

The rain slackened. Quiet, the dangerous kind.

Smitty didn't look up. "You're thinking about him."

"I am."

"Good."

Jenna's voice softened without losing steel. "We're almost there."

Max nodded. It felt like a step.

The phone vibrated—a number that didn't exist until it did. Four words: *doors open. masks on.*

Afternoon at the mansion would be a circus. Masks in place, called governance. Doors open to donors, cameras, and one man with a notebook and a coat that had learned rain.

"Let's go shut down a machine," he said.

They moved—light in step, heavy in purpose. Out into a city pretending not to watch. Under a sky the color of consequence.

Through streets where power wore a smile and truth wore good shoes.

The root was in the mansion. The bark was Trujillo. The tree had lived a long time.

It was ready for an axe.

38

Crossfire

The storm came on like a dare.

Jenna pegged the rental's wipers, but the rain still blurred the world into streaked knives of yellow sodium light. The warehouse crouched at the dead end like it belonged there—corrugated hide slick under a hissing power line. To the left: chain-link tangled with blackberry vines. To the right: a half-collapsed loading dock and a forklift's rusted skeleton. The night smelled of hot asphalt and old oil.

She killed the engine and let the rain speak. Counted beats between flash and thunder. Listened for the wrong sound—a foot scuff, a cough, the pause that comes with held breath. Nothing. Just storm. A sedan idled at the block's mouth, braked like it remembered something, then drifted on. Taillights bled out in the rain.

Hood tight, she slid out, kept to the building's shadow seam. The service door's keypad blinked under a plastic cover. She cupped it, punched eight numbers without watching her fingers. Soft thunk. She held still two extra seconds, letting her eyes adjust as the storm shoved in behind her.

Inside, the warehouse had been re-wired into a nervous system. Cables ran under taped mats. Folding tables groaned under laptops, radios, and open crates of silent, heat-throwing gear. A junkyard of ring lights—hers—stacked in the corner, domes tilted like fallen halos. The back wall's plywood skin had turned white-board: taped maps, red string crossing shipping lanes, grease-pencil notes that wouldn't erase when the power died.

A red LED clock blinked 11:03 PM like a wound that refused to clot.

On the main monitor: *Final decoy route uploaded. Confirmation pending.* Cursor pulsing like it had a heartbeat.

Lena from Homeland looked up from her terminal, hair in a knot that had surrendered hours ago. "Convoy's rolling. Manifests read clean. Vendor ID checks. Pull the barcode, you'll get refurbished routers and charity blankets. All hollow."

"Crossline Depot?" Jenna asked, tossing her damp jacket over a chair.

"Two enforcers staging. Same pattern as last time—cars opposite, no dome lights, windows shut."

"Good," Jenna said. Good meant predictable. Predictable meant someone else might have made it that way.

The crew moved like they didn't want to wake anything. Smitty hunched over a secure handset, chewing the same gum since sunset. Delgado bullied numbers on a spreadsheet. Halloran—Bureau liaison fluent in both polite and illegal—sat in the ops van outside. His voice bled through a speaker: "Five minutes to breach window. Assume no deviations."

Jenna paced, inventorying herself. Burner phone. Personal phone—dead, zipped away. Knife at ankle. Taser in bag. Head full of two lives and a third to carry both.

She yanked a map of the Arroyo Junction interchange from the board. The decoy convoy would pass under overpass B—a choke point where weeds survived on dust. Perfect for a squeeze. Better for pretending the squeeze wasn't planned.

Lena angled a thermal still. "Warm box at Mile 76. Car sideways against a ridge. Engine cold. No lights. Could be a sleeper. Could be a sensor."

"Ours?"

Silence. That meant no. Or worse.

Jenna circled Crossline Depot in red, then slashed it. "No later than 01:10. If they hold, we push. If they bolt, we shadow to county line. If they go quiet—"

"They saw the strings," Smitty said.

Her hands wanted to shake. She pressed one flat to her sternum. The bright JennaMorn persona would talk tides and patience. Storm-wet Jenna, inked with code words, just breathed.

"Visual on the enforcers?"

"Confirmed," Lena said, bringing up two pale ghosts with guns. Not nervous—bored. Dangerous that way.

"Okay. Time to set the trap."

SHE STEPPED into the van's hum. Halloran pointed to three monitors —convoy cams, chopper reroutes, a minimal map with dots crawling south. "Five minutes to breach. Unless they fall for diner steak."

"They won't," she said, eyes on the dots. *They trust me* stayed unspoken.

Her burner pulsed once—no chatter. Good. The other phone stayed dark. Better.

Then the storm did the worst thing it could. It stopped.

No wind, no rattle—just a pressure hush.

"I'll be right back," she told Halloran, slipping into the alley. Water roped from the gutters. The city's hum was distant and sullen.

That's when the wrong phone lit.

Her personal. The one that wasn't supposed to exist here.

NORA.

Jenna answered, voice soft enough to break. "Nora?"

Static. Then a lazy, bored chuckle.

"Heard you've been busy, sunshine."

Not Nora. A man. That kind of man.

"What do you want?"

"You've made a mess. Pretending's cute. Masks—cuter."

"Where is she?"

A gum-smack. "We netted a different catch. Busy friend. Big mouth. Brave, though."

"Nora—"

A muffled sound. Not a word—pain shaped into noise. "Jen—don't—"

The line died.

Jenna stood until rain found her again. The phone slipped, thunked against her shoe. She caught herself on the doorframe, ground swaying under her.

Inside: "They've got Nora." Her voice was wrong in her own ears.

Faces turned. Coffee spilled. Delgado swore in two languages. Lena's fingers flew. Halloran stepped in.

"Who?"

"Them. They know who I am."

"This changes the op," Halloran said. "We abort."

"No." The word came clean. "We finish. If we stop, they take more."

Arguments rose and died under that. Lena: "Push up three, shrink their window." Delgado: "Need a second decoy." Smitty: "No time."

Jenna: "No Nora." That ended it.

Lena: "Her way, then."

Halloran cursed, into radio: "Teams maintain posture. Green on sting. On Jenna's marks."

The night became a waiting room with knives.

Dots crawled south. Twice the feed froze. Twice it came back.

"Crossline in two," Lena said.

"Teams hold," Halloran.

DEA's Tasia: "Blue van ours. White Civic not. If Civvy moves, Blue tucks it."

Smitty: "Grid's a hum. Power lick will be local. Cameras live two minutes off-river."

"Two couriers alive," Tasia said later. "Burner phone, analog map. I want to kiss whoever kept them offline."

Ledger in pocket. Names unencrypted—because arrogance is faster.

Halloran: "We're good."

Jenna rubbed her eyes. Sparks bloomed behind her lids.

But no text. No ping. No Nora.

HEADLINES BROKE before sleep could try: Anonymous sources. Coordinated sting. No mention of ring lights or a woman who turned an audience into an ear.

At 03:11, steam from an old kettle. Delgado denying snores. Lena scrolling, frowning. "Nothing on Nora. Not in hospitals, not in noise."

Jenna nodded. No promises.

Three days smeared past. She ate when told, slept when she could. Dove into the under-web. Lit flares in places where favors slept.

At 02:08 on the third night, a mirror site coughed up a page that shouldn't exist.

Black background. White text. A still frame—cheap security cam, crooked.

Nora.

Bound, bruised, one eye swollen shut. The other—furious. Alive.

Captioned like a receipt:

**[INTERCEPTED TRANSMISSION // ROOK →
WREN]**

ROOK: got her in the box. sunshine's shadow.

WREN: clock her. let the stream queen learn time.

ROOK: tick tick. next cast is hers.

Jenna's jaw creaked. She captured the page three times. Zoomed on Nora's mouth—set, stubborn.

Be me in the fight.

She closed the laptop, reached under the table for the go-bag. Knife. Spare phone. Cash. Old ID. Taser charged.

On the whiteboard under the Crossline map, she wrote:

LINES MOVED.

NO MORE GHOSTS.

Smitty stepped in, saw the bag, saw the board. "When?"

"Now."

Delgado: "What do you need?"

"A wall. And a live wire."

Lena: "I'll build you both."

Halloran over comms: "We have one trace—industrial row, south docks, warehouse fronting as a yoga studio. Cute."

"Send the dot."

"You're not going in."

"I'm going through."

Beat. "Copy."

Jenna left the headset on the chair. Paused by the stack of ring lights. Not an apology—a promise.

"You crossed it," she told the room. "Now I do."

She opened the door. The night met her, warm and wet. A train horn moaned low, carrying until it ran out of track.

Jenna stepped into it.

No more decoys.

Only the crossfire she chose.

39

Under Duress

The rain pushed him sideways.

Max cut across the alley mouth with his head down and shoulders hunched, coat collar risen like the last good wall in a doomed city. The safehouse crouched between a shuttered print shop and a pawn store whose windows were blacked, faint spray-painted X's still ghosting under grime from an old hurricane.

He paused at the chain-link gate and let his eyes slow down. No headlights turning. No glow under tires. Just the plastic clack of a loose street sign and the low, wet hum of a city trying to mind its own business and failing.

His breath fogged. He slid a hand into his pocket for the cheap handheld scanner he'd started carrying again—an antique with a cracked casing and gaffer tape over the battery door. Tuned to nothing and everything: maintenance chatter, night-crew security, the occasional CB burst from a cab dispatcher misusing an old police band. He thumbed the wheel out of habit.

The storm flattened most of the sound.

Something still bled through.

[INTERCEPTED TRANSMISSION]

LLAVE: little blue two east, long shadow.

PEZ: copy. no light. Keep your eyes on.

Wrong channel. Wrong slang. South Texas border air, CB chopped with Spanglish. It hit the inside of his ribs like a song you hope you misheard.

He clicked off, counted three, clicked back on. Silence. Shut the scanner down, slid it into his pocket like it might burn him. Lifted the latch and slipped through the gate.

Inside, the air smelled of coffee gone wrong, wet concrete, and worry that had unpacked and stayed. The ceiling fan clacked crooked; every time the power hiccupped, the shadows traded seats. He bolted the door and moved to the back corner where a narrow bunk was buried under a yellow legal pad, a dead pen, and his own rain-blurred handwriting.

Contacts. Leak points. Safe numbers. Routes that failed. Names he'd trusted, names that turned to smoke when he needed weight. The page looked like a lake he'd tried to walk across.

He pressed a palm into one eye until comet streaks scratched the dark. Rain hit harder; the roof answered with urgency, as if someone had tapped the world with a ring. He couldn't remember a sleep that wasn't collapse. Couldn't remember a dream that didn't turn obituary.

Nora's name lived behind his tongue like a blade—making polite conversation impossible. Since the call—since Jenna's voice had thinned to wire and grief and the word *taken*—his own words had been rationed. He understood her silence now. She'd gone down into the cut, into the digital underworld that eats people whole and spits out their names as warnings. He'd stopped texting her lies like *rest* and *soon*.

The knock came sharp, in their rhythm: three, stop, two. He checked the cheap door-cam—rain-blurred man in a trench coat, hair plastered, chin raised like he remembered being taller. Ed.

Max shot the deadbolt. Ed stepped in, shrugging off water, the old coat slinging drops onto boards damp since the day they were cut. No pleasantries—just a manila folder and wet cheekbones, both set down as if they weighed the same.

"It's from the Zafiros," he said, voice rough with cold air and something deeper.

"I thought they cut us," Max said. It felt like a test—one you knew you'd fail and took anyway.

"Desperation breeds exceptions. They want immunity. For a price."

Max slid the folder toward him like it might bite. Top sheet: black-and-white aerial—compound scabbed into caliche dirt, fence line stitched like a wound, soldier-shadows walking their dumb ellipses. Date stamp. Annotations in Spanish—clean, field shorthand.

Under that: call logs in block columns, pen strokes getting meaner as the night went later. Under that: index. Offshore accounts. Numbers that weren't phone numbers—they were vaults without doors you could knock on. Currency flow maps: elegant and obscene.

He recognized some of it. That was the sickness. He'd brushed these names back when he thought his day job was printing and his night job was conscience. He'd filed pieces around the rot's edges and gone home imagining himself unafraid.

"This is real," he said. It came out hollow.

"They're not good people having a change of heart," Ed said. "Ortega's house is on fire. No one knows where to kneel. Zafiros aren't going to Hell with him out of nostalgia."

Max traced the fence line on the aerial photo with a finger that had learned to shake in private. "This where they're holding her?"

Ed leaned over his shoulder. "We think so. It's more than a jail—it's a vault. Route books, ledgers, transfer logs. They're consolidating. Classic firewall before a burn. This is their fire pit."

"They'll torch it when they smell us."

"Then we get there first. We don't need to hold it—just make a hole big enough the world can see through."

"We need to get to Nora. Tonight."

"Jenna?"

"She'll be there," Max said. He didn't know if it was hope or promise; his voice decided.

The burner jittered across the table. Max caught it before the second buzz.

"I'm here," Jenna said—static and wire. No sleep in her throat. He pictured her in a small room, too much blue light on her skin, another woman learning to be brave.

"They've stacked everything," Max said. "One place. Stronghold married to a server farm. We hit it, we cut their spine."

"And if it's bait?"

"Then we walk smarter than they think we can. And bring a can we can open quick."

"I want to be there."

"No." He remembered when you could tell someone to stay home and they did.

"I'm not asking." No defiance—just fact. He knew that smile; he'd worn it the day he printed a name that meant moving apartments.

He took it as agreement. "Zafiros gave us a key—Mateo Ruiz."

Silence. Then: "The colonel. The ghost hand."

"Wants exile. Trade—his map for his skin."

"Let him think he's cashing out. We'll take the map."

The line died. The room's hum returned.

They drove in an hour the city gives back to animals. The hacienda sat where the map promised—two miles off a road that had stopped pretending to serve anything but dust. Rain spent, the world sticky and shining. A dead mesquite tree scraped the wall in the wind.

Inside: air cooled, smelling of lime and old oranges. Furniture gone, taken by a family who left with heads down. Ruiz had chosen a table that didn't wobble and a chair facing the door. He didn't stand—just watched them enter with the patience of a man out of morals and miracles.

He didn't look like a kingmaker; that was the trick. Steel-wool hair, sun-ruined skin, hands too still. Eyes that measured rooms by the last good cover—and let Max see it on purpose.

"I made enemies on every side," he said evenly. "But I kept the truth. I curated it."

Max set a recorder on the table, slid it forward. Agents flanked, still as lawn ornaments. The wind slipped in, slipped out.

"Then talk," Max said.

Ruiz slid a scuffed flash drive from his coat pocket, set it down as gently as fever medicine. Tapped it once.

"Names. Documents. The lattice. Embedded assets—media, government, law enforcement. A list of my sins and your colleagues. Some wear your flag. Some wear their own faces for masks."

Max lifted the drive, felt its weightlessness.

"This starts a war."

"No," Ruiz said. "It shows you the one you've been losing."

Max asked for names. Ruiz gave them. Routes, facts, no decoration. A ledger with lungs.

"I want asylum. For my daughter. For me."

"You'll get what the law allows," Ed said—half line, half mercy.

Outside, the scanner in Max's pocket growled awake.

[INTERCEPTED TRANSMISSION]

MACHETE: la house is hot. la brunette's shadow's here.

LLAVE: clock 'em. coyotes don't run without noise.

Jenna wasn't here. She wasn't stupid enough to be. They still spoke like her shadow dragged light.

He killed the scanner, pocketed the drive, walked out with a chin the wind respected.

Back at the safehouse, rain was a rumor and the roof behaved. They air-gapped a trusted machine. The forensic tech—buzz cut, work-nicked knuckles—slotted the drive, exhaled through her nose like a boxer checking distance.

The files opened like a book whose last line you already know.

Thirty-seven officials. Three national journalists. A former senator with a hope-pitch smile. Dozens of shells named like head fakes. The lattice lit up like a nervous system under scan.

"Architecture," Jenna said on speaker, wire fuzz making her sound like a ghost with a throat.

"Self-healing," Max said. "You can't pull one brick and tell the wall it's not a wall."

"Then you don't pull bricks," Ed said. "You take out rebar."

Max stood at the table, letting the names pour through until they felt like a chant. Ledger initials reappeared in campaign disclosures signed by men laughing. Campaign dollars walked into clinics, walked out as poison.

"You collapse it in public," he said. "Print, video, testimony. Same hour. Everywhere. Earthquake, not tremor."

"Make it a mirror," Jenna said. "Make them see their faces."

He sat, moved the legal pad with its murdered plan aside. Opened a new document on the air-gapped machine.

He wrote like suturing a wound—spare, clean. Names from magazines, names in grease pencil on forbidden ledgers. Numbers threaded through sentences like rope. Present tense sharp enough to cut glass.

He wrote his son. Not the name. Not the date. Just *my son*—the way you write *oxygen*. No hospital smell, no tube's small-motor sound. Just infrastructure. The machine that carried poison, the hands that built it, the polished voices that excused it.

The sun pushed one color through cloud. He kept writing— Ruiz's drive braided into old reporting, sealed with corroboration his conscience could lift its chin to. Addressed the reader like a jury.

The last sentence arrived perfect. He saved—three places. Copied to an unlabeled drive, pocketed it, hand over the pocket. Tore the legal pad page, folded it into a shape that wouldn't stab.

The door shook with a knock that was more decision than request. Lena stood framed there—rain needled in her hair, colorless with adrenaline past its sixty-minute window.

"We've got a problem."

She held up her phone: grainy shoulder-cam feed. Smitty. In profile. Facing Ruiz. Something small in his hand, passed. Whisper into a collar mic.

[INTERCEPTED TRANSMISSION]

PEZ: the house is not sealed. Snake inside.

LLAVE: copy. Leave the door.

Lena's eyes were too wide. "He's been feeding intel."

The room thinned. The fan slogged another circle, not enough to keep life alive.

Max felt nothing for three beats. Then something colder than fury.

"Get him in," he said, voice low enough the table leaned to hear.

He didn't repeat himself.

"Now."

40

Calculated Risks

Max hit the curb hard, wipers thudding useless against a wall of rain. The storm had crawled in from the Gulf at dusk and refused to let go, turning Tallahassee into a smear of brake lights and flooded gutters. He killed the engine and sat a beat in the steamed-up cabin, damp wool and fatigue seeping into his bones.

The Gazette loomed a block ahead—no longer anonymous, all he had worked for—in the cross hairs of the Cartel. Evan appeared in his mind—this is what we have worked for—it is time to end this once and for all.

Collar up, he dashed across the street, taking the long way around—habit and paranoia having long since become the same thing. At the loading bay he stopped, scanning: no smokers under the eaves, no silhouettes at the corner. Only rain carving bright threads down stacked pallets and a lone sodium light beating a jaundiced cone into the wet.

He used the back stairs climbing to the Gazette's nerve center. Inside: heat, server hum, and stale coffee. Someone had a towel near the door; he wiped his face and listened—low voices, the click-sprint of keys, a cough that tried to be a laugh and failed. He moved toward the glow of Ed's office.

Jenna was already there, headset crooked, rain darkening strands of hair. In the antiseptic light she looked carved from concentration—eyes narrowed, mouth set, the influencer shine gone to ground. When she saw him, the steel softened by a notch he didn't deserve.

"You look like a broken umbrella."

"Storm likes me," he said, shrugging off his coat. "Or hates me. Same feeling either way."

"Ed's in the glass box," she said, tipping her chin toward the Gazette's glass-walled conference room, now mission control. "Ava's building the relay and talking to London and Berlin. Kyle is swearing at the firewall. We're an inch from go."

"And Smitty?"

"Coordinating logistics." He didn't look at him when she said it.

He followed her glance—Smitty hunched at the far row. She felt Max watching and offered a nod too quick to mean anything.

Max turned back. "You hear from Nora?"

Her face barely moved. "No."

He wanted to promise something that wasn't a lie. He settled for truth. "We finish this. Make them smaller. That's how we get her back."

"That's how we try," she said, and slid past him toward the conference room.

The storm rattled the roof. Somewhere across town a transformer gave up; the lights dipped, flickered back, and the whole room exhaled. The clock over the tech bay blinked 3:12 a.m. in wounded red.

Ed didn't look up when Max stepped into the glass box. Endgame stillness—that moment when a man's already argued with himself and lost. The draft on his screen glowed like a road flare: **THE MIRROR THEY COULDN'T BREAK.** Printed pages and cold coffee littered the table. Beside them, a steel frame with Hannah frozen mid-laugh.

"Storm broke the comms once," Ava said, eyes never leaving the lattice of network windows. "We've got redundancy now, but if they've got a kill switch on the backbone, the weather won't matter."

"They do," Ed said. He slid his phone across. The text on the screen was flat, bureaucratic: *Don't publish. They've embedded international signals. Release = blackout. Partial kill switch activated.*

"Not bluffing," Ava said. "Swiss VPN hop, Cold War birds repurposed for hand-offs. Trip it and we don't just kill a site—we shave hours off the power grid and freeze bank rails in half a dozen time zones."

"This is beyond cartel muscle," Ava murmured.

"It's architecture," Jenna said from the doorway. "We knew that."

"Ava, solution?" Ed prompted.

"Parallel relay," Kyle said. "Wide, dark, mirrored. Hardened nodes in twelve zones, thirty-plus outlets. If one fails, the rest replicate. If a packet burns, the next hops."

"And the worm?"

"I've ring-fenced the drop. If it bites, it hits our decoy nodes first. We'll feel it, but it won't get to bone."

Max dragged a chair with a scrape that pulled eyes. "Make them read it in breakfast lines. Watch it at stoplights."

Ed studied the headline one more beat, then nodded. "Global at noon Eastern. Dead if we have to."

The hours blurred—coffee to copper, screens to maps to faces. The newsroom became a submarine, outside world reduced to pitch and pressure.

At 3:37 a.m., Ava stiffened. "Outbound packet. Not ours."

Linda moved in. Kyle's knuckles cracked over his keys. A red line lit on the map, jumped a switch, burned toward a proxy.

"Where?" Ed's voice had an edge.

Ava pulled the trace layer by layer until the route snapped into a dotted line leading home. His mouth opened, closed.

"Say it," Ed said.

"Inside. Our C-sector node."

"Which workstation?" Kyle asked.

Kyle swallowed. "Smitty's."

The room didn't go quiet so much as stop pretending.

Smitty's chair creaked. "You don't understand."

"Put the phone down," Max said.

Smitty raised it like an offering. "I've been feeding them noise. Not our moves—their moves, back to them. Breadcrumbs. Kept them looking the wrong way."

Kyle yanked the ethernet. Ava threw his processes into a loop. Linda blocked the door.

Kyle's fingers stabbed keys; code scrolled. "You sent our building's grid. You gave them a heat map. That's not noise—it's a flare."

"They had my brother," Smitty said, too fast. "He's clean now, or was, and—"

"They always have someone," Jenna cut in. "You still chose."

Smitty's face twitched, then smoothed into defiance. "You righteous people and your perfect worlds. Out there, you deal or you drown."

"Out there," Max said softly, "I buried a son."

Smitty didn't look at him.

Max leaned over Smitty. "You're going to watch us finish. Then you'll give Ava every password, cut-out, handler name you've got. If I find out you so much as pinged a weather app, I walk you to the Bureau myself."

Smitty sat.

The storm ran its own relay overhead. Ava built the global drop node by node. Max juggled editors in half a dozen time zones.

Ed walked the loop: glass, whiteboard, lede, door. Guatemala flickered in his memory. Fall River. Hannah in the back seat of the Corolla.

He set a finger under his headline. "This is for you," he whispered.

4:17 blinked up. Linda poised over the master trigger. "Press and the storm wakes.

"Not tonight."

Max told Smitty quietly, "When the press hits you, you'll feel alone. That's the feeling you bought. Sit in it."

The phones shivered. Unknown Source: *Don't publish.* Eastern Europe's servers wide awake.

"They never sleep," Ed said.

"Three. Two. One."

Linda pressed.

Doha lit first, then Toronto, Berlin, Lagos, Seoul—independents making ladders out of fences. The worm lunged at the decoys, bit salted nothing, turned on itself. Ava's shoulders loosened—then stopped.

Unknown Source: *Kill switch armed. Publish = lights out. Final warning.*

"Too late," Linda said, pushing the redundancy wave.

The power line spat sparks into rain; the block became a constellation, then a street again.

Max pressed a palm to the glass. "Whatever happens, we made a dent."

"Make it a fracture," Jenna said.

41

The Cost of Truth

Rain hammered the steel roof of the security van like a thousand small decisions coming due. The AC coughed once, then settled into a wheeze that never quite cleared the humid veil inside.

Jenna sat curled on the bench seat, chin balanced on damp denim. The tablet in her lap stuttered blue across her face—graphs, packet traces, and a frozen frame of her own mouth mid-word from twenty minutes ago. Her livestream. Not a fishing tip or a quick-hit reel. A fuse.

She scrubbed back and watched herself again: shoulders straight, voice even until it wasn't, the comment stream sliding from hearts to static to hard questions. In seven minutes she'd broken her own rule—used her face to detonate someone else's life. No warehouse footage. Just her voice. The receipts: a philanthropic façade masking private-equity slush, ad-algorithms tied to shell fronts, contracts that never said *cartel* but did the work just fine. No filters. No edits.

A career had taught her to make a smile sound like proof. Tonight she'd turned it into a blade.

The van smelled of damp vinyl and old coffee; outside, the air was wet oak, diesel, and the storm's iron breath. Her phone buzzed beside the photo that always slipped loose from its folder: two girls, fourteen, a borrowed rod, mud on their knees. Nora's eyes—soft, honest, unprepared for war.

The message was clipped and ugly:

Unknown: She don't like heat. She likes the lights. Next time, we bring her back to block.

Attached: grainy photo, timestamped, Nora's stoop under streetlight wash. Blue pot on the step. No faces. Just proof.

The taste in Jenna's mouth went metallic and stayed. She slid the photo back into its folder and felt the paper catch skin. Every soft part of her life had become a lever. They knew it. She'd known it too, in theory. Theory didn't drip rain down your neck in a steel box at the edge of a city sharpening knives.

Earlier, they'd crammed into a hotel safehouse that smelled of sanitizer and old carpet—Ed pacing trenches into the floor, Ava's hands rabbit-quick on the keys, Max carrying the storm in on his shoulders.

"You went rogue," Ed said, voice low to make it land harder.

"I followed a lead," Jenna said, keeping hers level so it wouldn't break.

"You took apart months of choreography for a solo," he said. "This works because it's synchronized."

"They have her," Jenna said. "They took her because of me. Your choreography's just a slow bleed."

Ava tried to make the math hold. "We don't even know how they found her. Or you."

"We do," Jenna said, letting anger find a wire. "Santa Lucía—my old sponsor. They let a consultant plug into follower look-alike pools after I cut ties. 'One-time audit.' I ripped the metadata. They've been watching me move through my own reflection. Two watchers at two old brands I used to prop up for ten grand and a smile. Didn't have to hack anything. I left the door painted cute and *ask-me-how*."

Silence. Ed's jaw worked. Ava's knuckles whitened, then let go. Max looked at the carpet, then at Jenna. "So we're exposed."

"No," she said. "I am. Use that."

"How?" Ava asked.

"Give them what they want. Me out front, looking pretty, posting my little come-see. We lace it. Ava reactivates my old handles, baits the watcher pipeline. They lean closer. Then we tip the wheel."

It tasted like bleach, but cruelty aimed right still counts as strategy.

Ava unlocked the old account. *Jenna Morgan, Reformed Insider* returned from the dead with a carefully casual selfie. Caption: *Sometimes truth requires masks. Sometimes masks reflect truths others won't face. Tomorrow: no edits. No filters. Just the receipts.*

Four hours later: two million impressions, big-account amplifications, blue-check DM's offering to "help her come back after this nonsense."

Then the burner hummed: *Let's talk. 2 a.m. Hotel Astrid. Suite 906. Alone. Or Nora disappears.*

Ed said no. Max said they'd find another way. Ava asked for an hour to build a shadow.

Jenna went anyway.

She parked three blocks from the Astrid. Rain-dark coat. Polished-floor lobby. Old-money crown molding. Mirrors in the elevator—she didn't look.

Suite 906: heavy curtains, dim lamps, expensive art you didn't have to like. A thin man at the minibar poured a drink without looking up.

"You're late," he said.

"Clock runs when I say it does."

"Cute," he said, setting the glass down. A thumb drive lay on the table between them.

"I'm the cleanup. Loose ends used to be people. Now they're servers and reputations. Your team makes my job difficult."

"Cry me a river."

He smiled without teeth. "No threats. Just a transaction. Routes, rotations, who blesses which container with a diplomatic nod."

"What's the price?"

"Loud," he said. "No more whispers. Loud enough the banks

have to deny with straight faces while their hands still smell like cash and benzocaine. Do that, some of my clients lose a hand."

"And Nora?"

"She's alive. For now."

She took the drive and didn't turn her back until she had to.

DAWN CAME copper at the edges, then gray. In the motel safehouse kitchen, Ed waited with coffee, Ava with eyes ringed in sleepless circles, Max straight-lined by exhaustion.

Jenna dropped the drive on the table. "Insurance. Or a grenade."

Ava cracked it open. Routes, manifests disguised as donations, payment trails looping into procurement forms, names that chilled the room—diplomatic mail-drops, agency liaisons moonlighting as croupiers, a tech firm with OSHA posters over a war room.

At noon: secure line ping—*Nodes shifting. Internal leaks detected. Sweep now. Trust compromised.*

The circle that had felt like lifeline tightened into a noose.

"Trust will get us killed," Jenna said.

Rain hammered harder. In the window's steamed edge, she saw the two girls with the borrowed rod.

Secure channel: *Low light. Two shadows. Blue van. 'Camera girl' alone.*

"They're outside," Ava said.

Fifteen minutes later—three sharp raps. Smitty stepped in, soaked. "I'm burned. They know."

"They knew an hour ago," Ava said.

"I did what I had to. They had my brother."

"You sent them our breathing," Ed said.

"I sent them breadcrumbs into a swamp."

The steel door behind him thrummed—metal talking to weather.

"Out," Ed said.

"What does that mean?"

"It means you go to the room at the end of the hall and wait for the Bureau's questions."

He left. A minute later, the building shook—impact, not explosion. Lightning swallowed any flash. *Basement. Small door. Close it,* came the intercept.

Ava locked the building down. "If they want up, they come heavy or slow."

"We go neither," Ed said. "We publish and move."

"Move where?" Max asked.

He didn't answer.

Jenna's burner: *8 p.m. tonight. Marina. Bring your face.*

"They're not negotiating," she said. "They're scheduling."

Ava pointed at the drive's map. "If we catch these pallets live, we cut three heads off the thing. Make it too big to clean."

"Or get her killed," Max said.

"I can't wait for their mercy," Jenna said.

Ed: "We do both. Live drop and rescue. Assign what we trust. Lock the rest."

They turned the day into a hinge. Ava stitched the Astrid drive onto old drop architecture. Max called markers from lives he didn't talk about. ORION pinged: *Two nodes burned. Assume contamination.*

At six, Smitty made his own choice—out the door, down the stairwell. Feed went white, then black. A second camera caught the pipe, the hits, the collapse. They pulled him back inside.

"We have to assume every alley he knew is burned," Ava said.

"Then we live with none," Ed said.

One hour to the marina. Dummy streams to dead channels. Scanner feeds patched. Editors warned.

7:42 p.m., secure channel: *North dock. No sirens. Low lights. High water. Is the old man with her? No.*

"They want theater," Max said.

"Then we give them a crowd," Jenna said.

The van rolled in under pulsing streetlights that died one by one. Two blocks out, they parked. Rain was steady needlework.

At the dock's mouth, a figure leaned on a piling.

"You brought your face," he said.

"You brought other people's," she said, walking on.

Max kept high, Ava counted packet hops, Ed hovered over the trigger.

Blue's here. Face in frame. Hold, came the intercept.

"Where is she?"

"In the city that loves lights. Not here. Yet."

"You promised."

"I promised cause and effect."

He handed her a phone—Nora in a dark room, alive, eyes steady, date board in her lap.

"Where?"

"When your story goes live. Or she learns to love the dark."

In the safehouse, Ed said into his mic, "We publish regardless."

Ava's nodes bloomed green. Jenna lifted her chin.

"Say the line," the man said.

"No."

"Then say goodbye."

Footsteps behind her. Water shifted. Out on the bay, lights blinked out.

"Ed," Ava said.

He pressed.

The world lit—Doha, Lagos, Berlin, Toronto, Seoul. Headlines found throats.

The man didn't flinch. "Good. Now we can begin."

Her phone vibrated—pin drop, ten blocks away, a mirrored-glass building.

"Max."

"I see it."

She nodded. "Then we go."

Help / lights off, said the text.

She ran. Rain swallowed the sound.

Behind her, the man pressed a key. "Ahora."

Replies crackled in three accents.

The cost came due. The world didn't get smaller. It got sharper.

And the final battle hadn't even begun.

Barometric Pressure

Chapter 42: The Inner Circle

Tallahassee had never drawn much attention from the national spotlight—and that made it perfect. Miguel had chosen Florida's capital not for its politics, but for its blind spots. Between the decaying industrial zones, underfunded enforcement agencies, and a transient population of students, lobbyists, and government aides, the city offered a perfect smokescreen.

From the outside, his influence was hidden behind a chain of commercial fisheries, marina management groups, and boutique logistics firms that had quietly consolidated over the last six years. But beneath the paper trails lay the real currents: deepwater routes carrying synthetic fentanyl from cartel hubs in Sinaloa through Apalachicola Bay, then funneled inland through Tallahassee's network of distributors masked as "recreational outfitters."

It was all part of Miguel's genius—keeping his operations one layer removed from blood. He let others dirty their hands while he sipped coffee, reading defense reports that never named him.

But now the walls were bleeding. The safe zones weren't safe. And Tallahassee—the overlooked capital he once called a fortress—had become his final trap.

The cigar smoke curled through the skylight like a signal to no one, dissipating into the gray Florida dawn. Miguel Ortega stood alone in the atrium of the governor's Tallahassee mansion—the one he'd gifted to the current occupant in exchange for silence. The silence hadn't lasted. And now, the mansion echoed with absence.

Empty glasses from a midnight summit lined the kitchen counter. Unanswered texts blinked across Miguel's burner phone. The only reply that mattered had never come.

He crushed the cigar stub into a marble ashtray shaped like the state of Florida and muttered a curse under his breath. The world he built—systemic, sprawling, precise—was beginning to rot from the inside.

And the decay had a face.

His.

Sofia was gone.

He hadn't heard from her since the meeting in Havana. The moment she'd looked him in the eyes and said, "We're done playing by your rules."

He hadn't believed her.

But now…

Now the silence stretched like a noose.

THE CALL from Raul came just before dawn. Miguel recognized the tone before the words: clipped, urgent, strained.

"They've started moving product without authorization. Using alternate routes. Ones we didn't sanction."

Miguel closed his eyes. "Who gave the order?"

"Unknown. Could be Sinaloa, but—rumors say it's local. From our own. Your wife's signature authorized the account withdrawals."

Miguel said nothing.

"I'm heading to the Wakulla depot," Raul continued. "But if this isn't shut down within twenty-four hours, the federales will smell blood."

Miguel ended the call and stared at the blinking cursor on his screen. An offshore account just north of Curaçao had been accessed overnight. The timestamp matched the withdrawal Raul mentioned. Sofia had overridden his credentials.

For years, she had played the role. The diplomat's daughter, the patient consort. She spoke three languages, dressed like a senator's wife, and moved among politicians like water through marble.

But it wasn't patience.

It was planning.

And now she was the one pulling threads.

THE WAKULLA DEPOT squatted behind an abandoned seafood distribution center, tucked beneath layers of concrete and security footage no one ever watched. Miguel's convoy pulled in as a bank of clouds rolled over the pines. It smelled like fish and diesel and betrayal.

Raul met him at the gate, his shirt soaked with sweat.

"They diverted a shipment two hours ago," he said. "Came in under a conservation tag. Used a fake wildlife rescue outfit as cover."

Miguel raised an eyebrow. "That's Sofia's idea."

"Already scrubbed," Raul added. "But the inventory discrepancy will trigger audits."

Miguel walked past him toward the cold room. Empty crates, half-melted ice, and a residue trail where opiate shells had been transferred to unrefrigerated vans.

"She's bold," Raul muttered. "You always knew that."

"She's not bold," Miguel said flatly. "She's strategic."

There was a difference. Boldness gets people killed. Strategy leaves no fingerprints.

BACK IN TALLAHASSEE, Miguel entered the safehouse downtown where his inner circle had been relocated. Blackout curtains. Triple-encrypted routers. A floor plan Sofia herself had recommended six months earlier.

She had been building her own escape the entire time.

Paulo, the family accountant, stood by the dry bar sipping mezcal like it was church wine. "The accounts are bleeding. Funds diverted through a Panamanian shell, then rerouted through Tallahassee real estate trusts. All of it invisible on the books unless you know exactly where to look."

"Did you?" Miguel asked.

"I do now."

Miguel walked to the far corner of the room and sat in the high-back leather chair Sofia had once insisted was "too indulgent."

Maybe she'd meant it as a warning.

"How long?" he asked.

Paulo hesitated. "Six months. Maybe longer."

"Who else knew?"

Paulo hesitated again, then said, "Raul. Possibly Ava."

Of course. Raul had always been loyal—but to whom was less certain by the day. Over time, Raul had grown close to Sofia, especially as the internal struggles of his empire began to metastasize.

They thought he hadn't heard.

But Miguel heard everything.

BY MIDAFTERNOON, the air over the Panhandle turned swampy and thick. Miguel returned to the atrium, staring out over the manicured garden hedges that Sofia had redesigned last fall.

She'd said they looked too symmetrical. Too predictable.

She'd wanted chaos disguised as elegance.

Now he knew why.

A notification chirped.

A message from an encrypted contact named **Vega**:

"She made contact with your daughter. They met in St. Augustine. You're out of time."

Miguel's fingers froze.

His first daughter. Rosa.

The one thing he'd kept entirely separate from the empire.

Until now.

· · ·

HE CALLED SOFIA.

For the first time in weeks, she answered.

"Miguel."

"I warned you."

"No," she said calmly. "You warned the woman you thought I was."

"What are you doing with Rosa?"

"Protecting her. From what you won't admit still lives inside you."

Miguel's voice dropped. "You're making a mistake."

"No," she said. "I'm correcting one."

He wanted to scream, to issue threats, to call down men who'd buried enemies in limestone swamps.

But he said nothing.

She continued, "You think control is power. But power isn't built on fear. It's built on trust. And you have none left."

Then the line went dead.

HOURS PASSED. The inner circle began to dissolve. One by one, calls went unanswered. The encrypted network Ava maintained flickered out. Max hadn't checked in since the last transfer.

And then came the knock.

A single rap on the side door. Not protocol. Not secure.

Miguel opened it anyway.

Standing there was Santiago Vargas, the cartel's old diplomat, long thought exiled to Guatemala.

"Santiago," Miguel said warily. "You're supposed to be dead."

"I was," Santiago replied. "Until she gave me a reason not to be."

"She?"

"Sofia. She's building something. A future without ghosts."

Miguel stepped back.

Santiago continued, "I'm here to offer you a path out."

Miguel scoffed. "You think I'd abandon all this?"

Santiago held up a hand. "You don't have a kingdom anymore.

Just ruins. You want Gabriella safe? You want Sofia alive? Then step aside."

"And what do I get?"

"A plane. A clean passport. A quiet place to die without dragging your daughter into it."

Miguel stared at the man for a long time.

Then he looked back at the mansion.

And he knew Santiago was right.

Everything else was already gone.

He closed the door.

And began to pack.

But as he lifted the photo of Gabriella from his shelf, a flash drive clattered to the floor.

One he hadn't seen before.

Labeled in Sofia's handwriting:

For when you're ready to know everything.

43

Climactic Confrontations

The storm came in sideways—rain slung low and mean, hissing through longleaf and cypress like the Panhandle was one big lung drawing a ragged breath. Max Larkin shouldered into it, coat heavy, shoes sucking at the black mud, headlamp beam cutting fog and Spanish moss. The wetlands breathed their old smells—iron and rot, tannin and salt—and lightning stitched white linen through the sky far inland, behind the dark line of pines. A truck's taillights winked twice on the forest road, then went black. Good. The rest was on foot.

He crouched at the waterline under a blown-out oak and wiped rain from his lashes with the back of a hand still ink-stained from the newsroom. The small pistol Ava had insisted on pressed cold into his ribs. He hated the weight—and what it said about who he'd become—but he kept it. Not tonight. Not with a friend tied to a chair in a shack that used to sell live bait before the hurricanes took the roof and the new business moved in, quiet and ruinous.

"Camera?" Jenna's voice whispered in his ear, thin over comms. He could almost see her face in that stray-moon pall: lips set, eyes hard as bottle glass, hair braided tight to keep nothing stray from catching.

238

"On," Max said.

"Then breathe for me," she said. He did—one in, one out. "You're good."

Rain worried at every seam. Ozone and old sugarcane clung in his mouth. A mosquito whined past his ear; he didn't swat. In the van half a mile back, Jenna watched the heat map—two bodies in the main room, one smaller and steady in the back. A third flared cold and bloomed again with a cigarette. On her other monitor, a satellite tile from a rented node she'd paid for with the last of a sponsorship milled into deniability. Barely legal. Barely illegal. Perfect.

Khalil's voice came next—slow-drawl Gulf swagger over old Fed patience. "Bravo's set. Two on the porch, ten feet apart. Back door's got a broom handle through the latch."

"I'm left door," Ava said. "Clara on hall. Larkin on the girl—fast."

"Copy," Max said, breath smoking in the cold. The wind shifted; the shack on its pilings creaked like a man rolling a bad ankle.

Rain hammered the tin roof. Something small skittered over corrugate and fell. Max closed his eyes and saw his kid's bedhead, the geometry of his grin, the night-shift nurse in Tijuana touching his shoulder: *Overdose.* He opened his eyes on another word: *remedy.*

[INTERCEPTED TRANSMISSION]

—GULF/TLH x2.

—Blue coat, limp, weight L hip.

—Van in the pines, heat sigs: 3–4.

—Clock 'em. Let 'em cook till handoff.

The hair lifted at Max's nape. Storm nerves—or the way Jenna went quiet when she read something on her third screen and chose not to share.

"Keep it tight," she said instead. "We ain't got time for clean."

"Gator-tough," Khalil said. "On my mark. Three—"

Lightning came close, sawtoothing the sky and blanching the shack windows. Guards turned toward the flash. Khalil didn't count two.

The door blew—hinges howled, bodies forgot they were made

of meat. Max ran low and straight, boots slapping algae-slick boards. Ava ghosted beside him, shoulder-first through a seam of light and mildew stink. Inside, something barked—a gun, a shout, a chair leg—then Clara's muzzle flash shoved the dark back.

"Back room!" Max wasn't sure if he spoke it or thought it. He hit the hall wall with his shoulder, slid along bowed paneling to the door with the chair scrape, the muffled bravery under duct tape.

A boot to the lock. A room smelling of bleach and the old dead. Nora's eyes wide, hair matted from torn tape. She shook her head *no*.

"Yes," Max told her. "Jenna—got her."

The blade jumped in his hand when a shotgun blew a ragged hole in the kitchen doorway. Splinters rained. Ava swore—"Left!"— and answered with a controlled, surgical shot. Max sawed through the old gummy tape. Clara filled the doorway, laying down sound like a curtain.

"Eyes on me," Max told Nora. She nodded hard, breathing through her nose. He cut her ankles, tore the tape from her mouth in one jerk; pain made a sound in her throat.

"Up," he said, taking her weight. She was lighter than he expected—fear subtracts pounds, adds other heaviness.

Khalil: "Front secure. One runner to water."

Ava: "Let him run."

[INTERCEPTED TRANSMISSION]

—Runner to water is ours.

—Van's got two birds cold.

—Leave an off-ramp. We want 'em hungry.

"Rear," Clara said. "Now."

They came out into rain teeth, Nora between them. Levee grass slicked their ankles. The van's ghost-lights blinked twice—Jenna's signal.

"Almost," Max said. Nora stumbled; he caught her. Behind, the shack belched two more gunshots, then the noise men make when air leaves for good. Sirens far, rain near. He chose again to keep going.

"Run," Jenna said—not an order, permission.

They did.

The van was a low-chassis hum, warm plastic and coffee gone cold. Jenna slid the door, caught Nora in both arms, held her like she could compress a year's safety into three seconds. Nora folded in and made a sound braided of weight, shape, and relief.

"You're okay," Jenna said. "We got you."

Max climbed in, turned back. Clara popped two controlled rounds into the air. Khalil's silhouette filled the doorway, then shrank as the shack dissolved in downpour.

"Drive," Max said.

Halloran obeyed. Tires bit shell road, van fishtailing once before catching.

"Any pop behind us?" Khalil asked.

"Clear—for now," Jenna said.

[INTERCEPTED TRANSMISSION]

—Highway 98 cam dead.

—Eyes on 267 and Smith Creek.

—Salt truck rolling slow, tag ghosted.

—Tail two cars back.

Jenna's hand stayed flat on Nora's hair.

OUT BEYOND THE STORM, the other storm moved—money, names, signatures, silence—small decisions feeding the machine. In Tallahassee, one office light made a rectangle on rain-wet lawn. Miguel Ortega stood in it, cigar smoke making its own weather.

Sofia entered without knocking. Damp hair, Havana shawl, leather folio. She stayed standing.

"You're late," Miguel said without looking.

"I'm on time," she said. Rain underlined it.

He turned slow, choosing how to wear the moment. "You lied to me."

"Then we're even."

"You always mistook funny for soft."

Miguel gestured at the storm-lit lawn. "We built this house on silence. You brought microphones."

"I brought mirrors."

"Same thing."

She opened the folio—ledger, photos, message printouts, a hand-scrawled list like a kill-switch. She slid one photo toward him. Rosa, smiling into a wind not from Florida.

"You hid her," Sofia said. "I found her."

Miguel ground the cigar out harder than necessary. "What do you want?"

"Not to negotiate. To inform."

She tapped a page. "Curacao. Belize. Tallahassee trusts rolled into a Wakulla land bank under conservation cover you didn't invent. I've redirected enough to make you uncomfortable."

"You think this scares me."

"No. I don't spend verbs on your fear."

He almost laughed.

"You broke patience and care," she said. "So I'm breaking the rest."

"You never were a wife," he said.

"I was the scaffolding. You notice it when it's gone."

"You bought a governor," he said.

"I gave it back."

"You think you can run this better?"

"I think I can stop it—or set it on fire."

Thunder pressed on the house; the lights flickered.

"We have Nora," he said.

"Had," she said, holding up her phone. Miguel heard Jenna's voice from the van: "…we got you."

"You fed them that," he said.

"I fed them you."

"You'll die for this."

"I already did." She slid a flash drive, a motel key, a silver marlin charm across the table. "For when you stop pretending your hands are clean."

She left the door open; rain curled on the marble.

▭

IN THE VAN, Jenna pressed her forehead to the window. Nora slept heavy against her. Clara passed a blanket. Halloran drove.

"Phones?" Jenna asked.

"Burners only," Ava said. "Ghost accounts burned."

"You good?" he asked.

"Ask me when she's on a couch with bad TV and a dog."

Max pulled a sweatshirt from a tote, wrapped Nora in it.

[INTERCEPTED TRANSMISSION]

—Headed for town.

—Van plate spoofed; pinged twice on 30A.

—Girl breathing. Journal man on her six.

—We got time.

▭

IN THE NEWSROOM, Ed Harper stood at the glass, hand flat, catching thunder. He turned Hannah's photo face-down, then back up. The draft on his screen had been rewritten to muscle memory. Noon was the drop—global or nowhere.

Max came in wet, squeaking on the tile.

"You got her?" Ed asked.

"She's safe."

"Sit. Warm up."

"I'm filing."

The piece came fast—two parallel wars: backyard and boardroom. Nora's eyes. The weight of names. Rain as surveillance. A ledger that was sons, not numbers. Law as weather—falling where it chose.

Ed read. The copy desk handled it like stone. Noon came sudden, not creeping. Linda hit the send that lit thirty-two nodes. Phones rang. The kill-switch bit steel.

[INTERCEPTED TRANSMISSION]

—Drop went global.

—Sat worm met teeth.

—Switch didn't flip; lights only flicker.

—Clock's still ours. For now.

MIGUEL DIDN'T FLINCH when the lights dipped. He fed Sofia's drive into a dead-end machine. Folders opened: an empire's biography. He scrolled past paid and ruined men until a name stopped his face from remembering its place.

He made one call: "Phase Omega." In the Antilles, accounts unlaced themselves; contracts nullified; houses emptied. An endgame moved early.

In the van, Jenna let triumph pool once around her heart, then set it aside.

"Truth is," Max said, "we just put a match to ten miles of fuse."

"And the wind's wrong," Halloran said.

Jenna's phone buzzed: *she doesn't like heat—prefers the city—bring her home*. She set it face-down.

In his office, Miguel listened to rain find gravity, thought of Rosa learning to swim, thought of the marlin charm.

The door opened; Sofia crossed without her shawl.

"It's done," she said.

"I know."

"Then we talk about leaving." She set a ticket folder down. "Go like a man who understands rain—or stay like one who thinks roofs are forever."

"Take the house," he said.

"I'll burn it," she said.

They looked at each other in a moment that didn't try to be more.

"Rosa," he said.

"She laughs with her mouth open," Sofia said.

He nodded—bigger than thanks.

"You were never the worst man I knew," she said.

"You were simply real," he said.

She left an envelope in place of the tickets. "For when you understand planes are just houses moving too fast." She brushed the marlin charm and walked out.

[INTERCEPTED TRANSMISSION]

—Queen walked.

—King still aboard, water rising.

—Knights hungry; pawns drowning.

—Clock's got teeth now.

———

THE CITY MADE its noise again—sirens, slogans, prayers. Noon swept through like squalls. The governor's second statement came sanded soft. Calm didn't answer.

At dusk, Max texted Jenna: *you eat?*

gum and coffee, she wrote.

He almost typed *liar*, wrote *rest* instead.

Ed raised the blinds. "We go again tomorrow."

On the mansion lawn, rainwater found a new path off the step. Miguel pocketed the drive, marlin, and a key to a car he'd never be seen in.

In the van, Jenna checked Nora's pulse. Halloran took the scenic route. Clara counted heads and cased the rifle.

Max wrote three sentences no one would see, deleted them, kept the fourth.

Sofia's last text: *teach them the difference between rain and a leak.* Max replied with nothing but a radar image of concentric storms over the Panhandle.

The last light over the Capitol died. Somewhere between the wetlands and the mansion, two storms shared a wall.

Jenna's phone buzzed without a name. She waited five seconds —sometimes power is not-knowing—before reading:

[INTERCEPTED TRANSMISSION]

—Nora's breath steady.

—Van tagged sweet.

—Journal man's window light on.

—Smile for the storm.

44

The Tide Turns

Max hit the crosswalk as the light blinked white, heat lifting from the Capitol steps like a sigh. The Florida State Capitol rose ahead—pale stone, hard angles, its colonnade throwing long bars of shadow across a crowd with no reason to be anywhere else at four p.m.: tourists angling phones at portraits, staffers balancing boxed lunches with arguments, a school group clumping in matching T-shirts while their guide preached the Old Capitol's dome. Beyond the fountain, network vans idled, side doors yawning, cables snaking toward portable stages. In the gaps between chatter, you could hear the building's air intakes rumble—like the place itself taking a breath before the next round.

The old satchel hung on his shoulder, patched corner, ruined zipper, broadcasting "journalist" even when he wasn't trying. He'd shaved badly to look less like a fringe actor in his own story. Jenna's text had come five minutes earlier: *here. west colonnade. tourists thick. stay low.* The reveal would happen in plain view—only way to keep it alive. Arrests in crowds played like optics; silencers played like bad cinema.

Another buzz—his clean line, the number only a handful held.
[INTERCEPTED TRANSMISSION]

—white hat = east lawn, 2 o'clock. camera up. cargo on move. // tails see you. keep your head.

He didn't change pace, just slid in behind a family taking selfies, letting their slow drift carry him toward the steps. Heat off the stone flattened sound—arguments and laughter pressed into one big, steady river. Sweat gathered under his ribs; the jacket stayed for the pockets and the authority.

Second arch from the west: Jenna in the shade line, sunlight rimming her hair. Relaxed posture for the cameras, eyes set for war. Leather folio tucked under one arm, phone in her left hand. Ava leaned beside her, tablet hugged to her chest, looking like a state worker on break if you didn't see the heat in her gaze. On the step below, Nora sat near the governor's plaque, cap pulled low, the bruise fading under drugstore concealer. The humiliation was gone; what remained was an oyster shell—dull on the outside, razor-sharp on the edge.

Max took the column two down, set the satchel on the balustrade, Nikon up—not to shoot, but to *see*. Cameras made security watch you in the open, not the shadows. He panned left: two plainclothes by posture alone, one with a backward lanyard, the other bare-armed with an earpiece tucked like a tick. Far side, a Hill haircut pretending not to be one. Crowded enough for cover, open enough for a dare.

Their eyes met, skated off—two strangers who'd seen each other at the same coffee shop five times.

"You made good time," she said without moving her lips.

"Took the back way." He kept his tone mild, weather-casual. "You ready?"

"We're past ready."

"How bad?"

"Depends who you believe. Sofia says this is our only window."

The name hit his chest like a coin into a deep jar.

"Sofia's still—"

"Running her own game," Jenna said. "Today our interests overlap."

"Define overlap."

"She brings the match. We bring the oxygen."

College kids in polos drifted between them, docent booming about the pediment like it was a hymn. He shifted closer; Nora's eyes stayed clear.

"You're late," she said.

"Wanted to make an entrance."

"You always did." The ghost of a teenager's voice, then steel. "They're watching the west approach and the bus loop. Lots of shades. One waved to me like an old friend."

"Friendly town."

"Friendly until you ain't."

Ava's tablet thrummed. "Tier one in five. Tier two follows their denials."

"What's tier three?"

"When they realize the denials are bait," Ava said. "And we eat their lawyers for breakfast."

His phone buzzed again:

[INTERCEPTED TRANSMISSION]

—2 markers on your 5. lady in coral, man w/ boat shoes. half-step. // she's coming up the west stairs. sunnies off. blue dress. take air.

He felt the shift before he saw her—the crowd's school-of-fish tightening. Two cameras swung right. Security shifted weight to front feet.

Sofia Ortega climbed the west steps unhurried, blue dress reading *state business* on any broadcast, neutral bag at her elbow, sunglasses off to meet eyes and register. A faint smile, the kind that thanked donors. Not the gala-softness from the Mérida photo—this version had chosen a side and burned the bridge.

Jenna stepped half into the light, pulled by a line months in the making. Ava went still. Nora's breath leveled. Max stayed behind the lens for the extra second it bought.

Sofia nodded to tourists, thanked a man holding the door, let herself be witnessed as harmless. Only then did she pivot toward Jenna's shade.

"Daylight," she said softly. "Didn't think you'd do this in daylight."

"Sun's good for mold," Jenna said. "Figured we'd use the symbolism."

"Mold recedes. Doesn't die." Sofia glanced at Max. "You brought your scribe."

"Habit."

"Careful. Old dogs get shot for less." A beat. "Max Larkin. The long arc. How's the arc today?"

"Depends what it bends toward."

"Justice. Maybe survival. Maybe both."

She blocked the view with her body as she slipped a narrow drive into Jenna's hand—a practiced pass you'd miss if you hadn't lived in markets where men watched for hands.

"What's on it?"

"Names you know. One you don't. The one that tilts the floor."

Sofia's eyes swept the plaza, scanning cameras and black-shirted gimbals.

"You know what happens when an empire dies?" she asked, almost tender. "The tenders come out. They turn in receipts. Not because you're righteous. Because they're broke and angry."

"Worked for the Reformation," Max said.

"Worked because a printer got brave—and because the princes smelled advantage."

"You brought presses?" Ava asked.

"I brought the smell. And what I promised you."

Jenna didn't blink. "Say it."

Sofia smiled without warmth. "I'm not here to save Miguel."

The line went taut.

"And you're not here to bury him?" Max asked.

"I'm here to make sure he doesn't bury me. Haven't you ever wanted to win without blood?"

She let the pause do its work. Then: "Corday."

The name landed like a postcard flipped to its back—Michael Corday, the consultant who billed both sides for the bread. Months as a rumor on their map, a blank tile now burned with letters.

"You're sure?" Ava asked, already believing it.

"I don't say what I can't hold. Ask Miguel."

Jenna's breath came slow. "Okay. We do it here."

"Daylight. Big crowd. Messy sound. You won't get another chance to make it look like an accident when it's not."

Before Max could ask what she meant, his phone burned again:

[INTERCEPTED TRANSMISSION]

—blue dress = drop at 3:16. white cap near rotunda ≠ clean. // pickup on east ramp idling. stand tall. look like you belong.

White cap by the rotunda, smiling without his eyes. East ramp: black SUV tucked among state plates, windshield refusing light.

"Five minutes," Ava said.

"I'll give the word," Jenna said, eyes on the bright square beyond the columns. *Don't break*, she told Max without words.

He nodded. "Let's make some noise."

The noise had to be precise. He watched her step into the light, toward a local anchor with the Capitol framed behind. The whisper spread—*in-flu-encer*—and then she was at the mic.

"Receipts," she said. "And a small correction: this isn't about one bad man or one bad city. It's about an ecosystem. And we're going to show you how it breathes."

Ava hit enter. Across van-beds, graphics rolled—brand logos chained to shells, port maps, blurred faces. The crowd murmured.

"Who is Corday?" the anchor asked.

"Ask him," Jenna said sweetly, gaze toward the east lawn.

Questions stacked—evidence, Miguel's role—and Sofia finally spoke, voice soft enough to force the mics to lean in: "When a man forgets what he loves is not the same as what he owns, he loses both."

Tier two hit. WhatsApp exports, purchase orders, visitation records—ordinary until read together. The important things wore work clothes.

Then the crowd ripple, the sound of a dropped cane. Boat shoes pulled a weapon—but the Hill haircut stepped in, knocked it sideways. Security lunged. White cap drifted east. SUV stayed put.

"Tier three," Ava said.

"Drop it," Jenna ordered.

The last layer slid out—texts, orders, records, all dressed like chores. A blue-tie voice shouted *unverified*.

"We're interrupting careers that endangered children," Jenna said.

Then the question that hung over every room since the start: *We done?*

"We just started," Ava said.

Sofia exhaled. "Better than Miguel's birthday."

New ping:

[INTERCEPTED TRANSMISSION]

—heat ticked. pawn grabbed. rook sliding east. // wrap your work. tails crossing Monroe toward south garage.

Two suits in shirts that cost more than rent walking toward the garage.

"We should go," Max said.

"We should finish," Jenna countered—and did.

No button. Just the mics cutting and catching again, the crowd clapping and hushing in waves. Ava pulled back into shadow. Nora took Jenna's hand.

Sofia: "I'll take the stairs. You take the hall. Don't be seen leaving together."

"You shouldn't be seen leaving at all."

"Story of my life." A parting gift: "Your man with the Navy cap? Don't let him buy the first round."

"Noted," Max said, like a burial.

They peeled off like a school of fish. Max rode the crowd's momentum to the van. Jack glanced up. "Big, loud, righteous."

"Let's make it bigger," Ava said.

One last ping:

[INTERCEPTED TRANSMISSION]

—capstone set. heads turning. // eyes on your six from the garage. // she leaves clean if you do.

Through the lens, he caught Sofia at the top of the east stairs, head turned like she heard her name. She didn't look back. She moved down into the bright day like any woman leaving a meeting she'd won.

"Drive," Jenna said.

"Where to?"

"Wakulla. Then the office. Then D.C. Then wherever they think we won't go."

The van rolled. Behind them, a man in boat shoes sat cuffed, staring at the marble where his plan disappeared into comments. In a villa, a man rewrote a name. Somewhere, a girl named Rosa heard from a woman she believed.

Max pulled the laptop onto his knees, opened the confession file, and stared at the first line until he could stand it.

Structured and lethal, he wrote. Then he began.

45

Unmasking the Titans

The hum inside the *Tallahassee Gazette* wasn't the sound of electricity. It was animal—breathing, pacing, waiting to pounce. Ed Harper sat in his scarred leather chair while the newsroom flexed around him, every desk a fretted nerve, every monitor an open artery. Afternoon glare slanted through dirty windows and fell across a thicket of coffee cups, takeout boxes, and bulldog-clipped stacks of paper. A police scanner hissed in the background, dropping fragments of other people's emergencies. It made its own weather—one of those Gulf systems that rolls in stubborn and decides to stay.

Across from him, Riya Khanna hunched toward her screen, blue light glassing her eyes as she scrolled through the newest encrypted dump in their tip portal. Her stillness could fool you into thinking she was calm. She wasn't. Every so often she made a half-laugh that strangled into a whistle.

"They're naming bureaucrats now," she said, voice dry as cedar. "Not just CEOs with stock-photo headshots. Cabinet level. Motorcades."

Ed steepled his fingers under his chin. "Which means the real storm hasn't even started."

Since Jenna Morgan's colonnade livestream—since Diego

Mendoza stepped into the sun and handed over the keys—the city had walked like it had a fever. Protesters wrapped the Capitol in a chant-tight belt. Federal agents slipped in through service doors. Private jets baked on the tarmac without pilots. The shock kept hopping hosts: county offices, donor dinners, Sunday talk shows trying to give an earthquake a dictionary definition.

What sat in Riya's feed wasn't aftershock. It was bedrock.

She tapped her trackpad. "Signed MOUs between logistics subs and embassy intermediaries. France, Singapore, Brazil. These aren't gray-market handshakes—they're embossed, initialed, proper."

Ed leaned in, read the fine print, felt something cold slide in behind his ribs. "Export immunities. Diplomatic umbrellas. Jesus."

He stepped to the balcony rail and looked down: interns running copies like cigarette girls in a noir, analysts drawing string-webs across digital dashboards, two fact-checkers arguing in whispers about the year a committee sub-clause got renumbered. The *Gazette* had always been a stubborn regional with a mean streak for accountability. Today it was a hot node in a global nervous system.

"Pull the names tied to those MOUs," Ed said without raising his voice. "Cross-check with appointments, donor histories. Build a timeline that draws blood."

Riya's nod was already in motion.

They moved into the big glass conference box—the one once reserved for publishers and budget fights—and turned it into a war map. The whiteboard looked mugged: photos, arrows, acronyms, dates. At the center, the name that had gone from whisper to headline in a week: Monarch Syndicate.

Below it: cartel nodes sluiced through nonprofits, boutique logistics firms doubling as arteries, Tallahassee "recreational outfitters" that never sold a rod or reel. Jenna's ex-sponsors. Miguel's dissolved empire, still twitching. Not a web. A circulatory system.

"State first," Ed said, clicking the remote. A map bloomed: diplomatic ties, aid contracts, port expansions. "If we're calling out secretaries and ambassadors, we bring nails for the coffin and spare hammers."

Malik lifted a brow. "Retaliation?"

"We've been hit before," Ed said. "If we don't print this, it never happened."

The protected pipe began to sputter: ex-staffers, nameless interns, a whistleblower out of a South American capital. The shape shifted with each packet—wellness startups that weren't, ag-alliances moving anything but food, drone tech hidden in humanitarian grants. Each shard scraped another clean.

By three a.m., caffeine had gone sour on Ed's tongue. One name snagged in a matrix: Ragnar Åkesson.

"Why do I know him?"

"Norwegian trade envoy to the U.N.," Riya said. "Vanished after a Luxembourg mess."

"Holdings?"

Ten minutes later she had him in a labyrinth of an infrastructure fund: Honduras, Guatemala, two quiet Caribbean islands. A subsidiary popped: TriAxis Cargo.

"Florida hits," Ed muttered.

A headline anchored itself in his head like a barbed hook: *The Hidden Architects: How a Global Shadow Network Exploited U.S. Ports.* He wrote like soldering in a thunderstorm—small, precise burns.

By morning the bullpen had gone from tense to predatory. Jenna appeared on an encrypted call, fluorescents striping her face.

"Pushback's coming," she said. "Servers, subpoenas, PR napalm."

"We've got kneecap scars," Ed said.

Max's window flickered into the grid. He'd slept, but not behind the eyes. "Guardian and Reuters are ready to mirror. They're calling it the Digital Drop Doctrine."

Riya didn't look up. "Europol opened a quiet pre-investigation. Norway, Spain pre-warranting points of presence."

Ed tipped his chin. "Noon. Global drop. Full docs. The bones go public."

At 11:59 the depot servers whined like an old ship's engine room. At noon, the *Gazette*'s homepage became a fuse: **EXCLUSIVE: UNMASKING THE TITANS.** Tens of thousands of hits in the first minute; millions by ten. The site hiccupped and held. In

D.C., aides fumbled statements like hot plates. Two senators went dark. A New York fund paused trading.

A pebble-ping hit Ed's inbox. FROM: Unknown. SUBJECT: *You missed one.* Attached: a satellite shot of a warehouse on the Cyprus coast. *Check the registry.*

"Solar Meridian Holdings," Riya said, already beside him. The lineage felt designed to confuse God. "We're back at Åkesson."

"And?"

She turned the screen so the room could see. One signatory wore a familiar name like a string of pearls: Caroline Dupont. Former White House advisor, current board member of three compulsively clean foundations.

The board in the glass box went still.

"The corruption didn't stop at corporations," Ed said. "It was blessed in the chapel. Policy cover. Diplomatic grease."

NEXT HEADLINE: *The Hands Behind the Curtain.* The cursor blinked like a dare.

Jenna's voice in his ear: "Confession video. Bogotá embassy. Solar Meridian. Dupont. Friday. Geneva estate. Three European delegates, one U.S. senator. They think nobody will ever read it."

"We need someone on the ground," Ed said.

"Already pulled the trigger," Jenna said. "Max is wheels-up."

▭

MAX WASN'T AIRBORNE YET—HE stood on the mezzanine, hands on the rail while below, the paper grew wings. Ava Chen's corner had become a cockpit of packet-loss maps and mirror-node dashboards.

"We've got slop in the European backbone," she said. "If we don't spread the weight, we torque the frame."

"Spread it," Ed said.

"Already across Iceland and Seoul."

An intern skidded up with a printout: *The Guardian* was running a sidebar; *Le Monde* had grabbed the Åkesson block.

"Make them link the docs," Ed said.

Sirens somewhere. A helicopter too low. Max's phone buzzed: [ORION] nodes confirmed / Geneva estate validated / watch-word "Mistral."

"Pack light," Ed said. "If they spot you early, you're a headline, not the writer."

"I'll bring you something that bites," Max said.

By mid-afternoon, the office smelled of ozone and burned coffee. The traffic map lit up Tunis, Helsinki, Quito, Christchurch. Parents on lunch breaks and grad students at 3 a.m. pinched and zoomed through PDFs that would have bored them last week.

An [INTERCEPTED TRANSMISSION] scrolled across Ava's terminal: *Mistral parties secure // Friday window 2100 CET // blue room / lake glass.*

"They're sloppy when they're scared," she said.

"Or arrogant," Ed replied.

He felt the old panic scratching and the older resolve standing between it and the work. "Second package at five," he told Riya. "Lead with Solar Meridian. Dupont in the nut graf, Åkesson in the kicker. Clear but deniable—let their rebuttals do our amplification."

He found a minute for the photo on his desk—Hannah mid-laugh, hair plastered from play. Too many recitals missed. The only thing he'd ever been able to give her was the work.

The foreign-mirror clip came in grainy: embassy walls, a voice educated and exhausted. Solar Meridian. Dupont. Geneva, blue room, lake glass.

Ed stood. "We're past permission. We're in record."

"Max is already en route," Jenna said.

Ed made a slow pass across the newsroom, killing careless adjectives, trimming adrenaline from subheads. Truth didn't need perfume; it needed a spine.

A cart of fresh paper rattled by. "Press room says we're running extras," the kid said.

"Make sure the street boxes have real money," Ed said. "People need paper they can't unplug."

From his doorway he saw the bullpen—phones, faces, maps, murmurs. The titans had faces now. The names were entries in a ledger. The follow-through would live or die on the solidity of what they sent out.

He sat, typed the line that would bring a generation of evasions to heel:

When power launders itself through legitimacy and calls it policy, it ceases to be mere corruption. It becomes a design. Today we call the designers by name.

Save. Send to Page. The building exhaled.

MAX PACKED like he always did: batteries, the pencil, the paper map he trusted more than any phone. Call signs on a slip of paper no one else could read.

At security, the agent glanced at his press badge and looked away. In the boarding area, a TV without sound scrolled the *Gazette*'s headline under a lawmaker's moving mouth. A toddler laughed at a plastic airplane.

His phone buzzed once: *Mistral confirmed / glass room / lake side.* He typed *inbound* and went dark.

Group called. He filed in with the rest, Tallahassee spreading below like a palm holding a coin. The plane tilted, lifted.

He closed his eyes to sharpen the picture: blue room. Lake glass. Names like teeth.

He opened his notebook and began to write.

46

Echoes of Aftermath

Max Larkin stood in the stillness of his apartment, Tallahassee's skyline faintly etched beyond the fogged glass of his window. The buildings looked washed clean in the clear morning light, sharp-edged against a pale sky that held no threat of rain. Down in the streets, life moved with an energy that felt strange to him—too bright, too deliberate, like a city rehearsing how to live with its eyes wide open.

Inside, the hush was almost reverent. After months of adrenaline, coded calls, shadowed figures, and the constant knowledge that one mistake could erase him, this quiet felt both foreign and dangerous. The walls no longer hummed with tension; they breathed.

His notes still covered the coffee table—a chaotic map of names, bank accounts, offshore holdings, faces now etched into headlines. Scribbled arrows, coffee rings, and the smudged fingerprints of too many nights chasing threads through exhaustion. He hadn't touched them since the day the Capitol erupted with truths that could no longer be contained. That day had been a detonation. Everything after was just shockwave.

He moved to the kitchen, poured coffee he didn't need, and

stared at the framed photo on the fridge. His son—five years old in that picture, baseball cap, a toothless grin wide enough to eclipse everything else. He'd carried that image in his mind like a talisman through the worst of it. When he'd been cornered in parking garages, tailed through dark streets, or forced to listen as threats landed inches from his skin, it had been his face that anchored him. It still did.

The Gazette had transformed since the story broke. Once a haven for quiet diligence and the hum of old printers, it now teemed with federal liaisons, legal advisors, security consultants, and a flood of young reporters who looked at Max with something between awe and fear. He couldn't decide if he missed the old chaos or welcomed this new siege of truth. Maybe both. Maybe neither.

On the couch, he unlocked his tablet and scrolled through the news—stories from Brussels, The Hague, and Washington. International watchdog groups announcing joint investigations into cross-border influence trafficking. Financial crimes units in three countries reopening cases. And there—front row, calm but resolute —Harper Vale, seated beside whistleblowers and other journalists who had bled to get their stories heard.

He hadn't spoken to Jenna since the press conference. Didn't need to. They'd shared enough rooms where silence carried the weight of truth.

Finishing his coffee, he slid on his shoes and stepped outside. The morning air was crisp, still carrying the metallic scent of recent rain. Downtown had a pulse now—faster, sharper. Storefronts that had boarded up during the height of the corruption now stood open, their windows filled with hand-painted signs calling for vigilance and civic renewal. On one wall, a mural depicted clasped hands in every shade of skin, the Capitol dome in the background, and in bold letters: **Not This Time**.

He walked past the courthouse, its steps occupied by peaceful protesters. Handmade placards read: *Eyes Open. Don't Let Them Rebuild the Lie. We're Still Watching.* They weren't shouting. They didn't need to. The quiet conviction in their presence was louder than any chant.

Across the street, under the Gazette's sandstone rotunda, Ed stood with his sleeves rolled up, bellowing at a pair of interns about sourcing protocols. The old editor's voice carried over the street traffic like the bark of a drill sergeant. Max felt a reluctant smile as he crossed over.

"You actually came in on your day off?" Ed called, eyeing him like he'd caught him sneaking into church after skipping the sermon.

"I'm not sure I remember what a day off feels like," Max said.

Ed gave a grunt that could have been agreement or derision—it was always hard to tell. For a moment, they just stood there, watching the interns scatter. Then Ed reached into his satchel and pulled out a slim manila folder.

"Anonymous drop," he said. "Came in through the French consulate this morning. Codes, bank transfers, old naval logs. Some of the names from your last piece are in it. Could be noise. Could be dynamite."

Max opened the folder, flipping through the first few pages. The paper smelled faintly of salt and old ink. Tables of figures scrawled with handwritten notations. Wire transfers routed through Luxembourg, Marseille, Halifax. One typed memo, crisp despite the folds, bore the header: **Operation Rainglass**.

"You think this is real?" Max asked.

Ed shook his head. "No idea. But it's loud enough to matter, and quiet enough someone hoped it stayed buried."

There were photographs—grainy shots of shipping manifests, a dock at night, a face half-lit by a cigarette. And there was something else: a list of naval supply routes altered without official approval, and the signatures authorizing the changes. Max recognized one of the names. Not from the Capitol. From an older file. A cartel funding report. A name he hadn't expected to see tied to anything maritime.

"Guess I'm not done yet," he said.

As he started to leave, Ed's voice softened in a way Max hadn't heard in years. "Watch your back, Max. People like you... they burn fast."

Max nodded without looking back. He'd already felt the burn.

But in its place, something had returned. Something he'd thought he'd lost forever.

Purpose.

Back in his apartment, he spread the folder out across the desk. The details began to form into threads—naval supply chains rerouted through shell companies, private brokers with security clearances in both U.S. and European agencies. Some of the signatures belonged to people long thought retired. Others were still active in foreign ministries. And one diplomat's name glared up at him like a flare in the dark.

Somewhere, far from Tallahassee, the same web that had pulled him in was still alive. Still moving. And in its shadows, the people who had once used Miguel Ortega—*El Cazador*—like currency were tying off loose ends. Max didn't know where Miguel's road had ended, but the silence around his name told its own story.

Outside, rain began to fall again. Not hard. Not threatening. Just steady. Like the sound of a clock you couldn't stop hearing once you noticed it.

Max reached over and switched off the desk lamp. In the dark, the recording still played in his head. And beneath it, the words from that shadowed figure on the Capitol screen, just before the feed had cut:

"You think this is the end?"

He didn't smile. He didn't flinch.

He whispered into the quiet, "No. Just the next chapter."

Epilogue

Biscayne Bay breathed in slow, tidal pulses beneath a sky the color of pale steel—the same muted wash of light that had hung over the pier the morning Evan died. The air smelled of salt, brine, and that faint metallic tang of wet pilings, just as it had that day. Somewhere out on the water, a gull cried once—sharp, solitary—before the sound was swallowed by the hush.

Max drew a long breath, letting it settle heavy in his chest. The air here always carried memories—some welcome, most not.

It had been thirty-four days since the leak cracked Tallahassee wide open. Since Jenna stepped up to the mic and detonated decades of covert compromise. Since Nora came home. Since truths —once locked behind corporate vaults and cartel fear—flooded into daylight.

The world had shifted.

But Max still carried the weight.

From his coat pocket, he pulled out a familiar, sun-bleached relic: a laminated photo of a boy holding a red kite on a nearby beach. The boy laughed mid-stride, curls whipped by the wind. His name had been Evan.

He came here often to think—this quiet stretch of bay just miles from the school where Evan had once played baseball. Back then, before everything collapsed, Max sat on the bleachers with a pad and pen, half-watching the game, half-drafting op-eds he'd never send. Evan had been all elbows and smart remarks, a flash of speed in worn cleats.

Fourteen.

That's how old he was the day Max found him on the floor.

Fentanyl-laced Percocet. Bought off a kid two grades up. One pill.

One.

The paramedics couldn't save him.

Neither could Max.

Grief hollowed him; alcohol blurred the edges. But the edges always came back sharper. It took two years, three blackouts, two suspensions from the Miami Herald, and one failed suicide before he staggered into rehab and asked for help.

That was ten years ago. He hadn't touched a drink since.

But the ache—and the guilt—never left.

Max stared at the photograph until his vision blurred, then slipped it back into his pocket. The world had kept moving after Evan's death, but his had narrowed—first into the bottom of a bottle, then into this mission. The story that gave him breath again. The reckoning.

And they'd gotten it—at least the first part.

Tallahassee split open under the weight of truth. The press conference, the leaks, the raids—weeks of chaos, congressional stammering, and two high-level resignations. Investigators traced the cartel's invisible threads through branding firms, shell corporations, and lobbyist dinners beneath the state Capitol's marble dome.

Max had helped expose it—alongside Jenna, Ava, Jack, Nora… and Sofia, wherever she was now.

He never wrote for glory, never chased the Pulitzer buzz now clinging to his name like an unwanted halo. He wrote because it was the only way left to make sense of his son's death—murder, at the hands of the cartel's supply lines. If breaking one link meant fewer fathers got that knock on the door, fewer boys were sold a dream disguised as a pill, then the work mattered.

THE NEXT MORNING, mist clung low over Lake Ella. Two ducks cut slow ripples across the still water. Beyond the oak-lined paths, the city stirred: car doors closing, a jogger's footfalls, the faint whistle of a distant train.

Max sipped black coffee from a battered thermos, waiting for the sun.

Footsteps approached.

Jenna Morgan.

She wore a gray hoodie and jeans, hair pulled back. No cameras, no audience—just her.

"You always come here?" she asked quietly.

He nodded. "Helps me think."

She sat beside him. For a moment, neither spoke.

Then Jenna pulled out her phone. "Interpol hit the Belgium accounts this morning. Three shells down. The rest are scrambling."

Max raised an eyebrow. "That leak came from Sofia?"

Jenna's mouth twitched. "Still a ghost. But she's burning their money lines—quietly, strategically."

Max sipped again. "The story's not over."

"No," Jenna said. "It's not."

The ducks passed again, angling toward the far shore. Church bells chimed somewhere downtown.

"I think about him every day," Max said suddenly, voice low. "Evan."

Jenna stayed silent.

"He was smart. Smarter than me. Wanted to teach science. Said he liked helping people figure things out. I found a letter once—in his desk. Said he took the pill because it made everything feel quiet. Said the world got too loud. That's how they got him."

Max paused, the weight in his chest sharp as broken glass. "I've spent ten years trying to quiet that noise for other kids. Through ink.

Through truth. But there were days I wanted to die. Sometimes I still wonder if I've done enough."

Jenna reached into her jacket and handed him a folded sheet. "From Nora's journal. The night you published the first piece."

Max unfolded it. Shaky handwriting read:

They tell us to survive quietly. But some people survive by shouting. Thank God someone still knows how to shout.

He read it twice. Then again.

"I'm not done shouting," he said.

"Good," Jenna replied. "Because Brussels just found a new trail —Singapore. A biotech firm laundering through university research. Big."

"Bigger than Tallahassee?"

"Much."

Max rose, knees stiff. Sunlight broke through, gilding the dew-soaked grass.

He looked over the lake one last time.

"This started as a story," he said. "Now it's something else."

"A reckoning?" Jenna offered.

He shook his head. "A promise."

Max took out Evan's photo, let the light catch the boy's smile, then tucked it away. Zipping his coat, he turned toward the waking city.

His city.

For now.

The battle wasn't over. The cartel still moved in shadows. Bureaucrats who'd profited in silence were already hiring new PR firms to wash their hands clean.

But this time, Max Larkin would be watching.

And he wouldn't look away.